Peculiar Treasures

Peculiar Treasures

∞

A novel
by
Bernadine Okoro

Copyright © 2009 by Bernadine Okoro.

Library of Congress Control Number: 2008905835
ISBN: Hardcover   978-1-4363-5362-5
                 Softcover   978-1-4363-5361-8

All rights reserved. No part of this book may be reproduced or transmitted in any form or by any means, electronic or mechanical, including photocopying, recording, or by any information storage and retrieval system, without permission in writing from the copyright owner.

This is a work of fiction. Names, characters, places and incidents either are the product of the author's imagination or are used fictitiously, and any resemblance to any actual persons, living or dead, events, or locales is entirely coincidental.

This book was printed in the United States of America.

To order additional copies of this book, contact:
Xlibris Corporation
1-888-795-4274
www.Xlibris.com
Orders@Xlibris.com

Acknowledgements

I want to first thank my heavenly Father, Jesus Christ who resurrected my dreams of writing.

To my sister Stacy, thanks for all your time, help and advice in getting this book published.

To Vera and Petrolina, thanks for making me laugh and inspiring new ideas.

To my friends Andrea Harrell, Andrea Williamson-Floyd, Robert Young, and Keisha Murphy thanks for giving me your opinions and ear. To my sister circle, you know who you are, thanks for being there for me in the beginnings of our journey; the time we spent together was precious and is forever sealed in my heart.

Preface

There are things in life we often do not understand. Why were we born a certain way? How did we get into this family? Even our own personalities throw us a loop. We are born into this life ingesting preconceived notions of how we think we should live. Some notions come from our parents whether they tell it to us or not. Some notions come from society, media, and leaders. Other notions come from us. We project our fears, hopes, and dreams for a better tomorrow. Regardless, we enter this earth and we live day-to-day, meeting deadlines, dealing with bosses, friends, and family. We create products that help us communicate, work, and enjoy our life.

Then one day, this life we have created suddenly changes. It does not seem to be enough. We grow weary of the monotony. We groan at our tireless tirade of job duties and schoolwork. We look at fallen leaders with dismay, shame, and apathy. We seem almost empathetic of the suffering around us. Maybe we are too aware of it because we are powerless to control or contain it. There is a longing to feel safe. Technology seems to be the answer, but it further aggrandizes our isolation. Relationships, the first foundation we grew to know, are at best distant and dysfunctional. We look for peace. We want to belong. We want shelter from this world of rejection that we try desperately to shield ourselves.

Suddenly, as if we think we made the decision, we enter the kingdom of God. We surrender ourselves to the one called the Master Potter. He replenishes us with His spirit. He breathes new life and sets us on a new journey. We come into the kingdom not realizing that perhaps it is the beginning of our life. Now, the Master has the opportunity to shape and mold us into the image He means for us. As a gentleman, He presents us with choices, but He will not force us to choose.

Allowing us free will, we pick a direction, hoping it leads to the path of righteousness. Sometimes, however, we leave the path alone because it is too narrow. Our Father, as if He already knew what we would do, ushers us back into His loving, strong arms and reestablishes our path. Our preconceived notions, personalities, and ways of thinking fall under intense scrutiny. He refines us through pain and suffering. He shows us the "gift" He has placed in us. We may be aware of the gift, but hesitant; we do not know how to use it.

Thankfully, our Father loves us so much that He works with us tirelessly to show us who we really are. He teaches us what we should do with our gifts through service. He shows us His love through people. He gives us His vision of the kingdom. If we are willing to submit under his authority for a time, He makes what hidden, buried, or scattered dreams we have bloom into hope and promise. We weather storms of hardship, failure, and disappointment. We nearly escape oppression and depression. We lie thirsty in the wilderness, hoping we haven't been forgotten. We look for an oasis where we can drink. Thirsty for appreciation, love, and acceptance, we continue to tread through the desert until we are ready to receive what He has for us. We discover the Promised Land. We spy it. Our future beckons; fearful or not, we will enter. We open favor's doors and walk boldly into dominion. We know and accept our calling, our purpose, and ourselves. We enter into a new dispensation, a new way of thinking, a new paradigm. We enter into our "divine season."

Chapter 1

"Happiness isn't always a choice..."

Bible study took place at Faith and Victory International on a cool, autumn Tuesday evening in one of the fellowship halls, which featured a dimly lit peach-colored room adorned with Egyptian mappings. A cherry wood podium sat perched in the center of the room with a portable whiteboard just a few feet behind. A twenty-seven-inch Panasonic television sat next to the podium. Vicki Yohe crooned "Jehovah Jireh" softly on CD as the saints and the "ain'ts" began filling the room. Colleagues came in chattering like long-time friends; others weary from a day's work stumbled in. Stay-at-home moms, looking for a momentary break, a respite from home life, gathered their bibles and notepads, leaving their babies and husbands at home.

Simone Dusette sauntered into the room, wearing a pink sweater with a fitted jean skirt, and, careful not to show too much of what her mama gave her, took a seat in the back row near the door. She patted her texturized brown crop and retouched her makeup. Simone spent most of the day with puberty-stricken kids and she needed the comfort of some adult conversation.

Octavia Kalu charged into the room, wearing maroon pants and a cream top, reminiscent of her sorority days at the University of Chicago. Her mid-length bob swung from side to side. Her dark and distinctive bedroom eyes scanned the room for mental and visual space. She sat in the front row next to the wall.

Leah Decruz, carrying a camel brown leather knapsack, strolled in behind a group of yuppie business suits. Her honey golden skin, brown eyes, and brown-streaked hair could not mask the rough-around-the-edges, chip-on-her-shoulder aura that radiated from her being. She strolled in wearing an earthy, floral printed cap sleeve dress, black fitted bell-bottoms, and ankle boots. She found a seat in the middle row while eyes trailed her every move. Stragglers crept in haphazardly, praying for a back-row seat. Fifteen students, in total, filled the room.

Benevolence James opened the door, looked around, and paused. Broken spirits sat wounded and internally bruised, many needing care. Others stood in different corners kneeling, praying, and seeking solace. She closed the door, turned up the recess lights, and quieted the stereo. Benevolence James was a stout looking woman with cocoa brown skin, full-length tresses, and broad shoulders who displayed a no-nonsense attitude. She stood in front of the podium, wearing a green Kiyonna pantsuit with a pink silk blouse. She exuded a quiet confidence. Her voice was peacefully low, a mix of calming rain coupled with a forcefulness of lightning getting ready to strike.

"My name is Minister Benevolence James. I am a clinical psychologist. This class is entitled *Bondage Breaker: Breaking out from the Chains of Your Past.* For those who feel unsure, you are indeed in the right class. It is not by coincidence you came in here, even if you think you crept in just for a peek. God has called each of you here to help you in different ways. He desires to help you break out from the past and move into the future He's calling you to."

After a couple of minutes, everyone sat down as Benevolence distributed some pamphlets. Everyone stood for a quick word of prayer.

Yasmine Blue, the trendy-looking, caramel–colored latecomer, crept in andplaced all of her shopping bags in two empty seats near the aisle. Benevolence explained the classroom structure.

"We will be getting very personal in this class as we begin to uncover the things that have kept us bound in the past." Benevolence expounded.

"Nothing that is discussed in this room is to leave this room. Is that understood? We want to create an environment of safety and confidentiality that will allow the Holy Spirit to flow freely. It is the only way that healing can really begin. We will go over the syllabus. Assignments are essential! You will have scripture verses to memorize! It is your weapon against the enemy and his attacks."

After a few moments, Benevolence turned on the television. A video played; it showed a vicious argument ensuing between a man and a woman. The man yelled at the woman who spewed her venomous thoughts just as loudly back at her attacker. The man approached the woman, raising his hands toward the woman. His shadow loomed over her like the Eiffel Tower. The screen then cuts to an interview of a young black female talking about her current relationship with her abusive boyfriend. The room grew still. No one moved. Anxiety bolted out of the television and stood like soldiers watching its audience. Saints shifted in their seats. Someone coughed. Others muffled sniffles. Tension grew. One man spoke on divorce. Another spoke on abandonment. One woman spoke on sexual abuse. Another spoke on mental abuse. Benevolence stopped the video in midsentence.

Dead silence. *Did anyone dare breathe? Someone definitely loosed the cat out of the bag.* Confusion, wearing an orange jumpsuit, pranced around the room. He bellowed a brown stratus cloud of distraught that attempted to smother the joy remaining in the room. Many weren't sure what to think. Others sat in denial, refusing to acknowledge that the documentary was real. A few saints walked out. It was too much for folks to handle.

Benevolence assessed the collateral damage. She sprang quickly to action.

"Now I know many of you weren't expecting that. I brought the program to help you recognize the different forms of abuse. Abuse occurs in many ways. Many people experience different emotions because of abuse. It could have been in the past; but whatever it is, we are here to examine it and break all the ties that bind you to it. Amen?" She could literally hear people exhaling thankful sighs of relief.

"Amen. Now, I want you to arrange your chairs into a semicircle. We will go around the room and introduce ourselves." The new formation brought everyone even closer together toward the center of the room. Simone reluctantly scooted her chair into the semicircle, just close enough to have an easy expressway to the door. She was expecting a call, her routine phone call. Being in Bible study wasn't going to stop her from getting that phone call. She would politely excuse herself and attend to her business. She spoke first.

"Hi, I'm Simone. From St. Croix. Currently live in Maryland. I am an administrator for alternative high school in Hyattsville. Been saved for about two years. Been a member of Faith and Victory for about the same length of time. I just joined the women's ministry. I felt the Lord wanted me in this class but I'm not sure why. That's it."

Next, the trendy-looking latecomer spoke. She smiled all throughout her introduction as if she was on camera.

"Hey, everybody, I'm Yasmine. I'm from California but claim New York. I've known Jesus since I was eighteen. I am a fragrance chemist. I've been a member of Faith and Victory for some time now, about four years. I serve in the outreach ministry. I know my spiritual gifts. The Lord told me to come to this class. I'm just being obedient."

As other students began to speak, a knock rang at the door. Simone, being closest to the door, opened it, recognized who it was, and walked outside, shutting the door softly behind. The petite woman sitting up front began to speak. She repeated the same introductory pattern.

"Hi. I am Octavia. I was born in Sierra Leone but live in DC. I work for a corporate firm in DC. I rededicated my life to Christ almost four years ago. I've been a member of Faith and Victory for three years. I believe I know what some of my spiritual gifts are. I am taking this class just for information. It seemed important. I feel the information will prove useful to me at some point in the future."

Several men bravely spoke. "Cuties on duties" or rather "saints with weights" spoke about their upbringings and their work. Deacon Connor Davis, a tall athletic thirty-something brown-skinned man with green eyes, spoke. Many of the women perked up and gave him their utmost attention.

"Evening, my name is Deacon Davis. I'm from Chicago. Been at Faith and Victory for eight years and a deacon for two years. I am a correctional officer for Ward 6, a correctional facility for youth near Capitol Hill. God lead me to this class, primarily to help me understand the spiritual issues I deal with at work."

Leah decided to chime in. Her voice was a mixture of street and Trini accents.

"I'm Leah. From Trinidad but was raised in here in Silver Spring. I own Caribbean DeLite in downtown Silver Spring. Come and check us out anytime. Well, I guess you can say that Jesus found me about ten months ago. I like coming here to Faith and Victory. Been coming on and off for a while before I finally joined. I'm here because . . . well, I don't know. I was curious about the topic. We'll see . . . not sure what to expect tonight."

Leah cleared her throat.

"It certainly has been a lot to stomach right now." Her voice had a certain vulnerability and edge that seemed to echo the sentiments of everyone in the room.

After the last introduction, Benevolence opened her Bible and started the night's lesson.

"I want to thank you for being so open and honest. It may seem like a lot right now, but it will get easier later on. Open your Bibles to Philippians 3 verses 12-15."

A loud, wailing sound pierced the room. As everyone turned around, Simone had her head between her legs crying hysterically, as her cell phone fell like her dreams unto the floor. The semicircle opened. Benevolence rushed through the circle, knelt down, and whispered in Simone's ear. She carried Simone's limp, grief-stricken body out of the room. Everyone looked on in amazement. Many froze, not quite sure what to think. Class came to a screeching halt.

The whispers fluttered noisily. People gathered their belongings and prepared to leave. Deacon Davis sprang into action, rising in the middle of the semicircle. His six feet three inch frame quickly commanded everyone's attention.

"Folks, if you would quietly gather up your things, we will prepare to leave. Please wait for further instructions."

Octavia looked around at everyone in the room. She snatched her briefcase. Feelings of helplessness began to swell. She shrugged her shoulders. Unfortunately, it wouldn't be the last time these feelings would strike.

Chapter 2

"Love on a two-lane track..."

"I am running track for Morgan State." Simone Dusette responded confidently to her high school track coach. Her accent billowed out smooth confidence with each word. At five foot seven, one hundred thirty pounds, the athletically built senior was the talk of Eleanor Roosevelt High, being one of the fastest 400-meter sprinters coming out in five years. Simone was the oldest of two. She and her younger sister Sonia spent most of their childhood in the fields, playing with other kids or racing down the fields, whatever they could do; anything to keep active.

Her father, Darius Dusette, left when Simone was seven. Therefore, she took care of Sonia while her mother, Serena Dusette, worked two jobs, one as a midwife and the other as a housecleaner to help pay the bills. Between sports, Simone cooked and Sonia helped clean so that their mother rested from the hard days and nights of labor, she endured. Simone ran track, winning the state championships in the 4-by-100 and 4-by-400 meters relays, when the college coaches started courting her. Seton Hall, Hampton, Virginia Tech, Howard, and Morgan State were her suitors. Simone got a full-track scholarship from Morgan State. Serena Dusette moved the family to Maryland during Simone's sophomore year in high school to stay with her brother Kendall and his wife in College Park. This way, at least Simone knew her family would be close.

Morgan State was a historically black university infused with Baltimore city's culture: club music, ghetto slums, and city life. The athletic department wanted to rebuild Morgan State to its former glory. Fraternities and sororities stepped on the *yard*. Football games were en masse. Half-time shows began the "battle of the bands." College life meant freedom, excitement, and opportunity but with one unexpected twist, Tavian Giancello.

Simone met Tavian Giancello at the Morgan State Invitational. He, along with a group of his friends, enjoyed the normal banter as they crooned to the females in their tight orange shirts and midnight blue "booty shorts." The uniforms nowadays left nothing to imagination. Tavian spotted a curly-haired goddess jogging toward a blue tent. Simone was preparing to run in the first heat of the 4-by-100 meters relay. She warmed up in a small grassy area near one end of the orange-colored track before jogging over to the first aid tent to grab some ice. Her every movement replayed in his mind in slow motion.

"Kev, I'm going to get something to drink."

Tavian hopped up from the bleachers.

"Oh yeah, with all this booty flowing out here, a brother is getting thirsty. Needs some juice!"

Kevin boasted. He slapped hands with two other spectators in agreement.

"Why, don't you stop being so crass! Man, ya'll need some class!" Tavian defended.

"Okay, there he goes, Mister Rico Suave!" Kevin joked.

"But we all know, there's a dog underneath all that—vule' vu' bourgeoisie crap."

"Man, I'm just saying, there are better ways to talk to women, is all. I'll be back." Tavian was in his second year at Morgan State majoring in business administration. Being half black and half Italian, standing at five feet and ten inches, with hazel eyes, broad nose, and brown hair, Tavian looked like he'd just stepped off the *JC Penny* catalogue. He could pass for white if he wanted to, but his excessive "tans" and street language gave the impression that he belonged to "Soul Train" rather than the "A-Train." He excused himself from the banter and strolled on to the field. He tried hopping over the fence but banged his leg on the pole's edge.

"Ow!" *Dang! Now I need some ice.*

He approached the first aid tent with a slight limp.

"This tent is for athletes only!" exploded the nurse, who resembled a female Mr. T without the Mohawk haircut.

"But, I just want a small pack of ice." Tavian complained.

"I hurt my leg."

"Sorry. This is for athletes only."

"I'm an athlete," he lied.

"Can't run today." Tavian glanced at her nametag. *Martha*. He continued pleading but stopped midsentence when he saw Simone run to the line to grab some Ace bandages before her race. He quickly limped away. Minutes later,

Simone went to the first aid table. The nurse finished stretching the arm of another athlete who had shot put tryouts.

"Martha?" Simone inquired.

"Can I have another Ace bandage and a pack of ice—?"

"Ice," Tavian interrupted.

"She needs some ice." Tavian jumped in front of Simone to pick up the ice pack before Simone knew what was going on.

"Excuse me?" Simone demanded.

Who is this guy?

"You're running the 4-by-100, second heat, right? I thought I heard coach call you for warm-ups." He grabbed the ice pack and bandage before the nurse had a chance to bark.

"I'll just take this for her." He dashed out of the tent.

He grabbed the Ace bandages, tape, and ice and walked back toward the field. Simone walked past him and snatched the ice pack and Ace bandages out of his hand.

"These are mine, thank you!"

"I'm sorry," he whispered.

"I just needed some ice. She wouldn't give it to me. I had to say it was for you."

"Well, you can have the ice, I don't want it."

Simone turned, heading in the opposite direction.

"Can I have your number?"

It would be foolish to let this moment slip away.

Simone looked back at him for a moment.

"No. I don't give my number out."

Especially not to players like you.

"When can I see you again?"

"Who said, I want you to?" Simone challenged.

I don't even know you.

"Well, I'm giving you a choice in the matter."

"Are you giving all these other girls who are running out here a choice too?"

I bet he is.

"Nope. Just you. It's a limited-time offer." Tavian smiled.

"Well, I guess your time's up. Look, I gotta warm up."

Nice teeth. He is cute, but I don't want any foolishness.

Simone jogged off and met her teammates for their last warm-up. Her orange and blue sweatpants swayed in the wind. Tavian watched mesmerized, etching every inch of her frame in the contours of his mind.

He came to every home track meet to watch Simone. Like a detective, he found out as much as he could about Simone through friends; he did enough to wear her down to dinner and a "Friday night" flick. They became inseparable after that, much to the chagrin of many of the girls on campus. They had been going out for six months when Simone knew Tavian was the man she wanted to marry.

She later injured in her leg during her junior year, and it was a good possibility that she wouldn't finish eligibility. Simone began thinking seriously of a career outside of sports. She remembered an inspiring talk with one of her professors about secondary education and creating ideal schools. She geared her studies in that area and graduated with a degree in education. Later, she got her masters in administration with a concentration in curriculum and literacy development. Throughout college, Simone experienced two major loves in her life: track and Tavian Giancello. Nevertheless, eventually, she was bound to hit her first major crisis. She would need a special amount of stamina to win this kind of race.

Chapter 3

"Go to a place where I will show thee . . ."

"Octavie? Octavie, wake up. Wash up and come here."

"Yes, Daddy." Octavia dragged herself eight-year-old frame up and rolled her blanket and pillow off the floor. She walked out to the central parlor where her father opened the curtain door that led outside. He checked his thatch roof while looking up at the sky.

"I am going to the market to sell some items before I go to the fields. Your mommy is cooking back outside. I brought her new stones to put her pots on top. If it rains, bring everything inside. I want you children to go and get some roasted corn. Gather leaves, tomato, mango and coconut for me."

"Okay, Daddy."

Adolphus Kalu was a young miner with the voice of a chief tribesman in the village and the heart of a koala bear. In his patriarchal country, the chief tribesman maintained respect. He took honor in attending to his family and eldership affairs.

Each morning in the Seidu village before school, Octavia would gather potato leaves, cassava leaves, and fruits for her mother to cook. She had to wake her siblings, Omar and Sade, so that they would not be late for school. Omar, at seven, was strong and courageous like his father. Sade, at five, always took too long to wake up. She cried each morning, refusing to move from her bed.

"Sade, get up." Octavia pushed her shoulder.

"I sleep."

"Daddy said, get up and help us get corn." Octavia folded her arms.

"I don't want to." Sade turned over.

"You can sleep when you come back." Octavia pushed her shoulder again.

"No, I don't want to go." Sade shrugged.

"Sade, get up now!" Octavia squealed. They went through the same ritual at least once a week.

Sade would whimper and cry all the way outside until she reached the cornfields. They walked from the compound down the orange dirt road to the cornfields. Their work uniform consisted of a worn wrap skirt, t-shirt, and slippers. By the time Sade became fully awake, she would run through the fields into the rust colored street. Her job was to get the roasted corn on the road for their snack. After a couple of hours, they would bring the food in and dress for primary school. It took forever, it seemed, but Octavia didn't mind. She liked helping Daddy. She liked being in charge. Adolphus won the visa lottery to come to America. He ran into the house with the news.

"Praises be to our marvelous God! Everyone, come. Come! Sit down! I have an announcement!"

Everyone sat in the central parlor. Elizabeth Kalu, set the rice, fish and leaf sauce on the small table. She sat next to Omar. Sade sat on Daddy's lap. Adolphus smiled brightly.

"I have called this family meeting because I have something important to discuss. I have been given an opportunity, a very fortunate opportunity. We are going overseas! To America! We will leave by end year's time."

Elizabeth hopped up dancing and singing in Mende, *"God and His goodness has smiled on me."* Adolphus laughed, clapping his hands while singing along. Sade followed, clapping her hands. Omar and Octavia looked at each other. A mix of sadness and anticipation filled Octavia's eight-year-old mind, as she would be leaving the country land she cherished so much. She would miss running through the corn fields. She would no longer hear the elders tell their stories by the kitchen fire on Saturday evenings. It would all soon become a faded memory. However, the anticipation of coming to America would somehow win her over.

The airplane flight to Washington DC was the longest ride of Octavia's life. Eighteen hours, with layovers in Paris and Kennedy airport, was all it took to start a new dream for Octavia and her family. People were cordial. Passengers dragged luggage from port to port. During the layover, Sade and Omar slept. Octavia watched the orange sun flow out from the Parisian sky. There were other African families walking through the airport in a dazed excitement. Soon they would land in the nation's capital, Washington DC. Unfortunately, getting used to life in America was as easy as having a goat as your pet. Some days were better than others were. However, one thing that Octavia loved the most in school was learning black History.

Meeks Elementary held Black History Month in such spectacular fashion. The assemblies were combined with other musical events that often featured local DC artists. Social studies classes stacked the unsuspecting students with biographies of dozens of African Americans who made significant contributions to history all over the world. Every school day for twenty-eight days, they flooded stories of famous blacks, including George Washington Carver, Madame C. J. Walker, Harriet Tubman, Sojourner Truth, and W. C. Handy, into the minds of the youth sitting in the seats.

Octavia loved all of them. She learned all she could about African-American history. Octavia memorized every fact and every story. Stories of the inventors fascinated Octavia. They were so creative, making so many patents. Many of them did not get the credit, Octavia discovered. Sitting in Mrs. Taylor's fourth grade class, she would attempt to go over these stories, while her classmates, weary from boredom, talked and only half listened. She was always eager to hear the stories, even the ones she already knew. It gave her insight. They were artists, creators, and they went through a lot. Octavia often found herself imagining what it would be like to live in New York or Washington DC in the 1930s, during the "Harlem Renaissance." As she looked through the pictures in the books and watched videos, she saw how they lived with such style, class, and grace. It was evident in the way they talked, walked, and dressed. They carried respect on their shoulders and wore admiration on their sleeves. She wondered why her classmates did not share the same loving adoration.

While everyone was at school, Adolphus worked at Safeway as a grocery clerk and a cabdriver. Elizabeth worked as a part-time grocery clerk so that she could be home after school. She wanted to help pay the bills. They occupied a three-bedroom apartment on Eleventh Street in NW in the African Mecca. Neighbors were from Nigeria, Sierra Leone, and DC. Adolphus kept his eyes open to everything and everyone while earning his business degree at night. Adolphus Kalu loved order and obedience. It was Octavia's job to make sure that Sade and Omar were okay. They were a team. If Sade got in trouble, which was often the case, then Octavia and Omar got a beating too. They were supposed to look after each other. At school, the Kalus reigned. Grades had to be superb. Octavia was supposed to set the example. It was hard being the first. Kids ridiculed them a lot. Other kids called them names like *Kunta Kente* and *monkey*. Octavia just ignored them.

Kids are so stupid. They are just jealous because Africans excelled at everything they try.

The teachers called Octavia because she knew the answers to the questions in class. Between activities, she would sit and watch Mrs. Taylor arch her hand on the blackboard and write the homework assignments. Octavia copied her signature so that she could practice writing her name out with as much care and beauty as Mrs. Taylor did every day. Mrs. Taylor was a nice teacher who harbored a mean streak. Most of the kids were scared of her, and she preferred it that way. However, Octavia knew differently. Mrs. Taylor just preferred order and quiet, like Daddy. It was either order or terror.

Mrs. Taylor once gave Octavia a nugget of advice while writing the afternoon assignments on the board before sitting down for her quick nap.

"Octavia, this is a man's world. Women can only get so far. Therefore, you have to be better than the best. Be a team player, but you must be better than them if you plan on getting ahead . . . if you want to become powerful."

Mrs. Taylor enforced Black History Month throughout the year. In her class, if she asked you a question, you better have an answer. However, on Black History Month, she would quiz students on famous leaders. Every Tuesday afternoon in February, Mrs. Taylor distributed the quiz.

"Does anyone have any questions?" Then she glared at all twenty-one students, daring anyone to utter a sound. A few days later, she would return the papers. Octavia got 100 percent. Toby Olusemi looked over Octavia's shoulder at her grade.

"You make me sick! Why do you always get straight As? Make the rest of us look bad."

Mrs. Taylor chimed in, "Toby, mind your own business. If you would study then neither you, nor the whole class would have anything to worry about."

Octavia looked at the quiz later in the evening after finishing her math problems. She got the eerie feeling that one day she would be like one of those famous people they wrote about in the history books. Maybe she would patent an invention. She did not have the slightest idea how these thoughts entered her mind, but she entertained them as long as possible. Someday, her name, Octavia Kalu, would be in print in the history books as some famous African for the world to see.

Chapter 4

"Let me give you a glimpse of purpose..."

"Ms. James, you seem to have a knack for understanding people."

Vernice Cole, the school counselor, told a teenage Benevolence as she sat in front of her in the cramped, hot office, typing letters of recommendation for college. An island breeze pushed a few papers to the left side of the desk. It did little to cool off anyone. Venice Cole was raised in the old Martinique way, heavy into island traditions. She encouraged all of the kids at St. Martin High to do the same. In her late forties, she cherished the "librarian" look, her grayish brown hair tightly pushed back into a bun, gray suit with nude stockings, and nursing shoes. She spoke propaganda, which many misguided, ill-nurtured teenagers took as the gospel. A few bucked at her words. Benevolence was one of them. Benevolence let the breeze blow away negative thoughts. She waited.

"But I don't think that you need to go to the states to do what you want to do."

"Are you kidding?"

Benevolence laughed. Her chocolate skin, full lips, and deep brown eyes presented an image of defiance as she folded her arms and looked Mrs. Cole squarely in the eye.

"What do you suggest I do then, Mrs. Cole?"

Like I don't already know.

"Well, there are a number of schools here that could take care of your needs. Fill that appetite. And I'm sure there are gentlemen here who could suit your fancy."

"I'm not interested."

"Well, it doesn't have to be right now. Think about it. Trust me. I'm only thinking of what's best." Mrs. Cole smiled. Her smile revealed her laugh lines forming around her mouth. She used that smile to clinch the deal, sending any prospective graduate students away from state schools and back to the countryside. Benevolence stood up and gathered her knapsack.

"Thank you, Mrs. Cole. I'll think about it."

Benevolence walked out of the heat of Mrs. Cole's office, closing the foolishness of those words behind her.

Benevolence applied to Howard University, North Carolina A&T, Virginia Union, and Lincoln University. She was never good at following orders especially when it concerned her well-being. She could always detect when people's intentions weren't honorable. She chose Howard. Ever since Benevolence was little, she became a champion for the underdog. She developed the ability to negotiate for the underdog, though unsuccessfully at times, being the second oldest of four. Benevolence solved problems. She could be very resourceful when the need called for it. Most of her girlfriends disclosed their innermost secrets. The kind of secrets only told off the beaten paths walking home.

Her fondest memories were at home, climbing banana trees, playing soccer, and working in the pineapple plantation with her father. Being the youngest girl, they groomed her to be a proper young woman, but her tomboyish ways often overrode everything. Benevolence wanted fun. She ran track and played soccer. Soccer helped strengthen her legs, but her mother was concerned that Benevolence would suffer head injuries so Benevolence negotiated and focused solely on the field events, throwing javelin and shot put. Her abilities and strength grew, placing second in both events in the tri-city championships her senior year. When the prospect of college loomed, Benevolence was excited about the opportunity to come to the States. She went to her mother to discuss her options.

Valentina James, a stout woman with a strong voice, served as the island's "medicine" woman. She worked as a midwife for many years before she acquired enough schooling to become a nurse. Later, she would itch to mix and pound country "extracts" together in a mortar to aid the sick. All of the children worked in the store a few miles down the road during the summer break. The store had vitamins, supplies, food, island perfume, artifacts, and relics. Valentina James was in the store, grinding some leaves in the mortar when Benevolence decided to try her newest approach.

"Mummy, what do you think about me going to school in the States?" Benevolence inquired.

"Well, it sounds far."

Valentina continued to grind the leaves into pieces.

"What do you want to take up?"

"I want to travel and minister to people. I think I want to major in theology."

"That's good, dear, but I don't think you need to go to the States for that. We need help here."

She tapped the mortar to shake up her leaf particles.

"Mummy, there's more opportunity for me in the States."

"Yes, but with that major you will struggle."

She began to grind harder.

"How will you support yourself? Make a living? You can help others but help yourself too." She put the mortar and pestle down.

"Can't you stay here and help me with the business?"

"Mummy, we've talked about this."

Benevolence stood her ground.

"Bene, you are very resourceful. You could do both here. You wouldn't be so far away. Why do my kids all want to move away?"

"William's close. Florida is not too far. Besides, Francois and Rosette will probably do their studies here. C'mon, Mummy, please?"

Benevolence was not about to whine. She kept her voice even and calm.

"Talk to your father." Valentina acquiesced.

"I'll go with what he says."

She picked up the mortar and began grinding again.

Mummy wanted the entire family to run the store, but Benevolence had dreams of her own. Benevolence fell in love with Jesus at ten years of age. By the time she entered secondary school, the curriculum gave plenty of opportunities to learn other religions besides Christianity. When she graduated from St. Martin High, she decided to attend Howard University in Washington DC. Deciding that she still liked negotiating and helping the underdog, Benevolence majored in psychology. Howard University in the eighties was nothing but culture shock. It hit Benevolence like a stack of bricks. Nothing but black faces in all of her classes, all of the time. A few white professors taught classes but not many. "Black pride" stepped all over campus like a sorority. She savored all of the moments. Washington DC was "chocolate city."

Moreover, Howard had its own legacy, being the oldest black university in the country with its rich 141-year-old history and traditions. It boasted of notable alumni including entertainer sisters Phylicia Rashad and Debbie Allen, former Jamaican prime minister, Dr. Percival Broderick, gospel artist Richard Smallwood, Supreme Court Justice Thurgood Marshall, and chemist, Dr. Percy Julian. Many of the professors were alumni themselves. They continued to instill the essentials of the school's history and its presence into the students. It seemed, sometimes, they knew history all too well. Benevolence attended football games, basketball games, socials, and campus crusades with one of her roommates, Wilma Richards, a shorthaired, mocha-colored journalism major from Louisiana. Wilma's twang was just as thick as Benevolence's accent. Conversations, at times needed a friendly interpreter, but they soon adjusted. Benevolence's other roommate, Rona Roberts, was from Chicago. The political science major was pure grit on Howard's campus. Her afro puffs, bell-bottom pants, motorcycle jacket, and platform shoes gave her, as much presence as the other "fashionables" on campus, but it was the *Norma Rae* attitude that had many stand up and take notice. They were the dynamic trio.

However, when it came to campus crusade, Benevolence seemed set apart. She studied the Bible in her spare time and grew in evangelism. Later, she minored in religious studies. She grew in wisdom and patience. She studied leaders on campus. She met many leaders but few who would mentor, strengthen, and care for her. After four years, she graduated with a bachelor's degree in psychology but decided to stay and pursue her masters in divinity and counseling. Rona, her roommate, also stayed behind to pursue masters in fine arts. Benevolence went to her advisor to discuss her options, as she saw an opportunity for dual masters.

"Ms. James, I am afraid, that won't be possible. The course load is extremely heavy. Only few have done it and not always with the best results."

She tried to reassure Benevolence.

"Trust me; you'll be fine without the concentration."

"Thank you, I'll think about it."

Benevolence never heeded the warning. She tested out of three prerequisite courses with the help from the dean. It alleviated some of the stress. Benevolence pushed mentally through a strenuous three years. At Howard, God seemed to strengthen Benevolence, bringing her into maturity with her spiritual gifts, elevating her wisdom and pairing her with a group of pioneers that would forever change the way that she looked at Christian leadership.

Chapter 5

"Coming to your senses..."

"I paint because it helps me, but you guys . . . you can paint for any reason you want."

Twenty-three-year-old Yasmine Blue declared to her fourth- and fifth-grade students on the first floor classroom at Harriet Tubman Elementary. As a senior, Yasmine decided to take an independent study art class that allowed her to become a teaching assistant at the elementary school. Tubman Elementary located in East Manhattan, a lower-income section of New York City, was a melting pot of African, Puerto-Rican, Asian, Italian, and white kids, who came to an enrichment class twice a week for two hours. Yasmine allowed them to paint their cares away using watercolors, chalk, acrylic, and stencils. The kids were from urban schools with limited or nonexistent art programs, so they traveled from one end of the city to the other to get a glimpse, a taste of a new world contrary to their own.

Parents came in as Yasmine cleaned up. Curious mothers, fathers, older sisters, and brothers picked up used canvasses and knapsacks as they head out of the door. One of the younger fathers, Mr. Bennett, was particularly fascinated at the array of works painted by some of the children. He waited for his eight-year-old son, Robert, to put away his stencils.

"Ms. Blue, the work you do here is amazing. The kids definitely enjoy it."

"Thank you."

"Are you an art major?" Yasmine smiled.

"Sort of. I am biochemistry major at NYU. Studio art is my minor. I am more apt to mix chemicals than paint."

"That's interesting. Sounds like it should be switched."

"Once upon time, I guess it was."

In elementary school, Yasmine attended special classes with one instructor, Mrs. Tolbert. Yasmine wrote stories. She wrote her thoughts and poems in a journal as best as she could. They continued the ritual every day during the morning sessions at the Culver Art Academy in Los Angeles.

Then one morning, Mrs. Tolbert brought a box of wooden paintbrushes and a palette of colors. She asked Yasmine to help her decorate another classroom with some paintings she needed to finish. They pushed the desks to one side of the room, leaving an open space for a canvas and an easel. Mrs. Tolbert specified hues of gray, brown, orange, and blue in what appeared to be a montage of shapes, sizes, and objects in the painting. As Yasmine began to draw, a wonder came over her. Time froze. It was just a gifted young girl on a big canvas. She drew different shapes and intertwined them together as if they were family until they formed the image she saw in her mind. Mrs. Tolbert looked at Yasmine, curiously watching her focus. Yasmine's energy danced in between canvases like ballerinas.

"Yasmine, how are you doing?"

Yasmine, absorbed in her own painting paradise, did not hear anyone calling.

"Yes, Mrs. Tolbert? Did you want me?"

"Let me see what you've done."

Mrs. Tolbert came over to look at the painting. She picked it up as if she had suddenly found some lost treasure. She looked at the painting in amazement. She glanced at Yasmine and again at the painting.

"Yasmine, I am so sorry. I have been wasting your time. From now on, this is what we'll do." From then on, she read fashion magazines, wrote poems, short stories, essays, and painted. She spent most of the time painting. Yasmine was so absorbed in her own memories; she did not notice Mr. Bennett and Robert moving toward the door.

"I'll see you next week, Ms. Blue."

"Next week? Oh yes, next week. Mr. Bennett."

Yasmine met them at the door. They shook hands.

"You can call me Jason."

"Jason. Good-bye."

"Bye, Ms. Blue!"

Robert cried out. He ran in between them to give her a hug. Yasmine bent down and cheered Robert on.

"Great job today."

She whispered in his ear. Robert grinned. She stood up and looked directly in Jason's eyes.

"You guys have a good week."

"You do the same, Ms. Blue."

They walked out. Jason turned once more to steal a glance at Yasmine, only to find she was looking directly at him. He winked and walked away. Yasmine went back to picking up stencils. One stencil looked oddly familiar. There was an inscription from her father. She stared at it for a moment before placing the stencils and paintbrushes into her perfume-shaped container.

Yasmine was the apple of Jessica and Jeremiah's eyes. Her mother taught English and language arts in California's public school system while her father represented some of the state's biggest clients in the entertainment industry. Yasmine idolized her parents. Jeremiah Blue was a vision of brilliance, extravagance, and creativity. Yasmine was daddy's little girl. She would beg to go business parties with her father, as long as she did not become anyone's nuisance. Jeremiah had business dinners often, as it was the nature of the business and the best way to schmooze new clients. The Christmas parties seemed to be the best time of the year to wrap up loose ends.

One Christmas, when Yasmine was ten, Jeremiah decided not to take the family out for dinner. He picked up Yasmine from school earlier in the afternoon and returned quickly to the office to greet his partners and guests before leaving the party. Yasmine doodled in his office quietly. Unfortunately, the call of nature came, and Yasmine had to pee. She snuck out of the office down the hall to the bathroom, but not before, she saw her father whispering into the ear of some strange woman near the stairs.

He laughed. She laughed. They carried on like friends, or maybe even more than friends. He kissed her softly on the cheek and left to attend to some other guests.

What *was that? What was Daddy doing? Did Mommy know?* Suddenly, Yasmine remembered nature's impatience calling her and rushed into the bathroom.

Is Daddy having an affair? Will he leave us? Will he leave me?

Fear struck her ten-year-old mind as she felt life without Daddy would be impossible. Yasmine ran out of the bathroom and right into her father.

"There you are. I figured that's where you went. Let's go."

Driving later that evening in the car, Yasmine blurted out her fears.

"Daddy, are you going to leave Mommy and me?"

"Where on earth did you get that from?"

"Do you always kiss other women besides Mommy?" He blushed.

"Yasmine, I'm sorry. Sometimes, Daddy can be a bit too friendly. It is harmless. I want people to feel comfortable. That way if I need a favor, if I asked nicely, they will help me. No, I do not plan to go anywhere, not without my beautiful and precious Yasmine. I love you and your mother. Your mother knows I love her. She knows me. She knows my ways."

Jeremiah walked into the house. Jessica was in the kitchen with a glass of champagne while the housekeeper cooked dinner.

"Honey, we're back."

Jessica Blue walked out of the kitchen and into her husband's arms. He kissed her softly on the cheek and pulled out a small box. They walked upstairs. The next morning, Jessica came down the stairs, smelling like a summer's breeze, while Jeremiah came downstairs in a blue t-shirt and sweatpants. Yasmine ran down the stairs to the living room in a frenzy to open her presents. Dolls, brushes, Cds, videogames, and a portable Cd player were among the showstoppers. Yasmine could hardly concentrate on breakfast. She poured Golden Grahams into her bowl, while listening to Janet Jackson.

"Yazzy, we'll see you later okay." They headed in different directions; Jeremiah for his early morning run and Jessica to her Christmas soup kitchen. Yasmine and the housekeeper remained in the six-bedroom mansion. Yasmine gobbled down her cereal and stole away upstairs as soon as the coast was clear. Her mother's perfumed scent clouded the air. Yasmine engulfed the mist as she opened the master bedroom. She went to the dresser to check out her mother's latest editions. There were twenty to forty bottles of perfume, each having its own design, scent, and designation, staking their territory in the room. Yasmine picked up the newest addition left on the dresser. She held it briefly to her small nose. It smelled like flowers. Yasmine dabbed it on her skin, behind her ears and on her neck. She grabbed another fragrance from the shelf but heard the housekeeper yell from downstairs.

"Yasmine, are you ready? Please hurry. We don't want to be late getting to the ice skating rink. The lines will get really long today." Yasmine put the bottle neatly back in place. She snuck out of the room and closed the bedroom door.

Chapter 6

"Some actions speak volumes..."

"Leah is a very active child for her age but I don't think you need to worry. She'll grow out of it."

Dr. Nzinga announced. Leah's parents took her to doctor to see why she was so hyperactive at such a tender age of four years. She got into fights with the neighbors' children. They complained she played too rough. She harbored hour-long temper tantrums when she did not get what she wanted. She snatched items without asking, jumped off the furniture, and harassed her older sister Shah and brother Victor daily. Watching her turned into a full-time job. When Leah desired attention, she would cry for hours until someone finally decoded what toy, meal, or video she wanted. In daycare, Leah ran the other girls away, hitting, biting, and sometimes kicking the other children. At home, she ran around the house, screaming like a banshee, to the detriment of her siblings. Leah's parents endured more conferences at school.

"Mr. Decruz, Leah has problems completing her assignments and paying attention. She doesn't follow instructions very well."

The teachers observed and commented to Bernard Decruz who retrieved Leah from the daycare before heading off to the restaurant.

"Yes, my Leah is very active. I hope she has not been too much for you."

He apologized. He held Leah closely as teachers gave him news on her rants and tirades.

"Leah, come sweetie, come here."

Bernard called her later from the living room of their modest three-bedroom house.

"Daddy missed you today."

They would play *tickle monster* and laugh the rest of the afternoon until he left for work. Leah usually did not see him until the next morning.

Bernard Decruz came from India to the United States in the seventies. He worked hard as a chef to make a name for himself in the industry. Often, he endured thirteen-hour days pulling over eighty hours a week. When he met Rosetta, his Trinidadian princess, she was a junior at the University of Maryland in college, studying to be a nurse. Neither of their parents approved of the marriage for it was taboo to mix Hindu with Trini culture. Bernard Decruz had been raised in the Hindu religion while Rosetta was a nonpracticing Muslim. Rosetta became a Hindu. They married in Trinidad and eventually stayed for four years. They had a son, Victor, who was the mirror image of his daddy. A year later, a girl, Shah became the "twin" version of her mother. Two years later, Leah arrived.

The family returned to Silver Spring, Maryland. Bernard operated a small catering business that specialized in West Indian cuisine. He rented out space for many family celebrations and business functions. He spent long hours building clientele. Later he changed the business and called it Caribbean DeLite, which featured many of the dishes he learned to cook in Trinidad. Everyone chipped in to help. The children stacked plates quietly in the kitchen before going off to bed. Leah greeted the early guests with her mother while Bernard cooked. Business soon soared. Within three years, Bernard was breaking even and making some good money. He provided many luxuries for Leah and the family. Rosetta was inspired to finish her nursing degree at the University of Maryland. However, Leah often became the subject of intense conversation. Six-year-old Leah overheard her mother talking on the phone.

"Bernard, can't you come home early tonight? I really need some help with Leah."

"Rosetta, I will try. What is she doing?"

"Bernard, she really needs you. She only quiets down when you are around. Can I bring her there?"

"Rosetta, I can't watch her you know that. Where is Shah? She can help you."

"Shah goes to her room and waits until Leah sleeps before she comes out. They fight too much."

"I'll be home soon, I promise."

Leah knew then that she was a problem for her mother. Even though she grew out of her active stage, her reading issues persisted well into sixth grade. By junior high school, Leah had become a master at disguising her ways. She paid friends to take notes for her because she kept losing her books. She hung out with the cool crowd, ditching school and hiding from truancy to smoke weed.

It calmed her down. Often, she arrived to school late and sat in the back of the class. It never stopped her from making outbursts and anecdotes while instruction occurred. Instead of arguing with teachers at school, she found a way to get her homework in on time by staying up nights to complete it. Puberty struck Leah like lightning, swinging her moods from pleasant promises to cantankerous epitaphs, all the way to outright belligerent rebellions. She argued with her mother about anything and everything. To amuse herself, Leah immersed herself in fashion. Her wardrobe was chic, flashy, and very extravagant for her age. It only added to the friction that she created with other classmates who claimed that Leah thought she was *queen* amongst the peasants.

As much attention she received from her antics, it was always Daddy's attention she secretly longed for. By the tenth grade, Bernard decided that Leah should be home-schooled because her grades were dropping rapidly. For the first few weeks, it was rough. Her mother gave her assignments. She would briefly check in on Leah before attending to her own duties. Leah snuck out of the house to hang out and smoke. She needed to be anywhere but with her mother. Home schooling barely lasted five months. They placed her back into public school. Bernard Decruz encouraged Leah to pursue some extracurricular activities.

"Have you ever considered modeling?" her drama teacher inquired.

"No. All my parents care about is school."

"Well, the junior class fashion show is coming up, it'll be after school and you might be able to get your parents to come."

Leah broadcasted the news to her father.

"My daughter . . . a model?"

"It's for school, Daddy."

"For school? I never knew you were so interested in modeling. Since when?"

"Since now. Daddy, can I do it? Will you come to the show?"

Leah made sure that her father got his money's worth, as she strutted back and forth on the catwalk. He whistled and clapped for his daughter. At that moment, all Leah ever desired was to make him proud of her. She would try her hardest, but it never seemed good enough. Therefore, throughout her teenage years, Leah sashayed her way into situations while her father bailed her out.

"Leah, your father is sick. He had a stroke."

Leah remembered the dissonant phone conversation. She was a junior business major at University of Maryland. Her mother called that sunny morning at ten to drop the news. Leah was running late to calculus class. Leah was curt. Her mother was usually less patient. When Leah heard those words, a cyclone of grief hit her world, blowing away any safety or security she ever felt. Victor who had recently graduated from Cal Tech would look after the business until Daddy got better. Weeks later, Leah began smoking more and drinking heavily. She failed the entire semester and secretly dropped out of school. Leah was determined that she would handle things her way until Daddy got better.

"Leah, your father wants to see you."

Leah went to Prince George's Hospital. Bernard Decruz was the only occupant in room 204. Leah gasped. She barely recognized him. She had never seen him sick in her life. Her heart broke, as tears rolled down her face. She closed the door and ran into the bathroom.

I shouldn't have come alone.

After a few moments, she regained her composure and walked into his room. He was strapped to a monitor with tubes sticking in and out of his nose and body. He looked peaceful with his eyes closed. Leah sat down in the metal chair on the right side of his bed. His eyes opened briefly, sensing someone was there. He searched across the room, finding the apple of his eye. He smiled weakly.

"Sugar plum."

"Yes, Daddy?" she said, hiding sniffles.

"How's school?" Leah had taken a job as a waiter in the diner in College Park.

"Fine, Daddy," she lied.

"Leah, my beautiful Leah. I want the best for you."

"I know, Daddy."

"Leah?"

"Yes, Daddy?"

"I'm sorry. I love—" He could not finish. His voice died. She squeezed his hand and looked into his eyes, blinking away tears.

"I love you too, Daddy."

He smiled. He squeezed her hand hard. He closed his eyes and went back to sleep. With tears streaming down her face, she held on to his hand. She stared at the faint light shining through the window, hoping for another chance for her father to open his eyes.

Bernard Decruz died a month later. He left a will, providing a comfortable inheritance for the family. He gave the business to the children with some provisions. Victor and Shah wanted nothing to do with the business. They were angry. They were angry with Daddy for leaving this life so early. They resented the fact their father catered to Leah. Victor married and moved to New York. Shah stayed with her mother in Maryland. She became a public school teacher. Rosetta hired a managing company to run the business. She needed time away herself. Though the family was financially set, Leah wanted independence, so she continued to wait tables at the same diner. Leah served her grief on a platter. She was not a very good waiter. She screwed up orders or forgot about them. The bills always needed straightening out. She worked until she could will herself into becoming the best employee she knew. After work, she drank her grief to sleep. She missed Daddy every moment of every single day. No amount of cigarettes, weed, or vodka could dull the pain in her heart.

After four years, she became the manager. However, one partly sunny morning, she was serving coffee to a man who was somewhat of a celebrity, after covering a shift of a server who recently quit. Kendrick O'Riley, the son of Kenneth O'Riley, merged O'Riley's restaurant into franchises in other states. At six feet, 215 pounds, with cocoa skin, full lips, and eyes the color of midnight; Kendrick looked like a linebacker with glasses. He was charming but appeared a tad bit too confident of himself. Their meeting was uneventful. Leah later read about her newest customer and his chains of success. Kendrick O'Riley transformed the art of hospitality into a science using the latest technologies in equipment manufacturing. Even the architecture of the buildings had a certain renaissance flare. Kendrick, intrigued by the spunk of his saucy waiter, kept randomly stopping in. They exchanged numbers. They talked on the phone one evening after Leah closed up the diner.

"Leah, have you ever thought about going into the restaurant business for yourself?"

"Sometimes. I want to take over my father's business, but I'm not ready."

"Sure you are. I'll help you."

They began dating, and he mentored her. Kendrick showed Leah the latest hiring techniques, menu designs, and computer technology. Even customer specifications became commonplace to Leah.

After three more years, Leah took over her father's restaurant, Caribbean DeLite. Profits began trickling in like old times. Leah even cooked up possibilities of franchise opportunities in the near future. Everything seemed to be falling into place. One of the regular patrons raved about a church in Hyattsville with a good choir, young people, and a preaching bishop. Though Leah had never really been to church, she told Kendrick, hoping for insight. Kendrick gave his blessing. She attended a few meetings. The atmosphere was electric. She started coming more often. This was brand-new territory. After eighteen months of attending the services, Leah made a decision: she gave her life to Jesus Christ and became a member of Faith and Victory International Church. Leah's world simmered with new ingredients of hope and expectation.

Chapter 7

*"God can take a past problem and make it
a prophetic promise into your future..."*

With Bible study cut short, Benevolence gave out brief assignments and dismissed class. Many inquired to see if Simone was all right. The guys in the class walked all the women out to their cars, making sure they drove out safely. Leah, Octavia, and Yasmine stayed behind. Although strangers, they recognized each other's faces and their respective ministries on Sundays. Benevolence walked back into the room shortly.

"Minister James, is she all right?" Leah inquired.

"She's been through a lot. She is going to need some support. I would like, if any of you feel comfortable, to befriend her. You are all in the same class but I am not trying to put any pressure on any of you. I will give you numbers next week. Deacon Davis, can you escort these women to their cars? Afterwards, could you come back? I want to make sure that someone follows Simone home. It's not safe for her to drive under these conditions."

"No problem."

Benevolence left and went to the children's room. Grief slapped her in the face as she opened the door. She braced herself. Simone sat in the room, staring at the wall. Her dreams of happiness faded into the cumulus clouds that covered the mural. Benevolence sat next to Simone. She gave Simone a handkerchief.

"Do you need some water?" Simone stared in a trance.

"He left me."

"Who left you?" More silence. Simone stared into a fog. Her thoughts gathered slowly from the emotional rain that had just poured forth.

"Tavian dumped me." She breathed in sips of air.

"He dumped me tonight."

"Did he say why?"

"He's not ready. He says he's not ready. He does not know why, but he cannot marry me. He said that he loves me but he just can't do it."

Simone began crying again. Benevolence held her gently like a mother comforting a scared daughter frightened of a storm. Simone sobbed right into her arms.

"It's like a nightmare that I can't seem to wake up from."

Simone confessed to Octavia in her car weeks later. Two weeks after joining Faith and Victory, Simone gave her life to Christ with Tavian following a few weeks after.

"I never saw this coming. All of the planning, the monies we've spent. Almost thirty thousand dollars. I just cannot believe this. I got back eight or nine thousand back but the rest just went down the drain."

"Have you talked to him since?"

Octavia got Simone's number after the Bible study class and left a message. Simone had not quite connected with any of the cell groups or other church members. Her life revolved around school and Tavian. Tavian was her best friend, lover, and confidant. Now for the first time in years, she felt very alone. Reality had finally begun to set in. However, Octavia kept calling. She left messages, enough for Simone to notice. Two weeks later, Simone returned Octavia's messages.

Octavia spoke to Simone at church, but Simone would smile meekly and sprint out like Florence Griffith-Joyner after service. People bombarded Simone with sincere apologies. Others tried to coax her for the latest prayer gossip. Simone needed an ally. One Wednesday afternoon, Simone invited Octavia out to lunch. It lasted four hours. They walked to the mall where Simone met and fell in love with three pairs of designer-style boots that weren't on sale. Simone packed the boots and got into her 2002 black Cadillac Escapade.

"I know they weren't on sale but I just wanted them. Get in. I'll drive you to your car."

They chatted until Simone drove Octavia back to her car. She parked the jeep. Her heart exploded a canon of feelings. Octavia just listened. Simone poured from her belly rivers of frustrations, fears, and hopes. Anger and grief whispered constantly in her ear. Octavia did the best she could to comfort her. Two hours later, Simone and Octavia drove off in their respective cars. It was the beginning of a true friendship and, undoubtedly, more sisterly meetings in the black Cadillac Escapade.

Chapter 8

"Everything always looks good in the beginning..."

I have to get this job. I have to do well here. I know I can do this. Twenty-eight-year-old Octavia exclaimed to herself, as she strapped on the seat belt of her crimson 2003 Acura TL and began driving down Sixteenth Street. She thought of her conversations with Simone. She could not imagine what she was going through. Octavia had always chosen her career over men. She found relationships to be difficult and taxing. She found that men weren't receptive to the type of career that she envisioned for herself. It afforded less time for distractions.

After two years of disappointing venues in Chicago both personally and professionally, Octavia returned to Washington DC. Her father owned an African store in Adams Morgan, which he managed for years. The whole family still pitches in. Octavia had been temping for eight months as a patent paralegal. She prepared documents, litigation research, novelty searches, and patent filings. There was plenty of overtime but little travel except for the frequent visits back and forth to the patent and trademark office in Virginia. It was just a matter of time before Octavia began itching to manage her own caseload and not someone else's.

A Sunday search in the newspaper uncovered a new downtown position for an intellectual property associate at a firm called Huffman & Associates. Training is provided; opportunities opened to grow in a new field. It was located on K Street, near the financial district. She applied for the position.

It was a rainy Monday morning, having stormed all day Sunday and well into the night. DC morning traffic was monstrously backed up, and Octavia was already arriving later than her fifteen minutes "on-early" ritual. She would just make her ten o' clock interview with a few minutes to spare. She walked into the main building wearing a graceful, striped, silvery grey business suit, carrying her black leather briefcase. She signed in at the security desk while the security officer, a handsome Latino, handed her a visitor's pass.

"Ma'am, what floor?"

"Eighth."

"Ah *si*. Many go up there. Interview?"

"*Si.*"

"How you say, good luck?"

"*Gracias.*"

Octavia smiled. She instantly felt calmer. She took her badge and walked down the hallway to the elevators. Inside, the elevators boasted marble and gold molding along the walls. The doors opened like golden plates. Octavia checked her hair, which was a little damp from the misty air but still curly. When the elevator doors opened on to the eighth floor, Octavia charged out and turned right into two huge glass double doors. The doors appeared eight feet tall. A cherry oak wooden desk stood in the center of the room. A white woman, midfifties, with rimmed glasses and a librarian-style hair bun, wearing a pink shirt, greeted her between phone calls.

"Hi, can I help you?"

"Yes, my name is Octavia Kalu and I'm here for an interview."

"Oh yes. Ms. Kalu, have a seat and I will let Mr. Huffman know you're here."

Within a few minutes, a man, who mildly resembled Sean Connery, wearing khaki pants and a green Polo sweater came to the desk.

"Ms. Kalu?"

"Yes?"

"Come in. I am Roger Huffman. It is a pleasure to meet you."

He ushered Octavia into the main conference room. Murals paneled the high ceilings. The room was elegant, with lamp chandeliers, a maple wood table, plush leather chairs, stylish telephones for teleconferences, and the latest audiovisual equipment for video conferencing.

Wow, this room definitely gets a gold star.

Two other attorneys greeted Octavia. Brandi Nickels, a redhead wearing a black striped suit, immediately noticed Octavia's confidence.

Rod Cummings, the star struck young associate, immediately noticed Octavia's blackness. The firm didn't have many black attorneys, except Raymond Parsons, the first black partner to join the firm.

Most of the clientele came from government, nonprofit, and private practice. Huffman & Associates had many accounts in the city: SEC filings, antitrust cases, and tons of civil suits. They wanted to build their intellectual property department. This newly created department had the potential to add millions to their portfolio; they wholly took advantage of it.

"So, Ms. Octavia Ka . . . lu? Is that correct?"

"Yes."

"Tell me about yourself. Your resume is very impressive. I see you went to University of Chicago, my alma mater."

The other two associates nodded in obvious approval. Mr. Huffman explained the position. He looked everywhere, but at Octavia at times. Then he would stare into her eyes, trying to preview what she was thinking. Octavia did not shrink back. She liked the power he was trying to unveil. She stared right back.

"Ms. Kalu, we're developing an intellectual property department here and we need talented individuals like you to get it up and running smoothly. We're looking to bring more associates on board and a senior attorney to head the department. Brandi, here currently handles litigation."

Brandi saw her opportunity.

"It's a great place to work. You will learn a lot. Your background could fit well in here."

Brandi adamantly expressed the benefit of working at Huffman. She was happy for the prospect of another female on board. Octavia nodded. Rod felt it was his turn to speak. His words sounded practiced.

"Ms. Kalu, Huffman & Associates is an established firm with a strong reputation in the District. Our clients trust us. There are benefits that come with that kind of reputation."

Rod offered benefits for the position however; the prospect of a black woman coming on board was an idea he would have to accept. The interview lasted forty-five minutes. Everyone shook hands. Mr. Huffman led Octavia back to the receptionist desk.

"Ms. Kalu, we will be calling you next week to let you know what we've decided. Thanks for coming."

As Octavia walked out of the building, she smiled at the security guard. The nametag spelled Felipe. He nodded.

"Have a good day, *senorita*."

"Thank you."

Octavia felt confident she made the right impression. She hoped she would be greeting Felipe on a more permanent basis.

Two weeks later, Octavia walked into her Adams Morgan co-op to her kitchen with a ton of groceries when she saw her voice mail blinking with two messages. She placed the groceries on the floor near the fridge. She set the bottle of apple juice onto the kitchen counter before hopping over the ottoman to check her voice mail.

"Good Afternoon, this message is for Octavia Kalu. Octavia, this is Raymond Parsons with Huffman & Associates. I apologize for not being able to come to your interview but I have heard great things about you. Ms. Kalu, we would like to extend you an offer to come and work with our firm. I think you will be a crucial asset to this firm and we like to take the advantage and snatch up great talent when we find it. We will be sending your acceptance letter in the mail. We look forward to working with you, Octavia. Have a good day."

"Aah!"

Octavia cackled so loud she never even heard the second message. She danced around the living room, praising and shouting like an African wedding worshipper. After a few minutes of ritualistic praise, Octavia collapsed on her camel brown leather sofa, picked up the phone, and dialed.

"Hello?"

"Daddy, I got the job! Sixty thousand with benefits."

"Hey! You can give me some money now! That is good, baby. Did you doubt you wouldn't? Show them what you can do. They haven't seen anything yet. Go talk to your mother, the truck just came in."

"Hi, Mummy."

"Octavie, you did well. I am proud of you. You work hard. You always work hard."

"Thank you, Mummy. Mummy, how are you?"

"Well, Octavie, I'm okay. I have not been feeling well. I think it is a cold. I have to get more rest. Your brother and sister are fine. They miss you. You should come and see them more."

"Soon, Mummy, it will be soon. Let me get settled."

"You're not settled yet? It has been eight months. Please, Octavie, you have to look after your brother and sister. Omar is Omar. Sade? Well, Sade looks up to you, Octavie. She is not as strong as you."

Octavia heard glass crash to the floor.

"What was that? Adolphus! Let me go, Octavie. There is always something going on in here. Always a customer who needs something. They cannot find anything themselves anymore. We put everything in the same place, eh? Eh! What did they break? Octavie, let me go, okay?"

"Bye, Mummy."

"Bye, my dear." Octavia sat back on her couch and closed her eyes. She wanted this feeling to last forever.

Chapter 9

"Girl, you know me . . . with men, it's either feast or famine . . ."

Yasmine knew that moving to DC was a big step. New York with its bustling city life, frantic lifestyle, filled with off-Broadway theatres, music, and restaurants could compete and win easily over DC's cosmopolitan, "hanging with the Joneses" political lifestyle. However, Yasmine wanted to smell new experiences. Since Cadence Ivey, her best friend, landed a job in Capitol Hill in the senate page program, they would help each other ease the transition.

Washington DC is known for many things—its seemingly immaculate metro system, its politics, and its social atmosphere. Often its political and social atmosphere seemed to mix, particularly with the men. Some men were definitely more social than political and vice versa. No matter what the mix, the array of men that seemed to be available in DC would be an aroma that Yasmine would soon uncover.

Yasmine stepped on to the metro on her way to work. Three years in nation's capital, a twenty-six-year-old Yasmine Blue finally began to marinate in her Capitol Hill surroundings. Yasmine opted for the two-bedroom condominium as Cadence felt it would be closer to her job, and with both their salaries, they could afford the living and some amenities. Yasmine got assistance from her parents who felt that the Capitol Hill location would be suitable living. They paid the security deposit and gave Yasmine enough money to buy furniture. DC seemed to be shaping up, but not without a few surprises. Yasmine took a window seat right by the metro map. A business suit with dreadlocks sat across from her and winked. Yasmine smiled back and turned to view the continuous construction going on by New York Avenue.

The dating scene in the district was not too much different from New York's. At first, Yasmine was the wallflower waiting to bloom, waiting for the right man to pollinate her. With DC's men shortage and the plethora of men flowing in and out of the transient town, Yasmine soon found that she might be sleeping on opportunity. However, if there seemed to something that God could get her attention on, it would be the "Adams" he created. Italian, Brazilian, Mexican, Hungarian, El Salvadorian, Samoan, Jamaican, African, British—there were just too many "Adams" to choose.

Cadence says I don't know what I want. Only God knows. He probably wants me to leave them alone!

Yasmine soon thought about Simone and the drama from a couple weeks ago. She wondered how she would ever handle a breakup from a boyfriend, let alone a fiancé. She had always been on the left side of the equation: the breaker. She gave little thought to how the "breakees" mourned or how they handled the news. She no longer deemed the emotional investments any of her concern.

Yasmine's thoughts faded into the darkness of the tunnel. Her thoughts simmered on Kwame Jones, five feet eight inches, brown eyes, curly hair, full lips, and with Jamaican roots. He bragged about knowing the members of some of DC's most original bands. Yasmine often heard how rare it was to meet a native Washingtonian. She met Kwame during "happy hour" one Friday evening at the Java Café in northeast. A few of her co-workers wanted to check it out, and since they knew the MC, they invited Yasmine to come along. Friday was "open mike" night.

The MC, Jarrell Homes, a short stocky brother with long silky dreads walked up onto the metal stage, grabbed the microphone, and acquainted himself with the audience.

"Ladies and gents. Thank you all for coming out. You know how we do.

Tis Friday eve, and we'll here to conceive all the rhymes and rituals.
Are you ready to proceed?
Poets and Laureates shake things up
They don't give up
Till the rhythm shakes you . . .
Till rhythm bakes you . . .
Till it, till it, till it overtakes you . . .
Cause the rhythms be comin´
Like the river be flowin´
But you don't be knowing . . .

Betta´ check out each showing
Cause they'll have ya spinnin´ and they'll have ya grinning till you
think you're sinnin´
But you'll just be livin´,
On that DC high!
But let me go so those words can fly
My time is up, Let me hit the sky!
Ladies and gents, fly high. Fly high! Java Café."

The audience shouted and clapped as the MC stepped down. As the next performer took the stage, Sharon, one of Yasmine's more romantically inclined colleagues spotted some eye candy on her radar that spoke louder than the rhymes onstage.

"Yasmine. Girl, there is a tall glass of water staring your way! Whew! Just looking at him is making me thirsty."

"Where?"

Yasmine jerked her head over and then thought better of it.

Gotta be cool.

Kwame pimped over, and Yasmine literally had to catch her breath.

"Is this seat taken?"

As he walked over, light surrounded his entire body.

"No, unless you're going to take it."

Yasmine came back coolly.

"Kwame." He extended his hand in Yasmine's direction.

"Kwame Jones."

"Yasmine."

She accepted the gesture.

"Yasmine Blue."

Where am I again?

The conversation took off, and everyone else in the café faded like silhouettes in a background portrait. Kwame soon became the centerpiece. The next few weeks were bliss. They went out dancing, basketball games, poetry venues, and jazz clubs—everywhere. They became Siamese twins.

Yasmine found herself getting very intense in her relationship very quickly. Cadence and the others never really understood why. Yasmine felt the "love bug" and had to go with it. Unfortunately, all good things must come to a bitter end, and after three months, the honeymoon appeared to be over.

"Kwame is always in my face. Calling me or sending me crazy notes and e-mails. He's smothering me."

Yasmine complained to Cadence on the metro one day on their way home from work.

"I thought things were good between you two." Cadence cross-examined.

"It is. It was. I just think I'm losing my freedom. It just doesn't feel right anymore. It's getting too serious."

That was the end of Kwame Jones. Yasmine couldn't take it. She had to find some way to get rid of him, and fast. As it turned out, Kwame seldom attended church. He said it just to impress Yasmine. Sundays were always the Lord's time, so Yasmine made a point not to stay out too late Saturday evenings. Instead, she fellowshipped with the saints and hung out with Cadence and her girlfriends.

Faith and Victory International had a young, mixed congregation with a compassionate bishop and a spicy pastor. Yasmine always enjoyed the worship service. She had just joined the outreach ministry, which did prayer walks, soup kitchens, and evangelized the gospel out into the Maryland and DC streets. There seemed to be a strong magnetic pull toward the ministry. The magnet may have been Deacon Darius Baylor, a honey-colored southerner from Louisiana with a commanding voice and charm who headed the ministry. By this time, the warm and fuzzies were fizzing out of Kwame and Yasmine's relationship, and she wanted the Holy Spirit's permission to give her the "release." Yasmine's four-month-dating anniversary was approaching and Kwame arranged a special brunch on the Spirit of Washington. Yasmine enjoyed her brunch and broke it off two weeks later.

Kwame called Yasmine at home on that evening like clockwork. After the normal pleasantries, Kwame began his usual rambling. However, he could hear, understand, and finish his own sentences. Yasmine sat in her living room with a green Gap sweater and jeans, flicking channels on her twenty-seven-inch flat panel screen with the phone on speaker.

"Yazzy? Baby, what is wrong? Did I do something?"

"Yes."

"Tell me what I did so I can change it."

"No, I don't think so, KJ."

"You've been distant. What is wrong? Is it church, work? What is it?"

Yasmine had not even considered the thought, but now it was the perfect excuse.

"KJ . . . you know, I think this relationship is complicating what I need to be doing. It's as if we're . . . um . . . unequally yoked or something. Do you understand?"

Yasmine flicked the channels slower.

"What are you talking about? I go to church. I'm not a holy roller like you but I go. It didn't seem to bother you before?" Kwame whined.

"I just didn't realize it before."

Yasmine set the remote down and began filing her nails.

"I guess I was caught up. Look, KJ, I think it would be best if we took some time to, um . . . refocus."

Yasmine told him to stop calling. Afterward, she fasted for one week. She gave away all of her "Kwame" items. She called Cadence and others and profusely apologized for deserting them during her "suitor" period. Yasmine mourned by taking the girls to Ozio's in Dupont Circle and then to Blues Alley in Georgetown for some jazz.

"Doors closing."

The metro doors closed quickly. The doorbell chimed louder than usual or perhaps just loud enough to break Yasmine out her brief trip down memory lane.

"Next station will be Friendship Heights."

A melodic voice echoed from the ceiling. Yasmine jolted up as she heard the doors jam forward toward each other. She sighed and settled back into her seat. Thoughts of a new prospect stormed through the metro tunnel.

Byron Combs. Sophisticated, intelligent and bowlegged. Hmm, hmm, hmm!

Meeting Byron Combs seemed like a royal event. Yasmine had been in the lab early mixing lilac alcohols with a Spanish jasmine substance when Susan Walters, her supervisor, walked in with a six-foot, pecan-colored, Terrance Howard look-a-like dressed in a gray pinstriped, double-breasted suit that hung on him like a newly crowned king and his robe. He was absolutely too fine for words. As he walked in, it seemed even in the daytime, light surrounded his entire body.

"Byron, Yasmine is one of our most promising new formulation chemists from the crop of burgeoning talent we've brought in. In the few short years she's been here at Cyprus Pharmaceutical, she's made quite a name for herself. She has an instinct for scents. She's already on her way to creating a patentable fragrance. Byron Combs meet Yasmine Blue."

"Hello, Yasmine."

As Byron spoke, his rich deep voice roared with the sound of authority that made everything around him stand at attention.

"Byron. It is a pleasure to meet you."

Whoowee! Lord have mercy!

Their eyes locked briefly, and for a moment, it was heaven.

"Byron will be head of production." Susan beamed. "You two will be seeing a lot of each other and I expect sparks to fly!"

Byron smiled. He showed a perfect set of white teeth.

Jesus, I owe you one.

"It was a pleasure meeting you, Yasmine."

"Likewise."

Yasmine smiled. She wanted to watch them walk away until she remembered her precious experiment. She went to the fume hood and checked her distillation apparatus to see that most of the jasmine solution had almost drained completely away.

"Better get back to work, excuse me."

The doorbells of the metro chimed once more.

"Doors opening!"

Yasmine woke up just as the doors opened for Rockville metro station. She grabbed her purse and headed up the escalators.

Chapter 10

"If pain and frustration were grades, I'd have a 4.0..."

Caribbean DeLite was the misfit West Indian restaurant located in downtown Silver Spring in the 1980s. It was the neighborhood restaurant when downtown was not a neighborhood. Lunchtime was the most profitable time of the day. In the last few years, downtown Silver Spring had gotten a massive face-lift: new restaurants emerged, independent movie theatres moved in, and Borders bookstore arrived. Leah decided that Caribbean DeLite needed a new look.

Leah took care of much of the details, since Omar and Shah shied away from the business. While it had been a few years since their father's death, Leah hoped renovations would help her deal with her own grief and maybe move her forward. She brought in an artist to paint portraits of the "Trini island life" using warm colors inside the walls. She also installed 1940s vintage booths, a marble countertop bar, a fireplace, and French glass doors for the front entrance.

Caribbean DeLite soon transformed into the Western Indian art deco of downtown Silver Spring. While downtown began to breathe new life with other businesses, Caribbean DeLite flourished with new patrons with a twenty-nine-year-old Leah Decruz at its helm. Every morning had its own share of surprises. Leah was in the kitchen checking on the week's inventory when one of the senior chefs stormed into the kitchen.

"Leah, the inventory is late this week again!"

"Do we have enough food for this week's special?"

"I don't know. I can check, I think we can make it, but you need to talk to the vendors. I don't know what's going on but you need to consider changing vendors. We have a business to run! I can't be scraping and scrounging like this every month."

"Philippe, they've been with us for years. We can't just fire them."

"Leah, if I don't have my food right, I can't cook my specials. Simple as that."

"Philippe, please don't worry. We'll figure something out. Okay?"

Philippe stormed off in a rant as Leah's BlackBerry began to vibrate.

"Hello?"

"Hey, baby, it's me. Just checking to see how your morning is going," Kendrick sang.

"It's going."

"Are we still on for tonight? I've got a surprise for you."

"Hopefully, I don't want to close, but I have to make sure Philippe has everything he needs. The vendors are late again this month."

"Again? I thought you talked with them?"

Kendrick's tone changed.

"Things have been hectic. I never got around to it," Leah apologized.

"I'll take care of it."

"No, Kendrick, I don't want you involved. I can handle it."

"Are you sure?"

"Yes, Kendrick, I'll take care of it. I'll see you tonight."

Leah placed her BlackBerry back on her hip, left the kitchen, and went into her office. She picked up several colored Post-it notes off her desk: there is a flood in the women's bathroom; two managers called out sick; call Horizon foods about your recent order. Leah slammed the notes down on the desk, picked up her purse, and ran outside to the back for a smoke.

Leah seemed to have everything a girl would possibly want: a thriving business, a loving man, and the respect of a few good friends. When Leah met Kendrick, he was in many ways a big brother, mentor, and boyfriend all wrapped up into one. Kendrick was twenty-six, while she was a grief-stricken twenty-year-old server when they met in a diner a few years ago. Kendrick was heavily involved in his father's business. He was smart, older, and knew the Lord. He had this sense of confidence about him that was sexy.

Leah puffed out frustration from her Virginia Slims cigarette. Their relationship was a picnic, a roller-coaster ride, and a whirlwind fantasy all wrapped up in one. For the first three years, Leah and Kendrick's relationship was strictly professional. Leah was eager to learn more of the restaurant industry and was hungry to prove herself. Kendrick made the restaurant business seem like an art form. It was in his blood. She learned new recipes, built menu programs, visited restaurants, studied international menus, pricing, restaurant décor, and service styles. Leah remembered all of the mistakes she made and how patient Kendrick seemed with her. Memories of school failures flooded her mind. Leah stayed determined. This time she would not give up. She became Kendrick's protégé and later, his girlfriend. They had been quite an alliance in the past six years.

I wonder what he is up to tonight. Why can't I get the inventory straight? I hate going through this every week.

Recently, this season began with a mountainous share of overwhelming moments that left Leah feeling very "unchosen." Frustrated with renovations and distant relations with Omar and Shah, she baked away her feelings. She slept less, smoked and drank more, and often left her town house in complete disarray. Kendrick encouraged her, gave her scriptures to meditate, and helped her refocus. He hugged her tightly as she often collapsed onto the sofa from the exhaustion of the day.

"Leah, God has plans for you but it'll take some time for you to find it. Just go along for the ride. Don't worry, I'm here."

He kissed her on the cheek and rubbed her shoulders.

"I'll be there to take care of everything."

Leah smiled when she remembered those words.

I'll be here to take care of everything. Someone will be there for me.

Then, there were those times, when the grass seemed greener on the other side. One too many mistakes would set Kendrick off like a boiling teakettle. He was the consummate artist and perfectionist. Kendrick must have everything and everyone within his reach. He was used to it. Leah tried hard not to make too many mistakes when it came to the restaurant. She hired a part-time assistant to double-check most of the inventories and supplies when they came in. However, Kendrick seemed to have a sixth sense when it came to a problem with her restaurant. If he did not fix the problem, he deemed it an insult. As if, someone slapped him. For Leah, at times, it was too much.

Leah sat on the cherry-colored wooden bench in her "smoky" oasis. The fenced patio area looked out into the parking lot. The morning traffic simmered down. Cars honked occasionally back and forth down Colesville Road. Drivers honked at jaywalkers. At least, the birds chirped softer to each other. Leah took a slow drag and blew it into the air.

I hope the morning gets better than this. I cannot let the day spoil tonight.

Leah thought of happier times. She thought of her father. The way he'd call her name when she was younger. She heard echoes of his infectious laugh in the distance. She remembered the smell of his favorite cologne. A tear trickled down her cheek. She took another drag of her Virginia Slim, blew off the memory and the tears, and stomped the last of the cigarette butt firmly into the ground. She pulled out her compact from her purse, checked her hair and makeup, straightened her suit, and walked back into the restaurant with a little more confidence than she had five minutes earlier.

Chapter 11

"There is more that has been required of thee..."

"Good Morning, Faith and Victory International Church! Do you know what time it is? It's time to give God the highest praise. Hallelujah!"

Elder Johnetta Moore, a cocoa-skinned sister, with Senegalese twists wearing an autumn brown St. John jacket with an atrium skirt, stood at the silver podium. She belted out greetings with a voice as deep and boisterous as a trio of trombones ringing. She greeted the nine-hundred-and-fifty-member congregation during praise and worship on a crisp, windy September morning.

The 6,200-square foot refurbished church was a two-story redbrick edifice that snuggled into the residential, country tones of Hyattsville, Maryland. Faith and Victory International gave a renascent flare to the neighborhood as well as a property boost over the years. Freed slaves had built the church during the 1890s. The Victorian Romanesque building housed a thrust stage inside with flowers beautifully adorned at the corners. The choir section sat on left stage while the baptismal pool remained hidden in the center of the platform. Two sections of purple plush seating split the sanctuary, with television screens planted in various sections to help latecomers see everything happening onstage. The administration office, kitchen, computer room, and classrooms were located on the first level. On the ground level, the fellowship hall, visitor center, nursery, and bookstore surrounded the main sanctuary. For many anxious parents, the drop-offs to the nursery and Sunday school were a welcome treat. Recently, a new elevator installation from the main area to the first floor provided a "heavenly" access for the elderly and physically disabled members to get around.

Several of the ministers, deacons, and elders dressed in their Sunday finest, stood clapping, singing and dancing in the aisles. Octavia marched in quickly so that she could get a seat nearer to the front section. She spotted Simone a couple rows ahead. After a cluster of members funneled through the sanctuary, Cadence and Yasmine walked in and sat in the back. Leah came in escorted by Kendrick. Amazingly, their work schedules allowed them to worship together this Sunday.

"Good morning, Minister James."

A salt-and-pepper-haired man with a black shirt, blue silk tie, and black pants hugged a standing Benevolence before advancing to his seat next to her.

"Good morning, Elder Thomas."

"The Holy Spirit is moving in here already."

He waved his hands in the air.

"It's going to be a great day in the kingdom!"

"I certainly think so." Benevolence grinned.

I certainly hope so.

Benevolence sat down as the worship changed and became more melodic, more intense. She knelt down to pray, but she was not sure if it was in obedience to the Holy Spirit's request or her fatigue.

Thirty-five-year-old Benevolence James worked as a criminal psychologist at the Randolph Correctional Centre near Arlington, Virginia. She had just finished a double shift and had little time to change out of uniform before coming to Sunday's service. She served for years as a correction officer before being promoted to a treatment specialist then to supervisory program manager, which includes the psychiatry treatment center. She still serves as one of the supervisors of the 120-room women's facility, where once a month, she catches a double shift. Duties include inspecting the cells, rooms, locks, and fire hazards. She hated the rotations. She was always covering for another officer, which seemed often. She always ended up doing three rotations a month. The extra money came at a price. Her promotion could not have rode in fast enough. Now, she had the authority to reassign double shifts without fault. She needed to regulate her work schedule.

In the beginning, there seemed to be many good fruits of her labor. Counselees were young girls with broken hearts who met the Lord. They were gang members, prostitutes, drug victims, dropouts, and murderers who desperately needed rehabilitation. Getting their General Education Development, going to college, getting married, and having a family were no longer pipe dreams. Women started to believe they had a new chance at life. They even visited the institution chapel on Sundays regularly.

However, over the years, the penal system seemed to rot whatever good she aimed to accomplish. The women entering now were girls with criminal minds, hard times on their backs, and stony hearts. There were more black faces and Latino faces. They were more resistant than she remembered. Nowadays, she felt she bore no fruit at all. If she did, it was strange fruit. She wanted fewer caseloads. Benevolence's emotional tank was dry. Her mental tank could use an overhaul, and her "spiritual" brook needed freshwater. She was due for a nice long swim.

Benevolence felt an ache in her knee shoot up her left thigh. She realized she had been down for more than twenty minutes, and her legs had fallen asleep. When she lifted her head and rose up to her seat, Deacon Baylor was reading out the morning announcements in a rich Southern drawl.

"Faith and Victory is launching a new after-school tutoring program!

We need teachers for reading, math, science and Spanish. We also need ESL teachers for the adults and youth. Please sign up in the administration office. Let us not forget the marriage retreat that will be coming up at the end of the month. It is going to be a time of fellowship, refreshment and recommitment for you and your spouse! Slots are still available for those who want to sign up. Our singles bonfire will be this Friday. There will be food, fun and fellowship. Bible study and prayer will be this Wednesday at seven o'clock. Bishop Timms will continue his series on the 'Songs of Ascent: The Essentials of Worship.' I know I've been enjoying Bible study. Folks, come out. It will be a blessed time! That is all for the morning announcements. Guess, what time it is. It's offering time! Stand up and give the Lord some praise!"

The congregation screamed and cheered louder than a Redskins crowd at RFK stadium after a touchdown. Deacon Baylor read Psalm 84 from the NIV version of the Bible.

"Your tithe is the first fruits of thy increase. Tithes come from your gross paycheck not the net. If you want your heavenly father to meet the needs in your life, then you must first sow a seed. That seed will open opportunities for God to interfere divinely on your behalf. Sow a seed and believe with confident assurance that whatever you ask of Him according to His will, He has the power to give you."

As the congregation walked to the offering table, the musicians began to play. The mass choir got into place for a special selection. They sang a ballad written by one of the choir members. A cloud of praise enveloped the sanctuary. The congregation shouted. People fell to their knees. Many were crying, swaying, and singing their burdens away. Pastors glorified God. A sound, pure and heavenly, rang through Benevolence's ears. Soon weeks of weariness that sat perched on her shoulders lifted into the troposphere. Healing pervaded the sanctuary.

Benevolence stood up. She felt the awesomeness of His presence like refreshing spring waters, wooing and coaxing her mind. She eased her shoulders. Tensions in her neck ceased. Her hands and feet began to tingle. Benevolence tilted her head back, lifting her face toward the ceiling. Her smile grew. Thoughts that raced past each other now began walking at an even pace.

Thank you, Lord.

Benevolence sighed. She pulled on her jacket and felt her weapon still in place. She was "padded" even when she was off duty. She needed to keep watch. Demonic spirits were at bay, both spiritually and naturally.

Pastor Deborah Timms, a honey-colored sister with short black hair and strong African facial features, walked royally to the pulpit in her purple preaching gown. Pastor Timms was not just the wife of Bishop Timms; she was the only female associate pastor in the pastorate. Just in her early forties, Pastor Timms was one of the most sought-out pastors in Maryland. Her raspy voice gave her an electrifying preaching style. She had the authority and wisdom of a woman way beyond her years. Her messages evoked a "preceding" word, the type of wisdom that prepares disciples for a set of events yet to come. There was a divine timing to her messages, as if God opened up the heavens and proclaimed the following: *Children, some of you will see me in a new way but it will not be in the way you thought.*

Her voice rang through the sanctuary. It commanded everyone's attention, including the angels and demons.

"Good Morning, Faith and Victory! It is a pleasure to serve in this capacity. I am Pastor Deborah Timms, associate pastor of this wonderful ministry. I give honor to my Bishop Henry Timms, as well as the other pastors, elders, ministers, deacons and members of the Presbyterian board. Grace and peace be unto you all."

Pastor Timms prayed and began her teaching.

"God desires for you to have a passion for your life, a reason for you to wake up in the morning. He is waiting for you to give Him an opportunity to show up in your life, right in the midst of your circumstances. There are believers who believe that sitting in church every week is enough. They are blind, unaware. They don't realize they must seek God for the revelation that can change their life. They come here and they are asleep! They sleep on God, His word and His promises. Are they physically asleep? Well, yes. Some may be asleep right now. Look at your neighbor. If they are asleep, nudge them and say wake up!"

Whispers crescendo like waves through the congregation. Saints shook themselves awake.

"They may be asleep emotionally, mentally, even spiritually. When the revelation comes, they miss it. They never wrote it down."

The silence in the sanctuary room grew loud. Several amens echoed out from the congregation.

"Believers who think they will remember everything when tomorrow comes are fooling themselves. They pray once a week. They study the word once a week, if at all. Talking to God is nonexistent. They're asleep! To grow in the revelation of God, you must begin to process God's revelation as it relates to your life. God is looking for those who will hear His word and do what His word commands!"

Pastor Timms scanned the souls sitting in the front. Deliverance and wisdom drew up their swords. The angels left her side and went to work looking for ambushes. They were ready to strike the enemy. Pastor Timms grew more intense.

"Jesus needs people who will produce for the kingdom! He is looking for people who will be living witnesses. He is ready to pour more into you. There is more that He is requiring of you. He will use you to pour out into others and in return, you will be refreshed. He is looking for broken vessels. Will you be that vessel? The one that He will use?"

Pastor Timms repeated her last statement. She stared across the sanctuary, through the congregation, to the eldership. Her eyes locked in on Benevolence for what seem like a thousand moments.

"Will you be the vessel that He can use?"

A jolt from her left hip broke the gaze. She retrieved the phone and glared at the text message. When she looked back up, Pastor Timms had bowed her head down in a word of prayer.

Thirty-five minutes later, Benevolence stood in the foyer, greeting members leaving service. She spotted Simone on her way out and politely excused herself.

"Simone! Hey, how are you doing?"

Two months since the breakup, I wonder how she's doing.

"Oh, hi, Minister James. I'm okay."

I guess I am. Oh, please don't keep me longer than necessary. I don't want to have to start another conversation.

Disappointment, wearing a long black dress with a knapsack of negativity on her back, skipped beside Simone while twirling a baton. Benevolence gazed at Simone from head to toe. She scanned her for any signs of disturbance. Disappointment dropped her baton and quickly hid behind Simone.

She looks healthy. Not the slightest bit of fatigue. Unlike my own fatigue, that everyone in Oregon could probably see.

"Well, if you need anything, just let me know okay? Anything at all," Benevolence reassured.

"Thanks. I appreciate that." Simone fumbled for her keys.

"Um, I have to go."

Simone avoided crowds so that she could think. Not knowing whom to trust at church with her stuff, she kept her issues and frustrations to herself. As tears began tumbling through her eyelids, she got inside her jeep. Disappointment slid in the passenger's seat. Simone felt the minister's warmth but just did not know how to respond. She turned the radio to W104.1 FM and drove off. Simone drove up Drexel Street, away from the church and her embattled emotions.

Benevolence got into her blue plush-seated 2000 Nissan Pathfinder. Fatigue, frail, and weak sat confined to the top of the jeep with the wind blowing through her stringy strands of gray hair. Benevolence drove through the city but suddenly decided to take the scenic route home. She popped Vicki Yohe into the CD deck and began to hum softly to the music. As she drove through Seventh Street, the music softened, allowing her thoughts to wander into a trance.

Benevolence felt engulfed in a cloud. Fatigue heard rumblings. The music got louder. Benevolence pulled up along a residential street and parked. A ray of sunshine enveloped across the turquoise blue sky. Red-orange rays pierced through the heart of fatigue, disintegrating any remaining frailty she had left. The music got louder in Benevolence's inner ear, though she did not raise the volume. Benevolence entered the third heaven. Snapshots of visions impressed her mind. She saw women: their faces were fuzzy but familiar. She heard laughter, lots of laughter. She heard prayers on one side and saw warfare on the other. She saw glimpses of her house. The visions snapped brilliantly through her mind one after another. A warmness covered her being like a cozy fire on a cold winter's day. It seemed like God himself hugged her and whispered in her ear. As Vicki Yohe reached the height of the chorus, Benevolence began to cry. She had witnessed these images before. However, this time, they were more distinct. The images held her captive.

Yes, Lord.

Benevolence whispered, wiping tears from her eyes. She turned on the ignition and drove off. Angels carried the whisper, though barely audible, from this side of the earth to the highest heavens. They left swiftly so the assignment could begin.

Chapter 12

*"Obey me and keep my covenant; that you may become
out of all the nations, my peculiar treasure..."*

Hunt Valley, Maryland, had a small town quality that made it the perfect spot for the October women's retreat. Country homes filled the streets between hotels and long stretches of highway. Citizens seem to take the day as it comes. The pace treaded slower for the other "Marylanders" and "Washingtonians." Two hundred women decided to retreat from their daily life and their daily activities. The hotel treated the women like royalty. On the first day of the retreat, the women broke out randomly from general sessions into groups after a time of prayer.

Octavia, Simone, Yasmine, Leah, and eight other women gathered in a circle. Deacon Rachel Hammond, an evangelist from Richmond, Virginia, who worked for the State Department and Deacon Liardon, from Baltimore, an IT specialist and one of the music directors, led the circle. Everyone introduced themselves. Women spoke of their jobs, status, either school or professional affiliation, and membership at Faith and Victory. The various African, African-American, French, Jamaican, Cuban, Salvadorian, Indian, and Korean faces poured out greetings that displayed cultures from across the globe. Deacon Hammond entered the middle of the circle.

"Ladies, what are you looking to get from this retreat?"

"I want new friendships." one woman responded.

"I want rest!" another bolted out.

"Amen!" Everyone laughed and cheered.

"I want peace and quiet. No stress." another resolved.

"Uh-huh," the women echoed.

Deacon Hammond dove in deeper.

"Now, it may be a little difficult for some of you, maybe all of you, but I would like each of you to answer. What are your dreams? What have you been praying for God to answer in your life? Take your time. Whatever you say remains in this room."

She asked each woman to lay her dream out in the open, to lay her heart on the altar. Unsure whether the priest would bless it, sacrifice it, or condemn it, the women froze. Fear crept into the room, wearing a mustard-colored summer dress. She danced in and out of the circle, hovering around each participant, whispering smoky dust-colored doubts into their hopeful ears.

"You can't say that," she growled to one woman.

"Oh, now you know that dream is too silly," she snickered to another.

"You don't still believe that will come true now, do you?" she bellowed to several others. She snorted with laughter.

Confusion and terror pulled their seats into the circle, mixing their scents with fear. The demons seated behind the women then slapped fives with their paws. Deacon Liardon felt the hairs stand up on the back of her neck. She glanced over at Deacon Hammond. They nodded in agreement.

They're here. They need to leave. These women need a breakthrough. You are not going to keep them bottled up.

Deacon Hammond broke the silence.

"When I came to this conference, I wanted God to answer some specific questions concerning my family. I have this dream that one day, my immediate family is 'saved,' walking in God's will and somehow, they would be partners with me in ministry. We would travel together spreading the gospel. Right now, most of my brothers and sisters do not know the Lord. I am the youngest of five. One of my sisters got 'saved' two years ago after overcoming a cocaine addiction. We are very close. She continues to battle for total freedom. I continue to pray for her, for all of them."

The levees of anxiety broke. A tsunami of peace quaked through the circle, drowning terror and confusion in a massive wave. Fear hung on to a lifeboat sailing away from a narrow escape. Women revealed a cocoon of their dreams, their feelings about life, and for some, surmounting unhappiness that shadowed them each morning as they got ready for work or performed their various duties. Octavia sat quiet. She thought about her post-JD life. It had been a few years since graduation, yet there was an unsettling noise wrestling inside of her.

This is ridiculous. Of course, no one enters his or her dream job right out of law school. I've had some rough times but that's to be expected. I'm fine now. I'm where I need to be. Huffman & Associates. They're good to me. It's been good, so far. I just have to hang in there. Wait it out. Stay in control. Stay focused. Everything will work itself out.

"My dream is doing what I am doing now. I am content. I am in the moment. My moment is right now." Octavia sat back and assured herself and almost everyone sitting in the circle.

Octavia was selectively single. She was very particular about the men she dated. It was extremely hard to meet men in DC that captivated her attention. Many were often uneducated, unsaved, or uninteresting. Oftentimes, all of the above. The few that made it past the "resume" phase lacked drive or a sense of purpose. Their main goal was to get rich and live in luxury. She had no problems with the dream, but the chances of the lotto being their savior was as sure as one appearing on *The Price Is Right*. Romantic affairs usually dwindled after six months, with a disappointed Octavia conveniently making herself unavailable through work or various church obligations until the poor soul finally got the hint.

Right now, being at the retreat was a blessing, but sitting with all of these women talking about feelings and dreams, Octavia struggled to stay on the offense.

"Well, Yasmine, what about you?" Deaconess Hammond inquired.

"What are your dreams?"

"Well, I am not sure if I have an exact dream. I uh, don't want to sound arrogant but I try to live my life to the fullest. I want to be free to express myself and be happy, the 'happily ever after' kind. I know there are no storybook endings, so I rather create my own. So, if that happiness comes through my career, marriage, or friends, so be it. But, I'm not exactly holding myself to that, you know?"

A couple of women nodded in agreement. Simone sighed. She rolled her eyes, brushed some lint from her fleece jumpsuit, and folded her arms.

Spare me the psychological evaluation. Not like everyone can't figure it out anyways. I knew what my dream was . . . to be Mrs. Tavian Giancello. That's all. Everything else would have fallen into place.

Leah looked around the room. Everyone else looked engaged into the discussion.

All this mushy stuff . . . too many feelings too fast. I need a smoke. This is just too much. When is the next break?

"Leah, what about you?" Deaconess Liardon looked directly at her hand gestures.

"Do you have something to share?"

"Huh, what? Dreams. Um, let me think."

Leah rubbed her hands back and forth on her lap.

"I guess it would be too much wish that my father were still alive. I need more rest. More rest. I really wish I could go and get a smoke. Uh, I shouldn't have said that. Um, sometimes, life gets a little too frustrating for me. I'm not sure why. I deal with it, because I have to. I wish it wasn't always like that. I hate being so overwhelmed all the time. I just want to be happy. I want to be okay. Happy. Normal. Like everyone else."

Benevolence walked around the circles in the conference room. She eavesdropped on some of the discussions. She heard Leah's last statement, when the Lord spoke to her heart. She looked over at the faces in the circle. She wandered into her own thoughts.

Dreams are what you make them. Life is what you make it. There are always things that I can improve on. Like my job. My ministry . . . relationships. my health . . . my weight. Those are my goals. Right now, work is not something I want to think about, let alone ponder. My pager might go off just mentioning it.

Benevolence walked over to the back of the conference room next the exit. She went to the table and poured herself a glass of ice water. She checked her watch, 11:50 a.m.

Let me go and check on lunch. I hope it's something tasty . . . something with some flavor.

She walked out of the conference room and quietly closed the door. When all of the women said their piece, Deacon Hammond stood up, went to the podium, and addressed the different circles of women.

"Well, ladies, I thank you for being so honest about your lives. I know it was difficult even to admit your own doubts and unbelief. God wants you to know that He sees you all. He loves you and He wants to restore some things back into your life. There are treasures that you have lost. There are treasures that you will need to find. God wants you to know that you are His peculiar treasure. He will renew some promises in your life but He needs to lay out a new foundation. That foundation begins here. Let's pray."

While the women prayed, Deacon Liardon began humming a hymnal that led into a time of praise and worship. Women knelt to the floor in prayer; others swayed back and forth in worship like a gentle wind whistling through wheat fields. Tear-ridden faces cried out for forgiveness, deliverance, and salvation. Women offered up holy sacrifices like wrapped gifts, waiting for the Master to accept His treasures.

Later that evening, Benevolence went to suite after suite on a mission. She met Yasmine first, watching a movie. Benevolence sat on the bed.

"Hello, Yasmine, how are you?"

Yasmine lowered the volume. Cadence was in the shower.

"Minister James, I feel wonderful. So far, this retreat has been da bomb!"

"Good. I am glad to hear that. Listen, I would like to talk to you this evening at about nine 'o clock. In about an hour. Are you available? Can you meet me at room 345?"

"Sure, I don't have any plans."

Benevolence left for her next search. Minutes later, she approached Simone, Leah, and Octavia. They all came to Room 345, each showing up at least two minutes apart. Octavia was the last one to enter. She was surprised as the others to find themselves there. Simone was sitting on the bed closest to the window.

"Octavia, you know why we are here?" Simone whispered.

"I guess the same reason you're here. I figure that we're about to find out." Benevolence exploded into a big smile.

"Now, I am sure you ladies are all curious as to why I have called each of you here, tonight. Well, God has put it in my heart for some time now to start a mentoring program to build women already into the faith. I have been gathering the necessary information and have taken the program to the leadership board and they approved it last month. God had not however given me the women He wanted me to mentor until now. God spoke to me about each of you and said some strong things. He is very proud of you but He wants to challenge you to come up higher in Him."

Leah looked at Benevolence and began wringing her hands. Octavia looked at Yasmine cautiously. Yasmine was oblivious of the stares. Simone gazed out the window, shifting in her seat while stealing glances at Benevolence. Yasmine was only one who spoke.

"Well, for real, it sounds like it'll be cool, but check this out; I don't really know ya'll. I see you on Sundays but that's it. So, for real, I really don't know how this is going to work."

Benevolence responded to Yasmine and everyone else reassuringly.

"I know. So that is why, right now, I want to play a little game that will help us get to know each other better."

Chapter 13

"Sometimes, it takes being more than just acquaintances..."

A month after the retreat, the five women met in southwest at Benevolence's house for their first official meeting. Benevolence cancelled Tuesday night dinner plans to prepare for the meeting. She left work three hours early, cleaned the bathroom, wiped the kitchen counters, and mopped the floors. She vacuumed and dusted the living room and den. She scented her palace with lilac spring, one of the finest of Glade Plug-Ins products from the nearest Safeway. The leaves fluttered around the November breeze. The grass aged slowly. Temperatures dropped cold enough to sweep through the city as rush hour did at four o'clock in the evening. Benevolence plopped on the couch and turned on the four o'clock news.

All of this cleaning. Whew! I need a nap before everyone gets here.

Benevolence yawned at the news anchor reporting from Dupont Circle. With eyes fluttering, the words coming from the anchor formed into a huge garbled noise. Benevolence drifted off into an hour-long power nap. Hours later, around seven in the evening, the doorbell chimed. Benevolence changed into a Rinaldi multistripe velvet pants with a woodland suede top and boots and shook her hair out of her face as she walked up to the door.

"Hello, Octavia! How are you? You're the first one here. The others should be here really soon."

Octavia walked through the art-laden hallway. She carried her treats under her ivory jacket. She wore a long-sleeve cotton turtleneck, woven wrap skirt, and camel brown boots. She placed her grocery bags in the kitchen.

"Minister James, this is nice! Are you a curator too?"

Octavia took the desserts out of the handbags, placing the desserts on top of the counter, near the L-shaped bar that surrounded the wooden kitchenette.

Impressive.

She gave Benevolence a quick hug and walked out to the living room. Benevolence's home had an island flavor mixed with a taste of New York and DC all wrapped up like a tasty goat "roti." African portraits adorned the walls in the living room. Charcoal sketches and family photos covered the walls. A tan leather sectional engulfed the living room area with a small wooden end table in the center. A twenty-five-inch television sat on a metallic shelf with many textbooks and other decor. Floor plants covered both corners of the shelf unit. The door chimed again. Simone and Leah were pounding at the door.

"Hot food! Food's hot! Open up please."

"Excuse me for a second, Octavia."

Benevolence ran to the door.

"Okay! I'm at the door."

They ran around Benevolence and into the kitchen. Simone placed her masterpiece pepper pot soup on top of the stove, set it on warm, and slid into a purple plush bar seat on the other side of the kitchen. She took off her Benetton herringbone blazer, revealing the gauze knit top, corduroy skirt, and black Alicia boots.

"Is everyone here yet? I'm starving." Simone fanned herself.

"Not yet. We're still waiting for Yasmine. C'mon, I'll give you guys a quick tour."

Leah opened the oven and placed her secret recipe inside. She took off her full-length jacket, revealing a black double-breasted coatdress, and dumped her purse onto the empty bar seat. She ventured out to the living room. Octavia sat around the sectional, flipping through a book of artwork lying on the end table. She noticed a piece of artwork layered with some poetry.

"So who's the artist?"

"Sometimes, I write." Benevolence announced.

"When I'm in the mood. When I need to. Every now and again."

Leah leaned over on the sectional to take a closer look.

"This doesn't sound like every now and again work. This sounds real good. You could publish this, you know. You really could."

"I do shows on occasion. I really use poetry for other means."

The doorbell chimed one more time.

"I'll get it." Leah strolled up to the door.

"So what do you think will happen tonight?" Simone sat down and started flipping Octavia's unturned pages.

"I'm not quite sure. We'll have to see."

Octavia confessed. Yasmine looked refreshed wearing an olive green Victorian parachute jacket with golden linings, indigo blue jeans, and gold pumps. Being fashionably late was becoming her trademark. She brought out appetizers and spread them in front of the desserts.

"Is everybody here? I brought salad and juice. It is smelling like Negril up in here! Everything ready?"

The women started setting the table. Yasmine dropped one of the forks on the table, washed it, and set it back haphazardly. Leah studied her and quietly rearranged the fork to the right order.

"Yasmine, don't put that cup there, honey, it goes over here. Simone, could you fold those napkins this way?"

"Nice place, Minister James."

"Thanks, Yasmine."

"Yeah, it's like an island museum."

Octavia joked, pouring juice into the five glasses around her.

Benevolence ushered everyone to the dining table and said grace over the food. Simone picked up a biscuit and passed the breadbasket around the table.

"The pepper pot soup smells delicious!" Yasmine praised.

"Good choice for the appetizer,"

Benevolence agreed.

"We definitely put together a five-course meal."

"I've got room for the main dish."

Octavia rejoiced over the Ethiopian spiced stew. The stew was an orchestra of seasonings married over boneless, chopped, garlic-flavored beef sirloin poured over vegetables and yellow rice.

Soon the dinner conversation opened to careers, daily activities at work, and upcoming church events. Octavia talked delightedly about her cases and colleagues at Huffman & Associates. Simone complained about the new curriculum that the superintendent sprung on the charter schools to achieve her school's annual yearly progress. Simone lamented how she would motivate the teachers to use the new strategies. Leah briefly commented about the hustle and bustle of the restaurant business. Yasmine praised her job, her supervisor, and hinted at the anticipation of working with her new boss but gave no names. She didn't want to reveal too much too soon. Benevolence shared details about her directorial position at the correctional facility, including the realities of substance abuse, prison, and the types of women she counsels on a daily basis. At nine o' clock, the women retreated onto the tan leather sectional in the living room, feeling and looking fully satisfied.

"Ladies, what a wonderful dinner! I feel like you brought the island back here to DC. Can we move into the living room? You can bring your drinks, but bring those coasters. Be careful of spills."

As everyone settled on the sectional, Benevolence began.

"Now, that we are full let's take a moment and get acquainted. We'll be spending quite a bit of time together in the next six months. Here's a quick warm-up: first, I want you to share some qualities that you like about the person sitting to your left. Second, I want you each to share something that you think God is speaking to you about, possibly to work on for this season. One thing you feel is of significance."

Yasmine sat next to a despondent Simone with her hands crossed while Octavia sat next to a reflective Leah with her hands in her lap. Yasmine turned over to Simone and scanned her from head to toe.

"I like Simone's shoes and accessories. They always match."

Simone smiled. She gave Yasmine a compliment of her own.

"Yasmine is all right. I like her style. I am not sure yet, but I think I also like how outspoken she is."

Leah turned to Octavia.

"Octavia seems so intelligent. I like the confidence she carries." Octavia beamed.

"Leah has this street sense to her. She's tough. Yet, she has this grace, a sense of style. The girl can whip a meal together!"

Octavia patted her belly.

"My stomach thanks you."

Now Octavia pondered the second question a bit.

"The second question, well, I love my work. I love what I do at Huffman & Associates. I like learning the ropes. It gets challenging at times, the heavy caseloads, the research, but that's to be expected. Right now, things are good. I have no reason to complain. I am grateful. I can see myself excelling in this area, with this company. As a hobby, I manage plays. Been in love with the creative arts for a long time. I think the way that I see Christian dramas will change. Personally, I don't like them because they are too preachy and they don't appeal to secular audiences. I'm not even sure they really impact Christian audiences."

"I hear you."

Simone uncrossed her arms, smoothed her skirt, and sat straight in the chair.

"As you all remember, a couple of months ago, my fiancé dumped me. Well, I really don't believe that it's really over. Tavian hasn't called nor have I heard from his family except his uncle but there's something inside me that says he'll be back and we'll be married. People think I'm crazy for believing it, so I've stopped telling them."

"Well, I can see why!"

Yasmine raved, folding her arms in supportive defense.

"With what he did to you? Simone, you're still in shock. You'll soon know the real deal. You'll be okay. As for me, right now, my relationship with God is great. We talk every day. I feel that I am doing everything that He has spoken in my heart to do for this season. I have a nice place, a few good friends and a thriving career. I'm active in ministry."

"Yasmine, Simone is entitled to believe what she wants," Leah contended, between sips of juice.

"That relationship is important to her and if she believes it's meant to be, it's not for any of us to judge. Simone, I understand what you're going through. I'm also in a long-term relationship with a good man. He helped me continue my father's business. He's been everything to me. The restaurant industry is a tough business. I'm not even sure how I've been managing it this long. Lately though, I've felt . . . well, I'm not sure what's the word. I am always tired or bouncing off the walls. I've been distracted more than usual. I have been more restless and more frustrated about the pettiest things. I've always felt this way but lately it's been . . . well, on a good note, I'm recently engaged, I have a new relationship with God, and I'm looking forward to Him speaking to me. I want to learn more about Him. About this walk. Right now I'm basking in the moment."

Benevolence listened intently. She sat across the women and witnessed different visions as each of them spoke. The visions appeared as backdrops, like stage scenery behind the tan leather sectional. Their concerns were detailed monologues; each voice whether melodic or sullen conjured a setting that appeared just as distinct as the voice giving it life. When Octavia spoke, a small grey cloud began to hover over her head, with a huge hand trying to swat it away. Bodiless hands tried to shield Octavia's ears, but the smoky cloud kept passing through them. She walked around with silver chains tied around her ankles. The chains connected to a huge black boulder that rolled in the distance. Silhouettes formed in the shadows, watching her.

When Simone spoke, boxes upon boxes were being stacked on top of each other. Simone sat in the middle as the boxes began to form a fortress around her. Simone turned her cheek, but Benevolence saw another box appear in the distance. One box toppled over, spilling to the floor. Pictures of a family cracked into several pieces. Another box fell. More photos of couples. Different couples. Some looked like magazine centerfolds; others looked like family photos aged several generations. Soon jewelry fell. Stacked boxes began falling like dominoes.

Simone sat in the middle of the falling fortress, her face sullen. She appeared helpless.

As Yasmine spoke, men walked in and out of the living room like a revolving door. Some stayed for a minute and left, while others sat underneath her space. Yasmine had a remote control in her hand. As she pressed a button, men would talk to her. When she pressed another button, the men who previously were chatting with her stood up and left. Then, one man with his face hidden in the shadows swiftly came through the door and with a strong hand took Yasmine's remote. Yasmine frowned, looked up, and smiled. Then he grabbed Yasmine's arm. Yasmine frowned again, looked up, and laughed. A leg playfully kicked her. Yasmine frowned, looked up, smiled, and ran to an older man with the two-toned face. They walked off into the shadows.

While Leah spoke, Benevolence heard dishes dropping, voices, and pots and pans clanging together. The noise ceased. Leah paced back and forth. Strangers ran into the living room, pushing and shoving. Objects ran into the living room, pushing and shoving too. A man walks into the room. The strangers run out. The objects fall. The man takes a step toward Leah and reaches for an embrace. She stops pacing. Benevolence couldn't make out his facial features. The man embraced Leah, kissing her on the cheek. He sits Leah on the sectional where an image of panicky Leah superimposes over a calm Leah. From behind the sofa, he massages her shoulders, neck, and eyes. He doesn't remove his hands from her eyes. His smile grows into a scowl. Leah is shaking.

"Ladies, thank you for sharing yourselves with me. As I've said before, everything that goes on between us, stays between us. We want to build safety with each other. It will take some time, but I believe that if you allow it, it will happen. We are done for tonight. Let's pray."

With everyone seated, the women locked hands to pray. Shocked at what these visions showed her, Benevolence prayed for protection, peace, and guidance over these four women. She prayed for the journey each was embarking on. She knew they would need each other, and it was important they became more than just acquaintances from church. Benevolence prayed that God would begin to reveal to each of them the true desires of His heart. She prayed that His desires would be their desires. These women would become a part of God's leadership experiment. The various storms weren't brooding, but she knew they were coming. She prayed that the Lord would give each of them strength for the journey. They will certainly need it.

Chapter 14

"Maybe your heart is in the wrong place..."

Yasmine checked her e-mails. She read her early morning memos and daily astrology while listening to classical music. Yasmine's laboratory was her olfactory museum. She had shelves of natural and organic oils and scents stocked in rows in her lab. Her workstation was every mad scientist's dream: a gas chromatograph, mass spectrometer, and numerous distillation apparatuses. Yasmine turned up her radio. Memos, anecdotes, mentoring emails, were like "spiritual huddles," reminding everyone of upcoming assignments, new readings, and thoughts of the week to ponder. They were insightful and thought provoking. Yasmine needed the boost. She changed gears upon remembering her experiment. She needed to yield good results today. Yasmine prepped a perfume lacquer that brewed for eternity. It was the experiment from hell. It lasted several weeks too long. Her perfume refused to yield the right results.

"Ugh! This stinks."

Yasmine wafted the liquid to her nose and felt her small nose hairs singe. The mixture had a putrid odor, a musky, sulfuric smell Yasmine could not figure out. The lacquer volume was low. Yasmine looked through her notes. She flipped the pages rapidly to last week's data. She cursed under her breath. Earlier that morning, Yasmine brought her notebook to Sharon and some of the senior chemists. Some of them looked at her data and gave her suggestions. Few made unreasonable guesses as to why the mixture eroded such a pungent smell. Others were no help at all. Many secretly hoped that this experiment would unmask the "golden girl." Yasmine would be disgraced and dethroned. She would finally fall on her "Bunsen" burner. She scratched the notes out of her notebook, tempted to rip the notes right out the pad.

"Jesus!"

Yasmine stood at the fume hood with her notebook in hand. She wiped the fog off her lab goggles but could not wipe off the frustration brewing inside. She put the notebook down and picked up her gloves. She picked up the blackened lacquer, hoping for some inspiration on how to proceed next.

"Shouldn't be using the Lord's name in vain like that."

Byron stood by undetected, wearing brown slacks, brown shirt, and a yellow striped tie. Lust stood alongside Byron in his crimson colored suit. Byron looked as if he had just stepped off the cover of the GQ magazine and into her lab. He managed to announce his arrival and scare the "heebie-jeebies" off Yasmine at the same time.

"Ah!"

Yasmine jumped, banging her knee against the table. She almost dropped her discolored flask.

"Do you always scream like that?"

An intrigued Byron walked over, surveying the area. He stopped a few feet away from her. His voice sent shock waves through her body.

Yasmine flinched. Her anger blocked most of her pleasure. She placed the flask back into the fume hood and turned to face her accuser.

"Do you always sneak up behind people? You scared me. That is very dangerous. I could have dropped this experiment or even worse, hurt myself!"

"I knew you had nothing worth saving in your hands."

Yasmine belted out a laugh. She folded her arms.

"Can I help you with something?"

"Nope."

He folded his arms as a challenge.

"I came to observe."

"Well, right now, I'm kind of busy."

Yasmine, undaunted, turned away, lifting the fume hood up.

"I'm in the middle of an experiment."

"Looks like you're stumped."

Of all the times to pop up. There was no use in trying to cover it up. Half the company seemed to know that the "golden girl" had used up all her wishes with the perfume genie.

"I've been trying to figure out what happened. What's missing? I don't know why this mixture keeps coming out like this. But I'm sure that I've worked out the right formula."

"Maybe your formula is wrong."

How dare you? Down, girl, down.

"Can't be." Yasmine challenged coolly.

"I've calculated it repeatedly. It's correct."

"Are you sure?" Byron questioned, throwing more salt on the wound.

"I've gone to others. They didn't see anything wrong with it."

"What about your reactions? Did you look at them carefully? Did you produce any side reactions? Let me see."

Byron picked up her notebook and skimmed through the pages.

"Let's look at your molecular pyramid."

"My what?"

Yasmine hadn't a clue what he meant.

"Your fragrance pyramid, you do know there's a psychology to your fragrances."

Yasmine briefly remembered one of her boring training sessions. They blabbered on and on about the structure of molecular compounds. The main point was that her goal was to stack compounds together so that they could produce aromas. The aromas allowed the scents to change over time.

"Scents at the beginning of an application will be more volatile due to ingredients on the top and their molecules. But later, towards the end of the day, the faint heavier smell, such as musk from the bottom group will emerge."

"What are you talking about?"

Yasmine snatched her notebook back and looked over every inch of the last page. Byron smirked. He liked the mental "cat-and-mouse" game they were playing. He figured he would amuse himself a little while longer.

"I'm surprised at you, Ms. Blue. Surely, you know what I mean. There's a psychology to your fragrances."

Byron walked to the radio and turned the classical music up slightly. He walked to her shelves and picked out two oils, like a kid in a candy store. He stood in front of Yasmine, smirking. He was too close, too close for comfort.

"Your heart is in the wrong place."

"What?

"Your heart notes, the molecules from the composition. They aren't equally balanced. You've got three notes you need to balance: your head note, the more volatile component, your heart note and your base note, the least volatile."

Byron smelled the oils and set them on the workbench.

"Do you know what a pheromone is?"

"What does that have to do with anything?"

"Purely basic chemistry. Actually, it's a bit more advanced than that."

Byron took Yasmine's notebook and flipped a few more pages before placing it on the workbench next to the oils.

"Nice handwriting. Anyways, when pheromones react—"

Byron removed Yasmine's gloves slowly, gently massaging her fingers—

"They need a catalyst."

A sensual breeze blew in between the two of them. Byron lowered his voice.

"You know something that will allow the reactants to draw heat and bring them together."

He then put on the gloves, never leaving her stare. He pulled out a small pair of goggles from his pocket.

"Then they will release a scent."

He picked up the discolored liqueur from the fume hood. He wafted the smell to his nose.

"Right now, there's nothing. Well, maybe there's something. But there's nothing really gelling with the mixture."

Yasmine watched in amazement at the smoothness of this guy.

Was this sexual harassment, or foreplay?

She could not tell which was which.

"What about the environmental conditions?"

"That's not enough."

"But I'm using natural reactants."

"Still not enough."

Byron put the flask back into the fume hood. He then slowly but deliberately snatched off the gloves and set them on the workbench on top of the notebook.

"Ms. Blue, you need a catalyst that will produce heat. Good ole-fashioned heat. Enough heat to drive the reaction forward. You want your scents to mesh."

Byron headed for the door; his scent lingered behind.

"Change your percentages. Balance your notes. Then figure out what your catalyst should be."

Yasmine wanted to smear discolored lacquer all over his precious GQ suit and poke his "heart note."

Truthfully, she was glad she finally had a real solution.

"By the way, make sure you give credit where it's due, when everything works out, golden girl."

Yasmine just smiled as he strolled away.

What a jerk. He's fine, but he's still a jerk.

Weeks later, Yasmine and her colleagues headed off to a three-day seminar sponsored by the Cosmetic, Toiletry, and Fragrance Association in Atlantic

City. The conference held long laborious business sessions on leadership and management strategies for different science professionals to review the latest regulatory issues affecting perfumes. Some of it, Yasmine liked; other sessions couldn't hold toilet water. However, the latest trend seminar snapped her attention. After a long day, Byron took the whole team out to dinner.

After the restaurant, folks decided to go salsa dancing. Everyone had cocktails. Byron whisked Yasmine to the floor like dancers doing the "*pasa doble.*" He twirled her and caught her in his strong, muscular arms. Many noticed, but Yasmine didn't care. This felt so right. It felt so good to be near him. He looked so intently at her, piercing his gaze into her soul. After several rounds of songs ended, Byron, like a gentleman, led Yasmine back to her seat. He pulled out a handkerchief from his pocket and wiped his face. Yasmine fanned herself. There was more than just her "temperature" beginning to rise. Suddenly, he thanked everyone for their stamina throughout the conference and proceeded out of the door.

Who does he think he is? Whisking me off on the dance floor, and then leaving. I bet he gets a kick out of this.

Yasmine ordered a drink. Her colleagues also looked stunned. They continued dancing. At two in the morning, they walked back to the hotel. Yasmine flashed the hotel key card into the slot when a voice, deep and distinct, rang out.

"I'd thought you'd never get here."

Byron confessed, walking from behind the ice machine.

"What are you doing here?"

Lust opened his cape. A crimson fog condensed from his demonic being, spreading like wallpaper toward Yasmine's door. Suddenly as if he triple-jumped three doors down, Byron leaned Yasmine into the door, making sure she could not escape, meanwhile taking in every scent of her.

"I've been waiting patiently, but I don't think I can wait any more. You are just too tantalizing."

He suffocated any means of escape. The door crept slowly open. He bent forward, pulling Yasmine closer to him. Just one soft kiss was powerful enough to make her surrender all the control she had left. The door opened into her suite and into the next phase. Byron closed the door quickly.

Chapter 15

"Maybe you're running on empty..."

Octavia turned the radio to 105.8 AM. Usually, around 10:30 a.m., one of her favorite preachers came on. Hearing the word in the mornings helped clear her often-preoccupied mind. It complemented the research she needed to do, and it saturated her cubicle with a comfortable peace that allowed her to relax during the hectic pace of the day. Octavia reviewed cases on her overstacked desk when she glanced at an urgent note from one of the files and shook her head. She turned the radio down and picked up the phone.

"Hello. This is Octavia Kalu, from Huffman & Associates in Washington DC. There seems to be a discrepancy on my billable hours. What do you mean you can't retrieve them—I sent it last week. May I ask why? Are you serious? Can I refax it? Verification? Sure. Thanks."

Octavia rubbed her temples. She turned the radio back up. A gentle knock on the cubicle caused Octavia to look back.

"Hey, Octavia. Got a minute?"

Jason leaned against the cubicle. Gossip, wearing the same suit, leaned on Jason's shoulder, smirking. Octavia turned the radio down to a hum.

"Not really. They're billable. Plus, I need verification and clearance to be able to talk to you."

Octavia smiled, but she was dead serious. Jason Best was one of the other new associates. They clicked from the beginning. Jason was in his early thirties, wavy hair, caramel brown skin, and a small mustache. He had a good three months ahead of Octavia. Four new associates were added to the firm when Octavia arrived. Only two were African-American. Jason and Octavia became comrades, an unspoken alliance en route to senior partnership.

"How are you handling those trademarks?"

"I'm managing. Why?"

Octavia said between readings. Jason dumped a stack of cases on her already-stuffed desk and scooted toward Octavia.

"Don't you find it a little strange? The weight of your caseload compared to the other new associates?"

Gossip scooted next to Octavia on the other side. Jason sat back, flipping the pages of one case in his hands.

"Never bothered to check."

Octavia glued her eyes to her trademark application, looking at the specs.

What is he getting at?

"Well, some of my resources tell me that maybe we should. While we are here slaving, they're kissing up to senior associates and partners at lunches—and getting invited to sit in on court cases. Our cases!"

Jason was always complaining. He was gay and not ready to "come out" yet. It wasn't the best thing for his career right now. He hadn't made a name for himself, although it seemed that gay was "in" these days. Hazing new associates at Huffman was nothing new. Huffman & Associates are a part of the "old school" boutique. They were "old school."

Junior associates were linked with senior associates or partners. Either personalities matched, or they didn't. One had to figure out how to get along and get the job done. The firm's culture motto was watch associates like a hawk. Work em´ until they drop, quit, or can handle the caseload. Quitting was a sign of weakness. It did not go well in the legal community if people found out an associate quit a "prestigious" boutique like Huffman where associates would lie and die for a chance to work. Jason managed the best he knew how. He complained. It helped him cope. He got along well with some of the junior associates, but some of the senior associates and partners felt different vibes. The radar must be on. Octavia continued her defense.

"This ain't nothing new, Jason. You knew some type of hazing was going to happen. You can't just waltz your way to the top without putting in some blood and sweat. Just isn't going happen. I don't care if you're white or black. Those other associates will have their own challenges trust me. Don't worry. Hard work always pays off in the end."

Jason leaned closer.

"Octavia, have you looked around here lately? Girl, you're still wet behind the ears. You're still in awe of Huffman. All idealistic and stuff—but soon and very soon, clarity will come. I'm trying to tell you now because of all the new associates, you show the most promise and the most controversy—for some of the associates and some partners."

Jason leaned back, smoothing out his gray tie and gray shirt. Gossip copied him. Octavia turned around.

"What the heck are you talking about?"

"Look, all I'm saying is, be aware of your surroundings. Watch out for friends and enemies. People here, they talk. They are forming alliances. They're turning green and wielding their magic wands."

Jason waved his hand wildly. Gossip waved his paws.

"Let me go, I'm supposed to brief Mr. Weinberg before he goes to court. I haven't even had lunch yet." Jason took two files from the stack.

"Jason. Aren't you forgetting something?"

"No. I'm doing drop-offs. They just assigned foreign filing. It's only two. They need them by the end of the week. I'm sorry. Do lunch later?"

"A real quick lunch."

"All right. See ya."

As Jason walked down the hall, Octavia could hear him greet and politick all the way to the elevator. As the elevator bell chimed, her headache, which momentarily subsided, came bouncing back with a vengeance. Octavia began rubbing her temples.

So now, I have to watch my back . . . not again. I can't deal with this again . . . another firm trying to live up to the hype . . . but Huffman & Associates. They've been here for ages. Those kinds of antics should be dead and buried by now. I know right now might be rough, but there's perks. It's a good firm . . . one of the best. Huffman is my mentor. At least, he's becoming it. I can't focus on this right now. I haven't even made my mark yet. If Jason is right, maybe I need to get out of my bubble and check my surroundings. The caseload has been a bit much . . . Nothing I can't handle in time . . . I will manage. I have to. Jason's overreacting . . . just in case, maybe I ought to throw out a fleece.

Chapter 16

"When God made the highest mountains,
He placed some valleys in between..."

"Good morning, class," Simone began.

"Ms. Johnson and I will introduce a fun, new reading strategy to you. It is called metacognition. Metacognition is what we do when we are thinking about what happens when we read. Now, there are pipe cleaners on your desk. You will work in pairs. Pick a neighbor across, behind or next to you. Read the directions silently. You will make an animal and I want you to talk out what you are doing."

The students stopped talking. They stared at each other, and then back at Simone.

"Well, now that I've gotten your attention, let me show you how it's done."

Simone took an orange pipe cleaner from the front desk.

"Well, orange is my favorite color. I know the sun is either yellow-orange or red-orange. I love orange juice. Maybe there's an animal that is orange."

"You forgot to mention a screwdriver has orange juice in it." The kids laughed, and a few slapped high fives.

Simone directed her eyes at the person who made the response. Jose Mesina was one of Judea Charter's notorious masterminds. Jose, in a few short months, managed to plant stink bombs in the boys and girls' bathrooms, the cafeteria, and the gym, though no one has been able to prove it. Judea Charter was charged with raising the reading and math scores of the district's and Maryland's second- and third-time offenders. Judea teaches character education through nontraditional means. Some of the knuckleheads get it while others slide by. Simone decided to try Judea after six years as an English and reading teacher. She did one year as an administrator in Blade Senior High. She liked Judea's structure: 8 a.m. to 4:30 p.m. school days, Saturday intensive classes, summer expeditionary sessions and collaborative teaching. Math and science teachers teamed up, social studies joined with English, reading joined with arts, music, and drama.

Simone subbed for Ms. Lanier, who had been out sick for two weeks. She was coteaching with Ms. Johnson, one of the first year Prince George's teaching fellows. Even though they were starting a unit on metacognition, it was a chance to get back into the classroom, if only for a couple of days.

"Jose, since you seem to understand what's going on, why don't you try. Pick up your pipe cleaner and make an animal that has four legs."

"Ms. Dusette, I was just joking."

"Go."

"Um..."

Jose looked around the room. All tenth, junior, and senior eyes were on him. He did not want to fail. His eleventh-grade mind began calculating.

What could I make? It can't be cheesy.

He looked at Rachel Stevenson, a white girl from northwest, who came in for truancy and pickpocket offenses. He smiled. She scowled. He scanned her for motivation.

Brown eyes. Nice smile. Perky breasts.

"Breasts—Best—I'm going to make the best rabbit, kangaroo you ever did see. People think rabbits are dumb. They are smart. They let people take care of them. They act weak, so they can get lettuce, and food. Like Bugs Bunny. But as soon as they don't need you anymore, they're gone. Looking for another opportunity... the best opportunity."

He folded the ears and hands together. The orange rabbit silhouette appeared on his desk.

"Jose, don't you mean the 'breast' opportunity?"

A roar of laughter shook the classroom. Simone couldn't help but chuckle. Jose looked at Rachel and smiled. Rachel smiled and gave him hand gestures. Jose licked his lips suggestively.

"All right, class, enough. That's enough, Jose. Nice work. Now the rest of you work with your partners. No foolishness. Go!"

Simone surveyed the room. The students appeared to be having fun with the activity, talking loud and making boasts. The posters hanging on the walls of the classroom featured hip-hop characters drawn manga style. They were academic motivators. *Education on the brain*, *Get your read on*, and *Time Waits for No one* hung like graded papers. Few took the time to read the messages. Eighteen exiles, prodigal sons and daughters, lepers of the Prince George's school system, who failed the school system or rather the other way around. Judea was their last chance.

Trevor Middleton, an islander with a reputation to protect, and Andre Chambers, a braggadocios dreadlocked senior, started arguing.

"Son, that ain't no dog."

"Yeah, son, it is. Can't you see his tail? His feet? His ears?"

"Man, them aren't ears, son. They look like b—"

"Ms. Dusette, I'm finished. Can you see mine? I made a getaway truck."

"You mean a truck."

"No, I mean a getaway truck so that I can get away from these knuckleheads."

"Tiffany, you know that you love us. Don't even try it."

Rachel hammered.

"Rachel, mind yours. Okay?"

Nicolise Volkoff sauntered in like a celebrity, twenty minutes late. The boys screamed and cheered. Simone's guard jumped twenty feet high. The class seemed palatable before, but now, she had to leave for a meeting.

"Everyone, your projects look good. I've seen some very creative-looking animals and vehicles. Now, Ms. Johnson will take you through the next portion of our lesson. Nicolise sign the late board and sit down. I want to see you in my office after class."

Nicolise wearing a tight red sweater, tight jeans, and boots—slithered to her seat, looking like a candy cane ready to burst.

"Hey, ya'll. What did I miss? Hey, Tiff, Trevor. Hey, Dre."

"Hey, Nick."

Nicolise did not fit the stereotype. Half black and half Russian, she had a tough time fitting into the PG system after her parents divorced a year ago. Her mother moved to Hyattsville. After a series of layoffs, they became homeless. That was when Nicolise's problems began. She bounced from school to school until she got to Judea. Her tardiness continues.

Simone turned over to Ms. Johnson who turned beet red. She pulled her aside.

"Can you handle this?"

"Are you leaving now?"

"I have a meeting." Simone scanned the class.

"I will try to come back before the class ends."

Simone started to walk, but Ms. Johnson quickly grabbed her arm.

"Don't go." Simone looked down. Her shirt still had Ms. Johnson's handprint.

"Ms. Johnson, they can smell fear. Relate to them. You were in media industry. Use your expertise. Get them into it. Be yourself."

Simone turned back around to the class.

"Class, Ms. Johnson is going to continue with this activity. She has some items that need to be distributed. Trevor, Nicolise, and Rachel, come here please. Pass this out." Simone snuck out as the activity went under way.

Thirty minutes later, Simone walked into a zoo. Ms. Johnson was hiding underneath her desk. Kids were throwing paper balls at each other. The balls had objects protruding out. Simone radioed for security.

"I need someone in room 118 now!"

She flicked the lights on and off.

"Break this up!" Simone ducked under flying balls and other obstacles. One nearly hit her in the jaw.

"Jose, stop this now!"

Jose raised his hands like a conductor. Moving them in one swift motion, the balls dropped. Pencils dropped. Everything ceased. He dropped his hands. Ms. Johnson slowly eased up from behind her desk.

"Nobody move! Since there are eighteen culprits, there will be eighteen push-ups for each of you. Get on the floor. Find a space and move! Nobody goes anywhere until this room is spotless."

Mr. Muai, a medium-built cocoa-skinned man with straight teeth, walked in, observing the show. It seemed like PE rather than a developmental reading class.

"Ms. Dusette, I didn't know we had boot camp here."

He stood at the door smiling. His African accent was strong and thick.

"Well, some kids need a little extra care, some love and discipline." Simone moved closer to Mr. Muai by the door. It was the only unoccupied space.

"There's a staff meeting today. Principal Lester has some surprises. He's been cooking them up for a few months now."

"Really? I should let the math department know. Thanks for the heads-up. After the staff meeting, I figure we could get a bite to eat."

Mr. Muai offered candidly. Simone frowned and moved a few inches back.

"I don't know."

"You don't know how to eat?"

He smiled, not backing down.

"Well that's easy. I can show you. A genuine smile. Wow. You should do that much more often. I'll see you later. After the meeting."

Mr. Muai swaggered out.

Was that a date? Simone chuckled.

Well, it wouldn't hurt to get dinner. Probably pizza or something. We'll be talking about students. Math quizzes. No personal stuff. I can do this as long as there is no personal stuff.

Chapter 17

"Circumstances can push you to your breaking point..."

"Prison helps me with my problems."
One of the "juvies" retorted.

"I don't want to go back out there to society. In prison, I got a bed to sleep, food to eat, and at least a guard that pretends to give a damn. Out there, my mother is a junkie, and my father is invisible. I rather be in here. Call me a criminal, a delinquent. I rather take my three strikes."

Click.

Benevolence stopped the tape and jotted down more notes. The voice, raspy and harsh, had a sense of despair that echoed the spirits of the women who lived in the facility. Whatever strength one could muster, she held on for dear life. While so many feel hope slipping away.

Benevolence checked her calendar, quickly perusing her e-mails. Memos, industry readings, and devotionals composed her morning schedule: 11 a.m. counseling session, 12 p.m. tour, 2 p.m. counseling session, 3 p.m. new CO briefing, 4 p.m. meeting, speaking engagements, college reunion outing, mayoral council meetings, prayer.

She paused for a moment before clicking on the last e-mail. She had been slightly avoiding people, family included. Benevolence clicked on the last e-mail.

"Bene, it's uncle. Where you been? You were on me mind. You okay? I am praying for you. Call soon."

Benevolence smiled.

That's uncle. Always knows when to pop up. I need to call him. I need to see him. Very soon.

Benevolence sighed and rubbed her forehead.

Oh, Uncle. I know. I just can't right now. Please forgive me.

Benevolence clicked back to the industry news. Correction facilities were seeing an upsurge of women criminals and Arlington County was no different. Randolph Correctional Center's mission was clear: get young women back into society quickly but cost-efficiently. When offenders got sent to Randolph, it meant the judge was considering cutting them some slack. They still believed that society life was a possible venture. However, with the new governor in office, Virginia's budget called for a major overhaul. Randolph's budget got sliced 25 percent, making upward mobility, talks of renovations, and new programs a difficult conversation. A tinge of hope splurged when an official announced that a private company from Arizona was in negotiations to buy and manage the Arlington County Jail. Hope was beginning to funnel back into the facility. Talks of renovations resurfaced. New programs and positions resurrected. Arlington County needed to make changes. Randolph needed new leadership.

Things could be good again.

She wanted to believe it. A knock rang at the door.

"Ms. James?"

"Yes?"

"I'm Tiffany Carrington. I'm here for my morning orientation."

They shook hands. Tiffany was fully dressed in uniform, with her duffel bag and lunch bag all in tow.

She looks revved up, ready to go.

They proceeded out of the door.

"Where are you from, Tiffany?"

"Kansas. Just out of school. I did do six months at Kansas Corrections before coming here. I'm really excited. Ready to get my hands dirty, sort to speak."

Benevolence laughed.

Girl, slow down. All bright eyed and bushy tailed. Like I was. Ready to rehabilitate. Rebuild. Bring about hope. However, after ten years, things start to change.

"How long have you been here?"

"About ten years."

"Wow!"

"Let me show you around. Your orientation meeting is this afternoon. I'm sure you'll meet the rest of the staff."

They walked to the holding cells, puppy's nursery, visiting rooms, cafeteria, and gym. Benevolence pointed toward the library, main common area, chapel, garden, classrooms, and treatment center.

"There's a room I want you to see. It's small, but the work that comes out of there is remarkable."

They walked into a blue room. The recording studio had two booths. A paned glass window separated the booths. On one side sat a computer with recording equipment and a shelf of tapes and CDs.

"We record stories from the women to tell their children. Some are lullabies, some are short stories, some are poetry, but most are love notes to the kids. It's only open a few times a month, but when it is, it's packed."

Later in the afternoon, Benevolence met her counselee, a new transfer from DC. Benevolence opened the manila folder and began to take out her notepad when the guard signaled for the inmate to walk in.

She is younger than I expected. Could not be any more than twenty.

LaTasha Holmes swaggered in, handcuffs around her wrists. She was broad shouldered and muscular with a basketball build. She had long eyelashes and dark brown eyes that kept the sorrow and anger buried in her soul. She was pretty—rough but pretty. LaTasha surveyed her new surroundings, the guard, and Benevolence. She pulled out the chair, sat down, and stared at the wall. Moments later, though no one else saw her, Anger walked wearing a red and black jersey with the number 12 on it, red shorts with black stripes, knee-length socks, and sneakers tossing a crimson basketball ball back and forth.

Benevolence flipped through LaTasha's thick manila folder. She scribbled some notes.

"Says here you're doing time for a 2004 attempted murder conviction. You want to talk about it. You've done a year already it seems."

"What's there to talk about? You got it all there in the file. You can read, can't you?" Anger snickered.

"I don't always believe what I read. There are usually three sides to every story." Benevolence looked up at LaTasha.

"Whatever."

"Why did you get transferred?"

"I don't know. Those DC girls wouldn't leave me alone."

"Did you ask for a transfer?"

"Apparently, someone did."

There was more to this story than this girl is letting on, or that these files are letting on. I've got to get this girl to open up.

"Honestly, I don't think that you belong in here."

"Why? I know what I did. I knew it was a crime."

Anger stood up and started bouncing the basketball.

Bounce. Bounce!

"You could have plea-bargained. It was your first offense."

LaTasha wiped her nose with her handcuffed hands.

"The judge did what he had to do."

"Did you have any accomplices? You couldn't have done this all yourself."

"You'd be surprised what a person would do when they've been pushed to the breaking point."

LaTasha scowled and pursed her lips.

Bounce.

She sighed. Benevolence looked into LaTasha's eyes. LaTasha darted her eyes away. Benevolence shifted directions.

"It says here you were a star player on Anacostia's basketball team. Looks like you were going places. What position did you play?"

"Guard."

Anger felt a breeze. She looked around the room.

Where is she?

Anger slammed the crimson red basketball to the wall.

Bam!

Benevolence jolted slightly.

"Good position. I've always liked basketball. Were you a shot blocker?"

"I got some boards. Worked on it. Had my inside jump shot, a fade and was pretty good at three-point range."

"Okay. You held up backcourt, good at defense?"

"Of course."

"Always on your A game?"

"You know it."

"Prepared mentally?"

"No doubt."

"Practiced your free throws?"

"If you want to be the best."

"Constantly looking for your shot? Always a team player?"

"Always."

Anger looked confused. The volley of words spoken back and forth was coming too fast. She wasn't sure where the conversation was going. She could not deflect the basketball fast enough to stop LaTasha's train of thought, to distract her from what was really going on. Anger snarled and threw the basketball against the wall.

Don't tell her anything! You hear me? Don't tell her anything!

"Is that how your stepfather saw it? He looked for ways to make that shot. At you. He looked out for himself. He really wasn't a team player, was he?"

LaTasha cringed. She pressed her hands against the edge of the table. She looked at Benevolence. The game was over.

"That's not in my file. How would you know that?"

"It's not in your file. Why didn't you tell someone? You should have told somebody. There were reasons you lashed out."

Anger growled and banged the table. LaTasha banged on the table.

"You didn't think I tried to tell somebody? Nobody would believe me. Do you know how common this thing actually is around there?"

"Not even your mother?"

LaTasha bolted up. She went to the corner and started positioning her handcuffed hands to shoot imaginary free throws. One after another, LaTasha squared herself up. The room, in her mind, no longer resembled a prison but the state championship. The voices of crowds booed her at the free throw line. The Indians were up by one point. LaTasha squared her shoulders up. The clock suddenly transformed into a basketball hoop. LaTasha bounced the ball, raised her hands, and released.

Swish.

She heard roars. She smiled. She squared up her second imaginary shot.

Swish.

The roars got louder. LaTasha was in a trance of her own memories. The roars faded. She caught herself and just stared at her handcuffed hands.

"I needed a way out. I couldn't go back home. He'd never leave me alone. It had been going on since I was eleven. At first, it was just hugs and kisses. Sometimes he would kiss me on the mouth. It was uncomfortable. When I turned fourteen, he stopped kissing me. He started doing other things. I joined the basketball team so that I would get away for him. For a while, it worked. Then he started coming to the games. He hid in the crowds. When we would win, he would also score. He used to tell me what a good girl I was and how special I was. It made me sick!"

LaTasha threw up one last free throw in the air. In her mind, the ball bounced off the rim.

"He used basketball to get to me. I had nothing left. So life did not matter anymore. I told my mother. She refused to ask him. I couldn't tell my sister. I thought I had nobody. Sasha believed me, though. The Reds did. We were going to kill him."

Anger looked up at the ceiling and screeched in defeat. She vanished in a red pile of smoke. LaTasha softened. Her small brown face showed, for the first time, a scared little girl who finally realized the weight of her actions. She walked back to her seat, folded her hands on the table, and put her head down. Benevolence watched.

Breakthrough.

She began writing her notes when she heard sobs, muffled sobs. Benevolence got up and came around the table. The guard advanced toward the door, opened it, and stared. Benevolence raised her hand to stop him. A slight breeze flew in. The guard looked at Benevolence carefully, nodded, and stepped back. Healing slipped in. Benevolence knelt down and wrapped her arms around the desperate girl who took matters into her own hands. LaTasha fell into her arms.

"That bastard ruined my life."

Soon healing, wearing a turquoise blue dress, stood in the room. Her dress flowed briskly from the calm breeze of air blowing from the air conditioner. Healing blew a kiss. The cloud of blue smoke grew bigger and stronger until it engulfed the entire meeting room. Moments later, when the smoke cleared, Benevolence and LaTasha were still caught in an embrace.

Chapter 18

"Sometimes you don't even realize you're in jail..."

*B*eep! *Beep! Beep!*

The alarm blared four times before Leah smacked the buzzer to calm it down.

I just got to sleep.

Leah looked over at the alarm and answered it. The alarm had been going off for nearly an hour. Leah looked around her bedroom and viewed Saturday's clutter. Piles of clothes, food, and restaurant magazines were sprawled in different sections. It was an organized mess.

I have to call Dahlia today. I hope she's free. She's not scheduled for another two days.

Leah sat up, stretched, put on her rimmed black designer lenses, and unwrinkled her Saturday's to-do-list. Her lists almost kept her on track, when she remembered to do them. It was Kendrick's idea, one of the few that stuck. However, Leah often composed her lists when she was "on the go." *Grocery shopping. Cleaners. Two p.m. hair appointment.*

The phone chirped. Leah looked at the caller ID. The phone chirped again. Leah sighed. The phone chirped a third time. Leah took a huge breath and then reached for the receiver.

"Hello," Leah chirped as cheerily as she could muster.

"Leah, are you still sleeping? It's almost noon!"

"It's only 10:06 a.m., Mommy."

"Well, a young woman like you should be up and active. Getting prepared for the day. No telling what the morning will unfold. It's best to take advantage of it."

Here we go a lecture early in the morning. She's stalling. I'll just wait. I'm not asking this time.

"Well, I'm up now, so no more time will be wasted."

"Have you talked to your brother and sister lately?"

"Have you?"

"Well, you know how your brother is. Your sister is doing all right for herself, I guess. Everyone is trying to work for himself or herself. I wish we could all work together. Pull our resources together. Help each other out."

I knew it. Money. The tie that binds the family together or rather blinds.

Shah calls from time to time. Victor, her older brother, has been missing in action, dealing with his family, while her mother calls only to give the pity speech, long enough to siphon money out of Leah. Leah refused to sell the restaurant and split the profits. The family has since squandered their portion of the insurance. The restaurant remains the only source of stable and viable income, the only functional reminder of her father.

"What's the money for?"

"I don't want to get into the details over the phone. I just thought that you could come over to the house today and we could talk about it. It has been so long since I've seen you. How are you doing baby?"

Oh no, not today . . . I don't have time or patience for this. Leah sprung to her feet. She started pacing, getting herself ready for a battle.

"Well, I can't—not today. Not right now. I have a million things to do and I am already late for an appointment."

I can't handle this right now. Early in the morning? There's no way that I'm coming over.

"Okay, so what about 1 p.m.? Can you make that? On the other hand, Sunday at noon? Lunchtime?"

Leah grabbed the shirt on top of the bedpost and began wringing it around her arms.

"Mom, I can't come over."

"Why not?"

"I have appointments. They were prescheduled. I can't just break them just at the drop of a hat."

I don't want to either.

Her semistructured day already seemed to be unraveling.

"Figures. Your sister would have tried to see what she could do. She does try, you know?"

"Then, you go and ask her for the money! Look, I have to go. We'll have to discuss this later. Bye, Mommy."

Click.

Leah flung the shirt she arm-wrestled to the floor. Irritated, she stomped into the shower to wash off the guilt trip that her mother succeeded in laying on her. She turned on the steamy water, hoping to drain off the steam bubbling inside.

Why does she always do that? Compare me with Shah? After all these years?

Tears of frustration ran down her face. She mixed the cold water and let the warmth soak up all of the morning's heaviness. A few minutes later, Leah toweled down, searching frantically for her morning pack near the bed. With shaky hands, she fumbled with the lighter until she managed to drag out a long puffed ball of relief. She threw on a blue and white Nike suit and carried a bag of clothes to her trunk.

"Leah? Leah, is that you?"

Leah was at the register at Coleman Cleaners when a former college classmate walked in carrying a gray clothing bag.

"It's me, Sevara. Sevara Peders, well Brown now. From Maryland, College Park. We were in calculus class together. Girl, come here! Give me a hug!" Sevara ran to Leah. A surprised Leah welcomed the hug.

"It's been years since I've seen you. You look good! What are you doing now?"

"Well, I own a restaurant. My father's restaurant. I manage it now."

"Great! Are you still living in the area? We should do lunch. Take my card." The clerk interrupted.

"That'll be sixty dollars."

Leah handed the monies to the clerk and exchanged cards with Sevara.

"Sevara, it was really good seeing you."

"You too, Leah. Don't be a stranger. Let's have lunch sometime okay?"

Leah left the cleaners. Sevara Peders was a reminder of her past: the life before Caribbean DeLite. College. She never really thought too much about not finishing college. She mentally played back all of her teacher's comments in elementary and high school.

Daydreamer; lazy, but bright when she puts her mind to it; forgetful; excitable; short-tempered; needs to work harder; needs more structure.

Leah was not willing to go through all that criticism again.

I am still learning new things every day running Daddy's business.

She reasoned, walking toward the parking lot. It was the price she paid for leaving Maryland, and she would do it again.

Even with all my struggles and faults. It's an honor to live out Daddy's legacy.

Leah got into her car.

College was a lifetime ago. What would I major in now?

Leah drove to the supermarket.

She picked up items haphazardly on her list: rice, juice, tea, meats, and fruit. The grocery store was always a dance for her, constantly zigzagging out of people's way. She walked up to the checkout counter. Leah perused the Ebony and Essence magazines as the machine scanned her items. The front page of Essence caught her attention: *Women and Adult ADHD—What you need to know*. She stared at the faces. The women looked just like her. They could be anyone. She placed the magazine slowly back on the rack as the cashier waited for her.

"Miss, will that be debit or credit?"

Chapter 19

*"You get to see what God has for you when
you're connected to the right person..."*

Leah volunteered Caribbean DeLite as the spot for January's meeting. Everyone met early Saturday evening. Leah wanted to expose the women to the ambiance of her establishment. She began to look forward to the meetings. The company of these women thrilled her, though she had to endure the first two months of catfights, delayed e-mails, and women dragging their feet to make each meeting come together.

Surely, these "saintly" women would not dare make a scene in public, Leah hypothesized.

Wouldn't want anyone to lose their witness.

Leah smiled as she set the last few utensils in place.

Let's just see what happens tonight.

Leah's hip began buzzing. She took out her BlackBerry and scowled. She shoved the BlackBerry back on her hip. Moments later, her hip buzzed again.

"Kendrick, I can't really talk right now. I'm preparing for a meeting. They'll be here any minute."

Like I really feel like speaking to you right now.

"Baby, I'm sorry about yesterday. I didn't mean any of those things I said. Just had one of those days, you know. I know that I shouldn't have . . . you know."

"Yeah, I know."

I know you done gone crazy, is what I know.

"I will see you later, right? What time will you be home? I have something for you."

"I have my meeting tonight, remember?" *Glad for the excuse. Any excuse really.*

"Look, don't wait up. I'm closing up tonight. The girls might want to do something afterwards."

Normally, Kendrick would swing downtown and bring Leah home, but the arguments lately have left her feeling less than friendly with her soon-to-be husband. These telephonic rituals were starting to piss her off. Kendrick seemed to be changing right before her very eyes. He was turning into a monster.

"Look, the inspector just walked in through the door. I've got to go." Leah shoved the BlackBerry calmly back into her pocket. Leah shook herself off, turned around, and gave her model smile, walking toward the man in the foyer.

Garrick Oliver, a gray-haired stuffed shirt with glasses, stood around looking like he owned the world and everyone in it.

"Mister Oliver, good evening, I'm Leah Decruz. Welcome to Caribbean DeLite. We have a few treasures that I know you are going to love. Please come this way."

Leah sat him in a booth away from the kitchen and front entrance. She introduced her best waiter then nodded over to Philippe and his chefs to do their magic.

Ten minutes later, Benevolence and the women were led into a secluded area. With inside renovations 90 percent complete, Leah hoped accommodations would meet everyone's approval. Everyone sat down as the waiter came over to the table.

"Ladies, I'm so glad you are all here. Leah, thank you for donating your restaurant to us for the evening."

Benevolence beamed.

"Aren't we the lucky ones? We got the private dining room."

Yasmine boasted.

"This is nice." Octavia crooned.

"You have Chinese artwork and a screen door?"

"Ooh, a fireplace. I bet you get a lot of requests for this room."

Simone offered.

"You still managed to put booths and a cocktail bar."

Yasmine felt the smoothness of the countertop and gave the barstool a spin.

"No problem, ladies, thank you. I really hope you enjoy the food. I told Philippe to make something special. Excuse me, ladies. I'll be right back."

Leah went out into the patio. She needed more than a smoke. She lit quickly.

Can't be out here too long.

Leah ran through her "mental" checklist.

No foul-ups in the kitchen. Remembered inventory. Remembered supplies. Had my "to-do" list. Didn't botch anything up. Stay focused. For once, everything is going right. It's been hard, Lord, but I have stayed focused.

Leah doused the cigarette and put it in her special corner for unfinished "lights." One waiter introduced fried calamari and plantain as an appetizer. Moments later, another waiter brought out a smorgasbord of meats: oxtail, jerk chicken, curry goat, and curry shrimp and rice.

Forty-five minutes later, notepads and books covered the table.

"Did everyone finish reading chapter two?" Benevolence inquired.

"Let me hear your thoughts." Leah began.

"Well, I know that we talked about dreams and aspirations last month and what we think God wants to do, but this chapter was deep. It took me a while to absorb it."

Leah drank some coffee.

Simone scooped up a spoonful of orange sherbet.

"Can other people be a part of your calling? Your vision?"

"Simone, others can be called to your vision, but God sets those kinds of divine appointments. Yasmine and Octavia, thoughts?"

"What?"

Octavia appeared to be comatose.

"I'm sorry. What was that?" Benevolence chuckled.

"Sleepy? What about you? Any thoughts on chapter two?"

I have many thoughts . . . but I can't be concerned about that right now. I need to save my job.

"Uh, um the material was pretty interesting. I enjoyed it."

Octavia drank some water.

"And there's the usual response."

Yasmine crossed her arms.

"What was that, Yasmine?"

Octavia looked across the table at her opponent.

"What she asked was do you have something to share? And as usual, nothing. You just keep all that wisdom to yourself."

Yasmine accused.

"Ding! Round one. Here we go."

Simone scooped up more sherbet. She had good seats for this one.

"Quiet, Simone."

Benevolence warned.

"Now, ladies, you've been doing marvelous so far. Let's not spoil it." She directed her eyes on Yasmine then Octavia.

"Not here, not now. Please."

"Well, now that you've mentioned it," Octavia rebutted.

"I have a question. Can you be in your calling, if you're always dealing with warfare? Always struggling or covering your back, your assets?"

"About time!"

"Yasmine!"

Benevolence pressed.

"Good, Octavia. Now we're getting somewhere. To answer all of your questions: people can be 'called' to you. You can be in your calling and have warfare, but there should be peace. You should have a covering; spiritual parents who are praying for you. Understanding your calling can be overwhelming. It is a process. You may not even know what your calling is. All of this takes time. Now, you have many things stored inside of you . . . many gifts, talents . . . many blessings. All stored up waiting for the chance, the season to bloom. For anyone, it may require some sacrifices."

Benevolence drank some water.

"You might have to let people go . . . Others may have to be still . . . And still some of you, it's really a matter of who you'll trust."

Silence fell across the table. Simone decided she would break the contemplative moment.

"Tavian and I have met several times for lunch and dinner. I'm not drawing any conclusions, but I think he might have changed."

Octavia blurted out coyly.

"Where does Mister Muai fit in this picture? Please don't count him out yet."

Yasmine closed her book. There was a newsbreak.

"Mr. Who? What . . . there's actually someone else?"

Simone darted her eyes over Octavia.

"We just went out for pizza, Yasmine. It's nothing really."

Leah did not feel like discussing relationships.

"I'm praying for a good write-up from Inspector Oliver today. With renovations almost done, it could give us a big boost. It's been pretty sluggish around here lately, with winter season coming and all."

"The food here is great."

Benevolence defended.

"He shouldn't have any issues. Guess what. I'm organizing a women's basketball tournament. The tournament will be either in March or April."

"You deal with women all day and then come here? Man, that's a lot of estrogen. It's too much for me."

"Somehow, Yasmine, we get that. How are your 'conquests,' uh, I mean, perfumes holding up?"

Octavia gave Simone a high five.

Be holy. Forget the wrench.

"We're still testing, but one formula shows promise. Byron seems to like it."

"Your boss?"

Leah finished her coffee.

"No, Leah, her boyfriend."

Simone scooped up the last bit of sherbet.

"Well, actually, I guess both."

Yasmine confessed.

"Yasmine, that's slippery ground you're walking on."

Benevolence mentally planned for a talk with Yasmine later.

"Be careful."

"Well, he started it, minister."

Yasmine defended.

"And you could finish it, for the sake of your job."

"Octavia, there are other jobs."

However, there is only one Byron.

Yasmine, after a delayed reaction, refuted an earlier statement.

"Minister, what if Byron is a part of my calling? I think it is something worth discovering."

"Yasmine, aren't you unwrapping the package a bit too fast?" Benevolence didn't waver. Octavia whispered over to Simone.

"Has Tavian been back to church? Has he rededicated?"

"Not yet." Simone whispered back.

"He said he's got some things to work through."

The waiter nodded for Leah that he had taken care of the other half of the restaurant.

"Leah, have you talked to Kendrick about premarital counseling yet?"

"Minister, we have broached the subject. He's been busy. He feels we don't really need it . . . one source of our many arguments lately. But I'm sure we'll make an appointment really soon."

You retard! Why do I put up with you? What is wrong with you? You got ADD or something? Can't do anything right. If it weren't for your looks, no one would even deal with you. Just a mess.

Leah drank some water to distract the tears welling up in her eyes. She blocked the vicious wave of words from repeating another performance in her head.

"I need to check on the inspector, excuse me."

The women hugged good-byes outside of the restaurant. They were still breaking the ice, though the facades were being chipped away little by little with a butter knife.

"Leah, thanks for dinner. See you all on Sunday."

Octavia echoed.

"Yeah, the food was delicious. I have to come here more often." Simone buttoned up her coat. January's wind gusted through the parking lot.

"Yeah, everything was tasty. Thanks, Leah. Catch you guys later. It's cold out here!"

Yasmine headed quickly toward her car, three cars away from Octavia and Simone. They walked quickly and split into two directions. The cars honked and drove off. Leah began buttoning up her jacket and headed back into the restaurant.

"Whew! It's getting windy out here."

Benevolence got out her car keys.

"Leah, are you okay? You look like you got a lot on your mind."

"Oh god, I didn't get a chance to greet the inspector before he left. I hope all of the meals were okay. I knew I would forget something. I'm so stupid!"

Leah pulled out a Virginia Slim and lit before she remembered who was standing in front of her. Leah stepped away from Benevolence.

"Minister, I'm sorry. Do you mind if I smoked?"

"I didn't realize you did. What just happened?"

"I need to unwind . . . it's been an intense evening."

"Are you always this nervous? This wound up?" Leah blew out a puff of smoke.

"No, not always but most of the time. I forgot to check on the inspector before he left. We were having such a great time."

Leah looked at the cigarette; the stem disappeared.

"This helps me calm down. I know I should quit." She placed the cigarette to her lips.

"Have you seen a doctor, about the nervousness?"

"I did when I was younger. I think I remember my parents took me. The doctor told them that I was hyperactive and that I would grow out of it. I caused problems in school and had poor grades, so my mother had to home school me for a while . . . what a joke. She soon gave up on that idea and they placed me back in public school."

"Have you ever thought about getting another diagnosis?"

Leah stiffened.

"I'm not retarded! I am not stupid! I can do things on my own. I can handle this too!"

Benevolence moved closer. She looked at Leah tenderly and spoke softly.

"I did not call you stupid nor did I say you couldn't do any of those things. I just don't think you should be smoking."

Leah wiped the tears coming from her eyes with her shaky fingers and sucked in a wad of smoke helplessly.

"I can't help it anymore." she surrendered.

"I need this. I need to relieve the stress. I wish I had something else, but I don't."

"Let me help you."

Benevolence gently pulled out the cigarette from Leah's shaky hands.

"You're not alone. Let someone help you."

Benevolence stomped the cigarette out, held Leah tight, and said a quick prayer. It was enough to ooze all of the anxiety out of her body.

Chapter 20

"There are a lot things to forget in order to reach your potential..."

Benevolence pondered January's meeting at the restaurant with the girls, with Leah. She knew that it would take some time to get the women to trust each other—they focused too intricately on the details of their own lives. They could not see yet how to be their sister's keeper.

Lord, what will it take to get these women to become sisters? Is this not your will? Did you not call them together? I am not sure they like each other, but to get them to love each other? Am I doing the right thing here... continuing this? Benevolence stared into the computer screen at her daily e-mails. Suddenly, a new e-mail popped up and broke up the train of conflicting thoughts. "Spoken Word Opportunity—Please Read." Benevolence clicked the e-mail.

Bene, we just wanted to make sure you didn't forget about tonight. We know you are a busy woman, but please make the time. You haven't done any outings in a while... which can't be good. You have said it, but you DO need some rest... an outlet, a place to have fun and relax. You need to replenish. So having said all that, I expect to see you tonight. No buts—don't disappoint me now. Later—Jules.

Benevolence smiled. She almost forgot. Writing did replenish her. She had been meaning to do more engagements, but life lately had her dragging. Writing seemed to be one of the few activities that gave her strength.

Jules Tate still had a way of gently strong-arming her into new opportunities. Though their relationship fizzled out after a few months, they remained friends. He refinanced her house and occasionally accompanied her to poetry events. Rona and Jules tag-teamed her, and she fell for it. She had to comply.

Good. I need a distraction. Work was consuming. The women are getting restless here. More fights than usual.

February's weather blew in a chilly cold front through the metropolitan area.
Must be cabin fever.

The basketball tournament was scheduled to start in April. One of the correctional officers walked in.

"Benevolence?"

"Yes?"

"I got some mail for you. Just thought you'd want to know one of your girls gave their life to Jesus today."

"Who?"

"Not sure. Just heard some of the other COs talking. Maybe one of your ballplayers . . . anyways, the school is not pumping out enough graduates. The new board is talking."

"So soon? They just pumped money in here."

"They're always looking for a quick return on their investment. So who knows? The garden, recording studio, the school or puppy nursery might be axed if things don't change. They're looking at each one, to see if it's really useful."

"We really need those programs."

"You don't have to convince me. We don't have enough programs to keep folks going. It's the fact that these women leave and come back, that's the real issue."

The phone rang. The correctional officer left.

Who got saved? LaTasha?

The phone rang again.

"Hello?"

"Are you excited about tonight?" It was Jules.

"I'm getting there."

"You have your material ready?"

"Yes. I have a few on the shelf just in case there's an encore. I got something new I want to try. I will see what the mood is. Play it by ear."

"Now that's more like it. I'll see you later."

Benevolence nearly placed the phone back on the hook before it erupted again.

"Bene, you're ready for tonight?"

"Rona . . . what are you guys . . . a tag team or something?" Benevolence laughed.

"Jules just called, he said the same thing."

"Now for once, we're on the same page. He gives you more attention now than when you were dating."

"Shut up. I told you we are friends. Plus, I guess he wants to see me have more fun. Less work . . . more fun."

"Amen! But there are other things in your life."

"We've gone through this already," Benevolence reasoned.

"He knows that he's not in the place that he should be. It doesn't mean he's not trying."

"Well, going to church more than once a month would be a good start." Benevolence switched subjects.

"What time are you going to be there?"

"I can get there by six thirty. I will reserve seats. Are the girls coming?"

"I think so. I've sent out e-mails, but I don't know."

"Are they still clawing at each other?"

"Not so much outwardly . . . it's calmed down. They are just not congealing. They come together because they have to . . . not because they want to. I am not sure I made the right decision. I'm thinking about ending it."

"What? You've put so much time, effort and prayer into this. Don't these girls realize that? Are they that vain? If they can't see how much you're committed to them by rearranging your life, then maybe it really is for the best. Let me tell them. I guarantee it won't be in 'christenese'!"

Benevolence smiled.

That's my girl. Always got my back.

"Don't worry. I'm not really in control of this. I was just the vehicle to put the relationships together. Somehow, I have to believe the Lord is going to work things out."

"Okay," Rona sang.

"You sure you don't want me to say anything? It just seems that folks are just seeing their own reflections when they look in the mirror."

"Isn't that what they're supposed to see?" Benevolence laughed.

"Look, girl, I have to go. I have a session. See you later. Love you."

"Love you too, Bene."

Benevolence had an appointment with LaTasha. LaTasha had stood her up for the last two appointments. God's presence had fallen so strongly in the first session that it had surprised them both. Now LaTasha seemed to be dodging her. Did LaTasha get saved? Did she give her life to Christ? Benevolence checked her watch. LaTasha was twenty minutes late. Benevolence waited longer this time than the other meetings. She believed LaTasha would come if she could hold out just a few minutes more. Benevolence reluctantly closed her folder, picked up her notepad, and stood up when Tiffany, the new correctional officer, opened the door. LaTasha limped in. There was a fresh scar near her right eye and redness near her left jaw. She eased into her chair, wincing as she sat down.

Her new friend, bitterness, wearing black jersey, limped in and sat in the empty chair next to her.

"LaTasha, what happened to you? Who did this?" LaTasha stared at the wall and continued with the silent treatment.

Back to square one.

"You've missed two appointments. I thought we were getting somewhere."

"Been busy." LaTasha stared at the wall.

"Were you in a fight? With another gang member? What are you trying to do? Get yourself killed?"

Benevolence walked over to LaTasha, forcing her to look in her direction. Benevolence's perfume cinched LaTasha's nostrils. LaTasha winced and looked away.

"They were trying to take over our territory, but we took care of it. Besides, I'm already dead."

Bitterness smiled. Benevolence knelt down in front of LaTasha so that they were inches apart. It seemed all of professional tactics went away when it came to this kid.

"LaTasha, you're a bright young woman. You can still salvage the rest of your life. You do the right things and in a few years, there's the possibility of parole."

"Probation!" LaTasha winced again.

"So that I'll get out and do what? No one recruits convicts for basketball players. This isn't hoop dreams. Women don't get that kind of attention."

Benevolence wanted to be the first to tell her. Give her hope. She went back her side of the desk.

"We're organizing a tournament in April. I want you to play. Get a team together. Invite friends, family."

"Who told you I even wanted to play?"

"LaTasha, that kind of talent doesn't just vanish. What about your mother? Have you talked to her?"

"That bitch. No, I haven't talked to her . . . don't want to either." Benevolence felt anger rise up. She walked back to her seat.

"Don't disrespect her like that in front of me. She is still your mother." *Calm down, Bene, calm down.*

"It's her fault I'm here! Look, I see what you're trying to do, but that part of my life is dead. You hear me, dead!" she muttered.

"Just let it be."

LaTasha winced one last time as she raised her hand in the air. Tiffany came in quickly to escort her out. Benevolence looked LaTasha dead in the eye.

"LaTasha, basketball will always be a part of you. Just like your past. As ugly as your past is, what happened to you is not the real you. You discovered something real with basketball. Something wonderful. Now, I'm not asking you, I'm telling you. Discover it again."

Tiffany opened the door. LaTasha and bitterness left, staring at Benevolence.

Chapter 21

"Basically it comes down to this: hurt people hurt people..."

At Eve's CineArt Café, a restaurant and boutique-style entertainment center, the door opened and closed every two minutes. Patrons chatted at the smoothie bar. Friends met up with friends. "Wannabe" players stood in the corner, scoping out the "shorties." Octavia walked in and spotted Yasmine at a table, laughing and flirting with some man in a Brooks Brothers suit, while another woman chatted with them. The woman excused herself.

All right, Tavie, be on your best behavior. Do not let any of Yasmine's comments rattle you. Resist the devil and Yasmine will flee.

"Byron, my mentor is performing tonight and I want you two to officially meet."

"Good! Are the other ladies coming?"

"I'm not sure, but I think so."

Octavia strolled over smoothly to the couple, each step brimming with power. The men took notice.

"Hey, Yasmine."

"Hey, Octavia!" Yasmine greeted her with a pretentious hug. Octavia received her, figuring it was a show for the new beau.

Whew, he was fine!

"Octavia, Byron Combs. Byron, Octavia Kalu. He also works at Cyprus Pharmaceutical."

Byron stood up and shook Octavia's soft hands.

"Octavia . . . a very pretty name . . . Kalu, where are you from?"

"Sierra Leone."

"Wonderful."

The looks that Byron gave Octavia were pissing Yasmine off.

I guess Octavia is attractive, if you like the lawyer—Xena: Warrior Princess—I'll-bite-your-head-off type.

Yasmine prided herself in being primarily a lover, not a fighter.

"Byron, could you order us some drinks from the bar? You know my favorite. Octavia, what are you having?" She was eager to break up this flirtatious dance.

"A cosmopolitan is fine."

"Be back in a moment, ladies."

Leah and Kendrick walked in. Leah took the night off. Kendrick joined her in an effort to apologize from the spree of arguments running its course over the past two weeks. Leah knew she should forgive him, but being angry had its benefits. Anger was however, draining her focus in other areas. They came in separate cars and met in the foyer. Kendrick greeted a stiff-necked Leah with a warm hug and a kiss on the cheek. Leah soon recognized Octavia and Yasmine and sauntered over to the bar.

This is just what I needed . . . a good distraction. Please, Lord, do not let anything serious jump off between Kendrick and me tonight.

"Hey, ladies."

Octavia popped up and greeted Leah warmly. She liked Leah, her style, attitude, and toughness. Leah, though surprised, graciously received the greetings.

"Yasmine, Octavia. This is Kendrick O'Riley."

Kendrick shook both of their hands.

"Hello." Octavia recognized his name.

"Aren't you Kendrick O'Riley the restaurateur . . . your father owns a chain of restaurants across the East Coast. How's business?"

Kendrick smiled.

"Yes. Business is good."

"Where's Simone?"

Leah sat down next to Octavia.

"I'm sure she's on her way. Probably waiting on Tavian. We should go and get a table."

"Actually, she's here."

Yasmine nodded toward the door. She beheld the eye candy that appeared latched on to Simone's arm.

Ouch! So, this is the man that blew her off. I see there really is a thin line between love and hate.

Simone spotted them and waved. They walked over and made their pleasantries.

"Ladies, this is Tavian. Tavian, this is Octavia, Yasmine, and Leah."

The brothers introduced and shook hands. Rona walked over to the group.

Good-looking bunch of folk.

"I'm glad that all you were able to make it. Benevolence will be so pleased."

The crowd seemed electric. The MC strutted across the stage. Benevolence looked across the room. She saw the girls and their dates. Benevolence invited friends, colleagues, presbytery, and family.

Good, everyone is here.

Benevolence moved her neck from side to side. Jules noticed her tensing up. He began rubbing her shoulders and neck.

"Bene, don't be so nervous. It looks packed out there, but you're a pro. You are going to be fabulous! This is definitely your breakout crowd."

"You think so?"

"I know so. Something is definitely going to happen tonight. I can feel it. Are your girls here?"

"Yeah, right over there." She pointed over to the center of the room.

"They look like a sorority. No wonder."

"Don't start," Benevolence warned.

"Just playing . . . let me go and say hello."

"Come right back. In case they start early."

Benevolence checked her hair and makeup and took another glance at her suit. She looked ready for her first major gig. The room held all kinds of people. A strange kind of energy filled the air. Some of it disturbed her. These kinds of events drew in all types of people. Luckily, there was prayer cover and folks always knew when to turn it on. The MC picked up the microphone.

"Ladies and gents, welcome, to Eve's CineArt Café. Tonight is open mic night and we have a show for you. We have a few of newcomers and a couple of old settlers. Now folks, what do you do if you like what you hear?" The crowd clapped their hands and blew out whistles.

"Now, folks, what do you do if you don't like what you hear?" The crowd clapped softly. Others booed. Some were hushed.

"Now, we don't boo unless they're really bad. Just kidding . . . folks, we clap for everyone, make them feel better. It is hard work coming up in front of you people, with material that's close to my heart. It takes guts. Make sure you give everybody some love. All right, our poets are set back stage, show your love, not your rage for our first poet of the night, Johnetta Speaks!"

Several poets came on the stage. Some of the poets spouted out poetry served on a silvery crystal platter. Others handed poetry to the audience served in a brown paper bag. Poets cooed tales from spawned love to blue-collar blues. The MC ran up back onto the stage.

"Man, you guys are tough, at EC Cafe. I hope that this next poet will do it for y'all. Show your love, for first timer, Benevolence James."

Benevolence walked up onto the brightly lit stage. Beads of sweat trickled down her back.

"Good evening. The poem I'm about to do is called 'Fate's Hand.' I hope you'll enjoy it."

She fixed the mike, lowered her head, mentally counted to three, and raised her head slowly into stardom.

> "You came in by a Storm,
> Trying to transform—
> Me into the woman
> You knew I could be.
>
> Though I tried to hide it,
> I realize, I can't deny it.
> You wooed me with your promises
> Calling forth my destiny
> I try to resist not looking back
> Can't help it, my past seems attached to me.
>
> But Fate stepped in, grabbed my hand and we started to dance
> He whispered in my ear strength, giving me another chance.
> Stay close, hold my hand, and follow my lead
> Don't worry, I won't let you go, this is my dance too, indeed.
> We stepped left; we stepped right, swaying past through the night
> Fate twirled me and swirled me, ah what a beautiful sight.
> Dreams spilled back into my head, back into my heart.
> Giving me a new will to accomplish them; giving me a brand new start."

The crowd whistled and cheered. Benevolence bowed. They roared for nearly two minutes.

Encore! Encore!

The MC ran back on the stage.

"Man! You people found a winner, huh? We'll give you an encore much later." The audience booed and hissed. He liked the tease.

She is worth keeping . . . a moneymaker . . . she will keep a crowd coming in.

Later, Benevolence and a few old settlers did encores. The electricity in the room was enough to power the whole block. New fans stopped at her table. A waiter handed her a glass of ginger ale.

"It's on the house. You were great."

"Thank you, right on time." One man walked regally through the crowd. His presence seemed to brighten each pocket of the restaurant as he moved.

"Ms. James?" His tone was smooth and rich.

"I really enjoyed your performance."

"Thank you." Benevolence stood up and greeted her gorgeous new fan. He extended his hand. His skin appeared the color of cantaloupe; his smile was as bright as the sky. A mystique, which intrigued Benevolence.

"Darius Henderson. It is indeed a pleasure."

He took her hand, held it, and kissed it softly. A thunderbolt struck. She briefly closed her eyes. She opened her eyes and reluctantly released his warm touch for a cool glass of ginger ale. She drank it down to the ice chips.

"I hope to see you again."

He walked. Her fingers tingled. Benevolence wasn't sure whether the result was from her sudden thirst or from the sudden electricity of this chance encounter. He disappeared into the crowd. The girls hovered around her chair like rock star groupies.

"Benevolence, that was awesome!" Octavia crooned.

"I didn't know you did spoken word. Why didn't you tell us?"

"I haven't been writing like I should."

"Benevolence, this is my friend Byron."

Yasmine beamed.

"Benevolence, this is Kendrick."

"Benevolence, you remember Tavian, don't you?"

Simone offered.

Benevolence shook hands and greeted all of her newly found fans. She made mental notes of each man's handshake, facial features, and overall demeanor.

So, these are the men my girls are entangled with. Interesting.

"Your poetry is inspiring. It digs into the soul."

Kendrick admired.

"Well, put my brother . . . well put."

Jules knelt down and planted a kiss on Benevolence's cheek.

"That's the reason why we've got to book her on more shows. I think I hear, manager."

"Whoa, whoa! I perform one show, and you people got me doing road trips! One day at a time."

Benevolence stood up in a fake protest. Rona hugged her best friend and sat down next to Octavia.

"Forget Jules, he's exaggerating. Plus, he doesn't know you well enough to go all across the country. I'm the one that should be road manager. That's right, girl power!"

Rona laughed and slapped fives with all females in her vicinity.

"We've got to go. See you guys on Sunday."

Yasmine gathered her coat and purse.

"It was a pleasure, Benevolence."

Byron charmed. He helped Yasmine with her coat.

"It was fun. We should do it again, soon."

Simone nodded toward Tavian. They both got up and headed toward the door.

"Benevolence, it was a pleasure to finally meet you."

Kendrick pulled the seat out for Leah and helped her with her coat. He put his arm around her as they headed toward the door. Benevolence noticed Leah stiffen. She watched intently. Once the couple approached the parking lot, Leah pushed his arm off. Her latest companion, unforgiveness laughed, crossing her paws over her blue striped suit.

"Leah, you've been mad at me for weeks. I said I was sorry. You are being childish. This is ridiculous."

Pride, wearing a cowboy hat and boots strolled between the couple and sat on the hood of an Infiniti Q45. He winked at unforgiveness. She laughed.

"I'm being childish?" Leah laughed.

"You're ridiculous! I am tired of being your verbal rag doll when the world comes crashing down on you. Where did this come from all of a sudden? You need some help! I already have my own issues to deal with."

Leah began to walk away.

"You sure do."

Spite skated in a hockey jersey and jeans toward the car and slapped paws with pride. Pride scooted over, giving spite a front-row seat.

"What the hell is that supposed to mean?"

Leah walked back toward Kendrick. She and unforgiveness stood directly in Kendrick's face. Kendrick lowered his tone.

"Woman, don't you dare get in my face."

Rage came from out of nowhere, bumping both pride and spite off the car hood. He lit a cigar. Kendrick grabbed Leah by the arm.

"Leah, I need you to be there for me. Like I'm there for you," Kendrick said through clenched teeth. He looked around the parking lot, careful not to cause a scene.

"I help you organize the restaurant, your house, pay your bills, so that you can handle life. Who do you talk to about the inspector and how to change up the menus, or the latest reviews, inventory and supplies? Who?" Leah shifted her shoulder and gritted her teeth.

"You Kendrick."

Rage smiled. Kendrick released her.

"I just want some respect, that's all. I just need you to understand where I'm coming from. I am sorry that I fly off the handle sometimes. I've said some stupid things. I'm definitely less than perfect, I know."

Kendrick took her hand and tried to bring her close. His tone changed.

"Baby, please forgive me."

Unforgiveness refused rage's hand. She stepped back. Leah stepped back from Kendrick's grasp.

"Kendrick, we need counseling, premarital counseling. My pastor says we should have counseling before we get married."

"Your pastor? We can go to my pastor for that."

"Your pastor? Since when? You come mostly to my church when you're not working, which is mostly all the time. Have you made an appointment?"

"No, but—"

"Well, I have. Kenny, we really need this. Things are different between us for some reason. You're changing, I'm changing. I just want to make sure we do things right . . . that we're right for each other."

Kendrick's eyes appeared red. He grabbed Leah so quick she did not realize what was happening.

"Are you breaking up with me? It is that mentor of yours . . . putting all these ideas into your head. You've been talking to her . . . about our personal business."

Unforgiveness dug her claws in rage and pushed away from the fire surrounding rage's spirit as hard as she could. Leah forced herself away from Kendrick, standing almost five feet away. Fear grew in her heart.

"Kenny, we need counseling. We don't communicate. We argue."

"Is that what we're doing now? Arguing? Because I thought, I was trying to communicate with you. Trying to explain what happened."

"I can't keep going on like this. We're not getting anywhere. I'm going home. Alone."

Leah walked briskly to her car and drove off. Rage's fiery paws hit the car hood, sounding off a row of car alarms in the parking lot. Spite and pride vanished. Rage kicked the sidewalk. Kendrick threw his arms up, kicked the curb, and cursed. He paced back and forth. He kicked the curb again and then heard laughter. Rage looked in the window at the table where three friends sat laughing and joking. His gaze centered in on one particular face. Rage smiled. Moments later, Jules, Rona, and Benevolence walked out of the café at ten in the evening.

"Bene, you were fantastic! You started something. I just know it!"

"Yeah, the MC has me already booked for the next two Fridays. He's talking about paid gigs. Small, but it is a start. I'm going to need new material."

"All the more reason . . . why you need a manager. Well, folks it's been real. However, a sister has to get home. Get ready to work for the man tomorrow. Peace."

Benevolence and Jules walked Rona to her Hyundai Sonata and watched it speed away. Kendrick watched it too, from the other end of the parking lot. Rage leaned on Kendrick's jeep.

"I'll walk you to your car."

Jules took her bags, pressed the unlock button, and placed the bags in the backseat. Benevolence stood by the driver's side.

"You were amazing tonight, Bene."

Jules admired. Kendrick and rage looked on, amused at the exchange.

"Thanks, Jules. Thanks for everything."

"Benevolence, could I—"

Jules scratched his head and rubbed his chin.

"Yes?"

"Come to your church sometime?"

"You're always welcome, Jules."

He cracked a huge smile.

"Okay. Great. I'll see you then."

Jules held her in a tight embrace. Benevolence caught a whiff of his cologne.

Lord, I'm already wired. I don't need anything else jumping off tonight.

He pulled back in a nick of time. It started to hail.

"You better get inside. It looks like it's going to be nasty out here."

Jules opened the car door and watched until Benevolence strapped her seat belt.

"Bye, Jules."

Jules stepped back and watched her pull off before getting into his Lexus. Kendrick and rage pulled off moments later.

Benevolence was on Independence Avenue when she noticed an SUV tailgating her. The hail increased ferociously, coming down like marbles.

Man, get off my bumper.

Benevolence fumed. She moved over to the right lane. He later moved to the right lane. She sped up and made a right near G Street in southwest. The light was red.

People are crazy. I think I lost the fool.

Suddenly, the SUV rammed Benevolence in the back and pushed her in the intersection.

"What the hel—oh my god."

She swerved to miss the pedestrian running to catch the light and hit a tree near a dead-end street.

Whoosh!

The air bag exploded out of the steering wheel. Rage smiled.

"Oh my god!"

Kendrick banged his hands several times on the steering wheel.

"See what you made me do!"

He looked in the rearview mirror. Worry banged on the window, opened the door, and sat down in the passenger's seat. When the light turned green, Kendrick sped off.

Benevolence slumped over to the driver's side of the window. A black SUV speeds off just as she loses consciousness.

I need . . . to call . . . 911. I need . . . help. TE—X94 . . .

Worry placed her shaky, trembling claws on Kendrick's right hand, leading his hand to the cell phone in the cup holder. Kendrick pressed speaker.

"911. How may I direct your call?"

"There's been an accident."

Kendrick cleared his throat.

"In southwest. Near G Street. Hurry. The driver looks hurt."

"Sir, are you with them? Sir, sir?"

Click.

Chapter 22

"A lion has come out of his lair, to snare you and to lay waste your land..."

On Saturday morning, Yasmine and Cadence spent their day serving food at a soup kitchen near Seventh Street northwest, in the Shaw-Howard area. Yasmine found herself occupied with Byron so much that her appearances during ministry events were becoming nonexistent. When Deacon Davis questioned her one Sunday afternoon, Yasmine did not want to disappoint, so she scheduled Cadence and herself to an impromptu soup kitchen as a way of making amends.

However, others soon began to notice her sudden exclusivity. Yasmine even tried to weasel of out the February meeting, but Benevolence was not having any of it. Yasmine served the meat loaf with a smile.

"Have a good day," she greeted, handing a plate to young boy. The meetings, the women, the outings—she enjoyed them. It was just a matter of time. She could feel her guard coming down, brick by brick. She wanted to trust them, but a part of her wanted not to get too close. Yasmine's cell phone began singing in her pocket.

"Cadence, can you take over real quick?"

"Yazz, I already have the string beans and corn. It's going to slow us down."

"Real quick. I'll be real quick."

Yasmine ran toward the kitchen door, smelling of meat loaf and gravy. She propped herself up in the corner and lowered her voice.

"Hey, baby."

"Hey, yourself. Where are you?"

Byron was buttoning his canary yellow shirt.

"At a soup kitchen with Cadence."

"How long will you be there?" he said, tying his shoes.

"About an hour or so. What's up?"

"Go directly home and change. I will pick you up at 2 p.m."

He checked himself in the mirror one last time before leaving the hotel.

"What is going on?"

"You are too nosy. Have to go. Bye."

Byron's phone buzzed again.

"Byron, we've got to talk."

"Dallibeth, I can't talk to you right now. I have to go to a meeting."

"When then, Byron? We need to talk. It has been five months. If you want out of this marriage—"

"Dallibeth, I've got to go, I will call you later."

Byron hung up the phone and got into his Mercedes. Yasmine put the phone back into her pocket. She smiled to herself. She snapped her plastic gloves back on and returned to the line.

I done hit the jackpot is what I did. Early too. Byron is fine, sophisticated, intelligent and has a body! He is terrific in every way imaginable. It takes years for people to find the right one and I do it four months. So, he doesn't have a church home. That takes a while. You can't just worship anywhere. We'll have to work on that. Am I falling for him? I know we work well together. He can definitely tango in the bedroom, but does it mean . . . Am I in love? How does he feel? Until he says those words, I better—

"Yasmine!"

Yasmine looked at the hill of meat loaf she piled on to one patron's plate. He smiled.

"I'm sorry. I'll get you another plate."

"Stop daydreaming and get back to work!"

Cadence warned.

"When is our shift over?"

Yasmine rushed to fix three plates at a time. Cadence looked at her as if she had two heads.

"What shift? We committed for the two hours. We have one hour left. Yasmine, don't do this, I swear I will throw this corn at you."

"I have to leave."

Yasmine pleaded, scooping up gravy and filling the three plates.

"You said you had no plans. I thought you said we would hang out after this."

Cadence yanked Yasmine by her serving spoon.

"After all, you sign both our names up. I never gave you permission." Yasmine had only seen this side of Cadence a few times.

"I know, but Byron called. He has a surprise for me," Yasmine pleaded. Cadence released her and went back to serving corn.

"It's always about him. Do you have time for anyone else?"

"Yes I do, but this sounds really important."

"Yasmine, you really need to finish this first. You cannot just drop commitments like that. People depend on you. I am taking my break."

Cadence plunked a spoonful of beans in front of her.

"You can handle my beans."

Cadence threw her gloves off and walked away. Some of the staff looked at her and back at Yasmine. Yasmine turned back to the patrons as if nothing had happened.

"Do you want gravy on your meat loaf? String beans or corn."

The phone sang again on her hip. The line died after the fifth ring. The phone buzzed a text message. She served the last patron and went over to the corner to see one of Byron's love notes. However, this time, she got a different message.

"Come soon. Accident. Minister James is in the hospital."

Yasmine nearly dropped her phone. She removed her hair bonnet, her smock, and gloves. She washed her hands and grabbed her jacket. Whispers had spread among the ministerial staff. Cadence returned to a disheveled Yasmine trying to put on her coat.

"Look, Cadence, I have to go. Something happened to Minister James. She's in the hospital."

"I just heard. Are you going to be okay?"

"I'm going home first then see if I can make my way over to the hospital."

"You sure? You want me to come with you?"

"No, um. I'm ok. Let me just go home first. Cadence, um thanks. I do owe you. I promise, I got you."

Yasmine rode the Red line through the February wintry mix while her thoughts fluttered back and forth.

I hope she's okay. I hope it is not serious. I need to call Byron. He will have to wait. He will understand. She really needs my support right now.

Yasmine returned to her condominium and a few minutes later jumped into the shower. Her cell phone rang. She turned the water off before picking it up.

"Hey, baby, you're ready?"

"Byron, um, I can't go."

"Did you eat already at the soup kitchen?"

"No, it's not that. There has been accident."

"What? Are you okay?"

"I am fine. However, my mentor isn't. She's in the hospital."

"Where? What happened? Do you want me to take you to the hospital? I can drive you there. Open the door. I'm outside."

Yasmine threw on some clothes and opened the front door. Byron stood there, wearing a brown suede coat, a canary yellow shirt, and brown pants.

The brother looked fine all year long. Even in the dead of winter.

Lust circled Yasmine three times, creating a crimson cloak of dust clouds. Byron smiled, gave her a hug, and planted a kiss that melted all her immediate thoughts away.

"Where's the hospital?" He whispered.

"What?" Yasmine was still in his gaze.

"Yazz, the hospital . . . where your mentor is—"

"Oh, um, can we go a little later?"

Yasmine was out of sorts. She needed to get herself together.

"Are you sure?"

"Yeah . . . Where's my surprise?"

She snapped back to her old self. Byron smiled.

"In time, sweetie, you'll know in time."

He grabbed her hand, kissed it, and led her outside to the passenger side of his black Mercedes, his chariot. They drove off down the street and into their own wintry "bliss."

Chapter 23

"Your love towards Him should make you do things that take great courage..."

Simone, Tavian, and Octavia had tickets to the three o'clock performance at Dance Place in DC. The couple appeared attached at the hip for two months. Two months of late-night phone conversations, bowling, ice skating, movies, and other favorites—two months to start anew.

They walked inside the gray brick building nestled right into a historic residential neighborhood through the auditorium as many took their seats.

Twenty dancers came out onto the stage in front of seven dreadlocked drummers playing an arrangement of African beats. One drummer spoke with his African snare, and another with the base. One instrument weaved its way through cacophonic arrangement, shaped like a ukulele or mandolin, the small mahogany-colored guitar spun out harplike melodies. Tavian clapped his hands. He watched the women, the rhythm of their movements. One female dancer jerked, jumped, and kicked all through the routine. Her body twisted and turned, revealing a flat eight-pack with a tummy ring.

"Monie, I need to get back into the gym. I don't even have a pack like that!"

The director, a fifty-something dreadlocked warrior, jumped and kicked harder and longer than everyone like it was nothing. He never appeared out of breath.

"Yeah, that's right!"

The audience cooed the dancers on, following every story, seeing every tradition, and admiring all the new costumes. Children threw dollars onstage. One woman went boldly onto the stage and stuck the dollar to the drummer's forehead.

"Eh hem! That's how you do it!"

Octavia laughed and clapped loudly.

"She knows how to do it."

The drummers laughed. Simone and Tavian cajoled Octavia, who appeared ready to leap onto the stage herself.

"How come you never stick dollars on my forehead?" Tavian whispered.

"Shh!"

Simone nudged him playfully with her elbow, trying to keep from laughing. The drummers cupped up a syncopation of beats. They drummed loudly, then softly. The beats became heartbeats, each sound a distinct rhythm. The beats penetrated Simone's mind, creating their own space, their own wave pattern. She drummed up thoughts of Mr. Muai.

"I won't pressure you, but I can't keep you off of my mind."

Elijah said to Simone at Cheesecake Factory one afternoon, a few weeks earlier.

"Elijah."

Boom . . . tom . . . boom . . . tom.

"Yes, Simone."

"I can't—I can't do this. I'm not ready."

"That's not true. You're just not ready to be with me . . . what if he hurts you again?"

Elijah moved his left hand over across the table in search of Simone's.

"He won't."

Simone snatched her hand away before his hand could make contact.

"If he does . . . Simone, you deserve more . . . He better not or else—" Elijah raised his balled fists and began throwing punches.

"Put your hands down. You won't do anything."

Simone stretched to grab his hands. It was quite amusing. The man was defending her honor. She wasn't sure who would win. Tavian had a size advantage, but Elijah had heart. Elijah quietly receded. He took Simone's hand and kissed it.

"The man truly doesn't know the gem he has."

Boom . . . tom . . . boom . . . tom . . . boom.

"I think this time he does. Time will tell."

Boom . . . tom . . . tom.

The audience clapped and roared out whistles and screams at the end of the first act. The theatre manager announced a ten-minute intermission. Simone snapped out of her trance. Tavian got up from his seat.

"Do you guys want a snack, or something to drink?"

"Apple juice and an oatmeal pie for me." Octavia announced.
"I just want a bottle of water." Simone offered.

The show lasted two hours. Afterward, Simone, Octavia, and Tavian stood in the main lobby, talking to some of the performers.
"Simone thanks for inviting me. This was wonderful."
"Tavie, thanks for taking the extra ticket. It was fun."
"Next time, Octavia, you should bring one of your friends."
Tavian stood behind Simone and helped her with her jacket.
"Don't worry about me, Tavian, I'm fine."
"Now, I can hook you up. Just say the word."
Tavian chimed in and smiled.
"Good-bye, Tavian." Octavia glared at him.
"Monie, we'll talk. I'm going to work for a few hours."
Simone and Tavian walked toward the parking lot. Fear sat on the park bench in the parking lot, looking through yellow-colored binoculars at the couple. As they approached Tavian's car, Tavian scanned the area. When the coast seemed clear, he grabbed Simone close and kissed her tenderly on the lips.
"What was that for?" Simone panted.
"Not that I'm complaining or anything."
"For being you, for being the woman that I love. These two months have been the best months of my life. It has taught me a very important lesson. I don't want to spend any more time away from you again."
Tavian pulled Simone close to him, close enough to hear his heartbeat.
"Tavian?"
"Yeah?" He sighed.
Should I talk about this now? Lord, can't it wait? The man just poured out his heart. I could just fall out right here ... in the parking lot. He can be so passionate, so tender.
Simone backed away from his hypnotic embrace.
"Let's talk for a moment."
Tavian opened her side of the door and ushered her inside. Fear got into the backseat. She sat up real close, filling up the space between the driver and passenger seats. Tavian got inside, turned on the ignition, and drove off.
"Monie, what's up?"
Be careful how you word this, Monie. Things are going so good now. Don't blow it. You could still have everything you want: a future, a life, and kids. Just let this be.
"Tavian, can I ask you a question?"
They stopped on a red light near Michigan Avenue.

"Sure."

"While we were separated, did you see anyone?"

"What do you mean?" Fear coughed.

"Where you dating anyone?"

"No." Tavian coughed.

"Not really."

"What does that mean?" The light turned green.

"Monie, why are you bringing this up? I thought we cleared everything. Did you talk to Bishop Timms about us? About what happened?"

"I didn't have to. It was already on the gossip bulletin."

Fear led Tavian's hand to the radio. He switched stations very quickly.

"Monie, do we really have to talk about this now, I'm really in a good mood. I just want to enjoy this moment."

Simone turned the radio off.

"Then when, Tavian, when? I didn't want to bring this up now, but eventually we needed to talk. I've enjoyed these last two months, but it's been nagging me and I have to get it off my chest."

Simone took a deep breath and then plunged in.

"You have never apologized for all the hurt and pain you caused."

"Monie, I apologized to you. What are you talking about?"

"You haven't apologized to Bishop, to the deacons or ministers. You haven't talked to anyone. You and Deacon Davis used to be good friends. What were you doing all that time? What were you doing for four months?"

Fear blew yellow dust around Tavian. He rubbed his head.

"It was a bad time for me."

Tavian looked straight ahead.

"Look, we shouldn't be stuck in the past. I promise it won't happen again. It's over now. I'm back. Things are sweet. Let's not spoil that."

Simone continued her press.

"Tavian, where are you, spiritually? These last four months, have you thought about getting baptized, about getting rededicated?"

Tavian glanced at Simone. The car stopped at the red light.

"Simone, you really have to do this now?"

"You walked out on me. We were planning a wedding. We had two more counseling sessions. You took off without so much a word. No one knew where you were! Now you reappear out of thin air and everybody is supposed to forgive and forget? No one is going to say anything to you. No one has forgotten."

"Including you."

Tavian drove what seemed like the longest drive down Eastern Avenue.

"Tavian, do you realize how much pain you've caused? How much you have hurt my family and me? We attend the same church, yet you barely speak anymore."

"It's really your church. I don't feel comfortable there anymore."

"It used to be yours too."

"Monie, please, let's not ruin what's left of the day."

"I want you to see Bishop Timms. Rededicate your life. Settle things." Tavian pulled the car into the parking space of Simone's condominium and turned off the ignition.

"Who the hell made you priest?"

"Tavian, if we are going to be together, there are a lot of issues we need to straighten out. You can't just run off when life starts caving in all the time."

"I like life just the way it is right now."

Selfish bastard.

Simone flung open the car door and marched over to her condominium. Tavian parked the car and ran after her. Fear sat in the backseat. She pawed open the door, watching the whole fiasco.

"So, as long as I change and accept you and your ways everything is fine. However, anything that you have to do to change isn't. Tavian, you really don't get it."

Simone looked at Tavian. He was in a fog. The same fog that she had seen a million times before. It was the "fog" over their relationship. Simone grew tired of the fog. She wanted to see the relationship more clearly.

"Tavian, I don't think I can go through this again . . . I just can't."

"Monie, we're ok. I hate it when you get this worked up."

"Tavian, please don't call me anymore."

"Simone, don't do this."

Simone took off the engagement ring. She only started wearing it a few weeks ago. She was still getting used to the fit.

"Tavian, I'm different now. I love you, but I'm not sure that's enough. I am trying my hardest to be the kind of woman that God would be proud of. I can't pretend anymore."

"Pretend?"

"There's been a sharp pain in my soul. A hole in my heart. It's been there for four months. You were gone and I was here. I dealt with all the whispers, all the side comments, the gossip, and the ridicule. All the nights I couldn't sleep or eat. I knew it was my fault. You come back, and you cannot even honor me with this one request. Make amends . . . Prove your love . . . I've been a fool."

Simone turned the key into her door.

"Simone."

She went inside. She turned around and faced Tavian.

"Don't call me anymore. Do not come by. Just leave me alone."

She gave him back the ring. Tavian cupped the ring in his palm. She closed the door.

"Simone. Simone!"

Tavian banged on the door several times. Simone and disappointment walked into the bedroom with tears streaming down their faces.

Chapter 24

"You can be connected to someone and be in bondage..."

Simone met up with the women briefly in the lobby one Sunday afternoon. The huddles were becoming a regular routine.

"By now, everyone should be aware of Minister James's situation. I'm not sure of her current status or if anyone of you have had a chance to go to the hospital, but I thought we could pitch in and see if we could be of any assistance."

"What did you want us to do?"

Octavia opened her journal, ready to take down any notes.

"Well, I'm not sure,"

Simone concluded.

"She would be better able to answer that. We need to go to the hospital first, together. To show our support."

"I'm not fond of hospitals."

Leah shifted her purse from her right shoulder to her left.

"It's not exactly everyone's favorite place."

Yasmine rolled her eyes upward.

"Hush!" Simone warned. The administrator now stood in front of them.

"Here's the deal. We need to put differences aside and come together as a team. A real team. We won't have our fourth monthly meeting in the usual format so we need to adjust. We'll have to ask how we should hold meetings, if we do at all. We'll wait and see how she feels. She has poured herself out to us in a very short period. We need to acknowledge that. God wants to see how we'll respond."

"So the judgmental stuff needs to stop. The fighting, the wisecracks . . . all that. Okay? Can we do this?"

Leah belted out with sudden courage.

She looked directly at Yasmine.

"Oh, so I'm the sole culprit."

Yasmine glared back at Leah.

"No, you're not." She directed her gaze over in Octavia's direction.

"I'm willing to try it."

Octavia put her journal in her purse.

"But I can't be by myself." Octavia negotiated.

"Simone?"

"I'm willing."

"Good, I am too. So, it's settled."

Leah shifted her purse back to her right shoulder. "I'm heading over to the hospital later on. Does anyone want to ride together?"

"I'll ride with you." Octavia picked up her belongings.

"I have something I have to do first," Simone added.

"Me too, but I'll be there later," Yasmine reassured.

Leah stayed behind in the lobby after the brief meeting with the women.

That went extremely well, Leah thought, relieved that everyone felt united on the issue. It was the first time since they got together that a conversation went by without verbal backlash. There were more pressing things to worry about. Leah walked into the sanctuary. Her hands trembled. She couldn't keep still.

A smoke would be so nice right about now. Bermuda would also be nice right about now.

Normally after service, Leah drove quickly away so she could satisfy her cravings. She was careful not to reek of smoke before coming into the Lord's house of prayer. Lately, she felt a twinge of guilt at having to satisfy constantly her nicotine habit.

Lord, I know you do not like me smoking. It calms me but I know it's not good for me. I just get so nervous sometimes. I need your help and your strength. Tell me what's wrong with me so that I can quit.

Leah continued praying. She felt a sudden warmness come over her. She could feel herself loosening up. Her head became lighter; her hands stopped shaking.

Kendrick was to meet her for their first appointment. He had finally agreed to premarital counseling. After weeks of arguments, fights, and silent treatments, both wanted a truce. Though Kendrick initiated some of the verbal battles, Leah had a way of holding out longer. She began avoiding him. She closed up the restaurant more often and refused rides home to arrive in the wee hours of the night. She rose up early, ran errands, and returned to the restaurant. She even slept there when it got too late. It offered a convenient wall of distance from Kendrick.

Kendrick walked into the sanctuary. He could walk into any room as if he owned the place. Coming into the sanctuary today, Kendrick was unsettled. Worry walked in behind him with her paws behind her back. Kendrick wasn't at church due to work obligations. He liked the worship services and the sermons, but he had not placed much priority on religion recently. He grew up in a working household. They praised work and success. When he found the Lord, it was through the experience of a former girlfriend. Being saved changed some of Kendrick perspective's in the world of work, but there were areas of his life that still needed God's spice. Kendrick, as successful as he was, had issues cooking inside of him. Ever since deciding he really wanted to be married, with a family of his own, Kendrick waited. He waited for a family that he could lovingly dictate terms to. He waited for a family that would love and respect him. He waited for a family that would not criticize him as his father did. He pressured Kendrick. He bullied him into manhood. He demanded that Kendrick be the best at everything. Kendrick had no room for failure.

Now on the brink of happiness, Kendrick felt it slipping away. Kendrick scanned the sanctuary like a lunch menu. Leah was kneeling on the floor with her head bowed down. She looked peaceful. Kendrick's guilt crushed up against him.

She needs to know ... what I have done. Can I tell her without jeopardizing everything? Why couldn't everything stay as it was?

He rubbed the back of his head and looked at his watch.

Let's get this over with. I will find another way. I can't tell her now. Not yet.

He took a step closer. Kendrick felt queasy. He stopped.

Don't back out now. If you do, you are a punk. C'mon, be a man. Do not let your woman punk you. You are in charge. Woman was made for man. It's in the Bible. Do what you have to do to keep your house together.

His father's voice interrupted his thoughts. Kendrick flinched as the memory of an eight-year-old boy walking into his father's empire flashed through his mind. His father commanded everything in his path: chefs, managers, waiters, even the food critics. All with a smile. A calm control. However, at home, with his mother, it was another kind of control. With Kendrick, there was another type altogether.

"Leah," he whispered gently in her ear.

"It's time to go."

She wiped her face and looked up into his eyes.

"I didn't hear you come in."

"I didn't want to disturb you."

He helped her to her feet. She grabbed her coat and purse nestled underneath the pew. They walked around to one of the small conference rooms. Leah knocked three times. Deacon Davis answered.

"Yes, can I help you—Leah! Come in."

Deacon Davis looked at the man standing behind her.

"We're here to see Bishop for premarital counseling."

"Oh yes. Come right in. I'll let him know that you're here."

They sat in a painted sky blue room with wooden sconces covering the edges of the walls. Miniportraits of multimedia artwork from some of the members hung on the walls. One portrait hung of a black Jesus kneeling in solitude while a floating angel stood watching in the distance.

"Interesting paintings."

Leah commented. Kendrick could not stop staring. The angel seemed to be looking right at him. He swallowed and turned away.

"Yeah."

Bishop Timms, a tall, burly figure, who looked like a defensive back for the Washington Redskins, walked in. His wife, Pastor Deborah Timms, entered, followed by Deacon Davis. Leah and Kendrick stood up as if a judge entered the room.

"Leah, hello. I am Bishop Jeffery Timms. This is my wife Pastor Deborah Timms and Deacon Connor Davis, whom you guys met at the door earlier."

Bishop Timms shook hands with Kendrick. He sat at the head of the table, which were elbows away from Kendrick. Deborah Timms took the seat that faced Leah. Deacon Davis sat in the corner. Leah and Kendrick sat back down.

"First, I want to say, I've eaten at both of your establishments," Bishop Timms exhorted.

"The food and service have been excellent."

"Thank you," Leah and Kendrick chorused.

"I understand that this is your first appointment. Are you recently engaged?"

"About five months now." Leah answered.

"Have you set a wedding date?"

"I'm hoping for a summer wedding."

Kendrick chimed. Leah looked at Kendrick and smiled.

"No, we haven't set a date yet."

"Okay, have you set up premarital counseling sessions yet?"

"With all due respect, Bishop, I think we're just fine."

Kendrick affirmed.

"Bishop, Kendrick doesn't want to go to counseling . . . of any means." She finished her sentence in Kendrick's direction.

"That's not true," Kendrick defended, trying to save face.

"I'm here now. Isn't this counseling?"

"What did it have to take to get you here, Kendrick? What did it cost you? Me?"

Bishop Timms wanted to settle everyone down. He glanced over at Deacon Davis and his wife. Deacon Davis began praying silently.

"Everyone calm down. You are still in the early stages of your engagement. Some people have short engagements. Others have long engagements. However, no matter the length, there is a process. It is always good to discuss and have premarital counseling. People take counseling for granted. It gets bad publicity. Premarital counseling helps couples see what kinds of ideas and attitudes they may have about marriage. It helps them think beforehand, the types of issues that will come up in marriage. Issues such as finances, children, education, retirement, illness, are important to discuss. Most of all, you need to understand God's design for marriage. What roles and issues will you, Kendrick, need to know as Leah's husband? Leah, what roles and issues will you need to know as Kendrick's wife? Let us go to Genesis 2:19-25."

Leah opened her Bible and slid it closer to Kendrick.

"Kendrick," Bishop pondered, "where do you fellowship?"

"Um, well, I come here with Leah . . . uh, sometimes. Sunday has been hard because of the restaurant. I fellowship at another church, but uh, haven't quite found my home yet."

"Make that a priority, Son. You need a true spiritual foundation, a place where you serve and can grow. Be accountable. You need to be planted in a church where you can grow in the word of God. Where you can grow and flourish. God desires to speak to you."

"Yes, Bishop."

"Let us read Genesis 1:26."

While everyone read silently, Deborah Timms whispered in her husband's ear. He nodded several times before switching subjects.

"You see, God had something in mind when He created the idea of marriage. His goal was that man and woman would come together and become one in the spirit. They were made to help each other, to become partners. Before we go any further . . . Pastor Timms has a few questions."

The room started shrinking. Kendrick cleared his throat.

"Kendrick, tell me about your childhood."

"It was a good childhood, I guess. Didn't want for anything. Had the best clothes, toys, schools, you name it."

"Yes, your father is a pioneer, one of a few black restaurateurs in the country. He worked hard to get to where he is today. However, allow me to be more specific. Did you have good relations with your father and mother?"

"I was my father's protégé. I admired my father. His business sense. His tenacity. His determination."

"Your father is a very successful businessman. A man with drive. Energy. It takes a unique kind of energy to create. To be successful. If his employees didn't see the vision, it was his job to get them there, right?"

"Of course."

"No matter what it took?"

Deborah Timms continued probing.

"And your mother? How was your relationship with her?"

"I love my mother. I would do anything for her. She is a kindhearted soul that wouldn't hurt anyone. She worshipped my father. They love each other very much, even now."

Kendrick felt defensive.

"What are you implying?"

She didn't miss a beat.

"Did your father ever hit your mother? In anger, or frustration? By accident?"

"Excuse me?"

Kendrick demanded.

"Abuse can come in many forms. It's not always physical. It can be sexual, emotional or even mental. Emotional and mental are harder to detect but they can inflict just as much damage. I think more damage. You see, words have power. They have the power to heal or kill. A soul, or spirit can over time, be so damaged by constant criticisms, ridicule, and rebuke that it buckles, they buckle underneath. People become self-protective. Sometimes you can vow to get yourself in power so that you will never have to subject yourself to that much pain. But then life happens, and you find yourself repeating the same cycle."

Like a prosecutor, Deborah Timms asked again softly in a tone that aimed at the truth.

"Did your father ever abuse your mother? Speak of her unkindly? In front of others, or you? Have you ever watched him helplessly badger her? Call her names, criticize her, or even humiliate her right in front of you? Could you hear it in your room between arguments?"

Tears streamed down Leah's face. Deacon Davis came over and gave her a few tissues. He led Leah out of the room. It was becoming clear what was going on. Kendrick bolted out of his chair.

"I knew it! I knew this would happen. Blame me. Blame everything on me!"

Kendrick creaked.

"My time is up anyway. I have another appointment. Where is Leah?"

"Kendrick, sit down!"

Bishop Timms said sternly. He looked Kendrick dead in the eye. He was serious. Kendrick huffed once more and sat back down. He could not look at anyone. Leah walked back in and sat down. Bishop Timms took over.

"Leah, let me ask you, how often do you two have Bible study together? Have times of prayer together?"

After a long pause, she offered a response.

"We used to pray together. A long time ago. I was young in the Lord. Then our work schedules got hectic."

"Kendrick, have you ever thought of picking it back up? As a husband, you will be the royal priest in the home. Jesus teaches you how to lead. He will teach you how to lead Leah and your life together in marriage." Bishop Timms looked over at Leah.

"Leah, when did you meet Kendrick?"

"Right after my father died. Almost nine years ago. My father left the family the restaurant to manage. After he left, my world collapsed. I did not know how to run a restaurant, but I wanted to honor his name, his memory. I did not know many things. I was a mess. Kendrick was a godsend."

Deborah Timms whispered again in her husband's ear. He nodded. Leah looked at Pastor Timms. She felt a connection. Leah knew she would not try to hurt her. Leah's hands began to tremble.

"Leah, honey, what effect did this have on you and your family? I imagine you were in college when your father passed."

"My mother froze. She stayed strong long enough to handle the funeral arrangements but after that she shopped and began drinking. She slept a lot. Shopped a lot. He left us a lot of money. The restaurant is the only thing that has not been squandered. I refuse to let my family touch it, but it doesn't matter because no one wants it."

"How's your health? That's a mountain load of stress for a young person to handle."

"I was a wreck. If it wasn't for Kendrick—"

She reached for his hand. He grabbed it thankfully.

"If it wasn't for Kendrick, I don't know. I dropped out of college. I put all my effort into the business. I was in over my head. I was always overwhelmed."

"Kendrick came in at the appointed time, it seems. Like a father figure in some ways. But, Leah, do you regularly go to the doctor for checkups?"

"I try to do my annuals."

"Have you gone this year?"

"Not yet."

"Nine years, that's a long time. A lifetime. You can know a whole lot about each other. Strengths and weaknesses. Particularly weaknesses. You both are in the same line of work. Same struggles, experiences, families, and even legacies. Has it ever been too much for you, Leah?"

Pastor Timms was reaching for something.

"Sometimes."

"Ever feel heavy or burdened? You think that whatever you're doing is stupid? Didn't make any sense?"

"Don't call her that. She is not stupid. She just gets confused, distracted sometimes. She can't handle things by herself."

Deborah Timms looked at her husband and Deacon Davis, then back at the couple.

"Kendrick, do you always make outbursts like that?"

Bishop interjected.

"No." Kendrick looked at Leah, took her hand, and gently kissed it.

"Leah's been there for me like I'm there for her. She knows me."

"As your verbal punching bag."

"You've already condemned me."

The battle was on between Deborah Timms and Kendrick.

"Am I on trial here? Is this your idea of a counseling session?"

The battle of words roared on between Kendrick and Deborah Timms. She was not about to retreat. Bishop Timms asserted himself into the conversation.

"Kendrick, there seems to be a cycle in your life. Your father bullied you. He bullied your mother. It is emotional abuse. He used words to assault you and words to praise you. Somewhere in this spectrum, you are hurting and you continue to hurt. I think you know what he did. It is power over what is perceived as the weaker vessel. You could not describe what it did to you but he always made you feel bad. You have worked hard to prove him wrong, to please him. You feel in his eyes, it's just not good enough. You swore you would never allow yourself or anyone around you to control you like that ever again, right?"

Bishop looked Kendrick directly in the eye, man-to-man.

"You have to acknowledge some things in your life before you can break the cycle."

Bishop Timms said a prayer.

"We thank you, Holy Spirit that you reign in this place. That you are the spirit upon waters. We thank you, Father, that your presence is with us and you will give us rest from our labors. I thank you for your revelation and guidance in this meeting. I thank you, Lord, for the gifts of the spirit that went forth. I ask you, Lord, for the repentance of sins and forgiveness. I ask that the Holy Spirit guide and direct Leah and Kendrick's relationship. I ask that the Holy Spirit lead and guide them into all truth. I ask that the Holy Spirit infuse courage into both of them. I ask you, Lord, to reveal whatever darkness is hidden and bring it to light. May Kendrick begin to grow as he abides in your presence, in your care. I thank you that Kendrick is a new creature in Christ. The old things in his life have passed away. We pray that you will direct Kendrick to a church home where he can hear you clearly. May he begin his journey with you and become one with you. Show him who you are, Lord. In Jesus' name. Amen."

He ended the prayer with safe-travel mercies for everyone.

"Let's schedule another appointment in two weeks."

Deacon Davis opened the conference door. A beaten-up, defeated spirit crawled out of the room. Bishop Timms put his hand on Kendrick's shoulder, trying to comfort and encourage the embattled groom.

"Kendrick, there's help . . . but you have to want it. A real man is someone who learns how to walk in love . . . not in anger."

Chapter 25

"What does any soul want: to be taken care of . . ."

Byron drove Yasmine to a classy four-star restaurant by the marina near Arlington. He led her by the arm, like a princess into the foyer. The maitre d' greeted them both. He was very familiar with Byron.

"Mr. Combs, it is nice to see you again. Your table is ready."

Yasmine raised an eyebrow.

"You come here often?" Byron scratched his head.

"Sometimes, for special occasions . . . people remember me here . . . I try to leave good tips."

Byron ushered Yasmine to her seat. He took off his jacket, took out the bottle of champagne sitting in the bucket of ice on the side of the table, and began pouring it into Yasmine's glass. A waiter soon appeared.

"Hello, my name is Ramon, and I'll be your waiter for this afternoon."

Yasmine looked out into the marina and saw the Potomac River. She looked at the arrangement of the table, her silverware, then around the restaurant. Everything seemed staged, like a production. Yasmine waited for her next cue. She placed her hands on the table and leaned over in Byron's direction. She focused all of the attention on her "leading" man.

"What are we celebrating?"

Yasmine leaned in, resting her hands on the table.

"Do you love me?"

Whoa! Where did that come from? Those three little words. No warning. I need to be careful how I answer. He wants me to say it. Has he said it? Well at least not in daylight. Maybe we can say it together. Quick, turn it back on him.

"Do you love me, Byron?"

"Ladies first . . ."

"Can't you tell?"

"Tell what?"

"That I do?"

"Yasmine, look me in the eyes and tell me you love me."

"Byron, c'mon, we've been together for four months. Can't you tell by now?"

"You're chicken. You're afraid."

Byron dared and gently poked Yasmine in the shoulder.

"No I'm not." *You bet I am.*

"Yes you are."

"Ridiculous."

You are right. You do it then, take the pressure off.

Yasmine poked him playfully back. He kissed her hand and smiled.

"Okay, since you're chicken, I'll start. Yasmine Blue, I love . . . you . . . your hands. They are so soft. I love you . . . your eyes . . . so dreamy. I love you . . . your mouth, so sexy."

He whispered it so low, she did not hear it.

"Marry me." Yasmine gasped.

"Marry me," he said in a deep, huskier tone. He brought out a two-carat ring. It appeared small for a man of his tastes. It also seemed smaller than the one Yasmine fantasized that she would wear. She could always seduce a bigger ring later on.

"What?"

Byron slipped the ring on a dazed Yasmine's finger, quietly demanding a response.

"Say that you love me."

"I love you . . . your walk. I love you . . . your smile, so sexy. I love you . . . your scent, so musky. I love you, Byron."

She whispered. He leaned over and delighted her with a kiss.

"Ready to order?" Byron winked.

"Appetizer or dessert?" Yasmine offered.

In the evening, Yasmine sat on the sofa, looking over her brand-new ring.

Mr. Bryon Combs . . . Mrs. Yasmine Combs . . . Not bad . . . Not bad at all. I have to call Mommy and Daddy. Tell them the good news. I think Daddy would like him. They are cut from the same cloth. They could play golf. Oh, Cadence will be my maid of honor.

The phone rang.

"Byron? I am so excited. I can't wait to tell—"

"Yazzy, it's Daddy."

"Daddy! I was just thinking about you. I've got some wonderful news for you and Mom . . ."

"Yazzy, sweetie, I didn't want you to hear this from anywhere else . . . Your mother and I are getting a divorce."

A bomb suddenly exploded in her ear.

"Yazzy? Yasmine? Are you still there?"

"What?"

A ten-year-old Yasmine appeared from across the room. She came up and sat on the arm of the sofa on the other end.

"I didn't want you hearing it from the tabloids. I wanted you to hear it from me."

The phone fell to the floor. The older Yasmine felt the wind knocked right out of her. The voice on the other end of the phone still called out.

"Yazzy, Yasmine? Are you still there? Yasmine!"

A ten-year-old Yasmine sat helplessly watching the joy from her "older" self fall to the living room floor.

Chapter 26

"In this walk, you may be persecuted for my name's sake..."

Benevolence was rushed in an ambulance to George Washington University Hospital. She had suffered a concussion and a broken right leg. There were other minor bruises. The doctors x-rayed for any internal bleeding. They wanted to make sure there weren't any grave injuries. The hospital called her parents. Benevolence's mom screamed. Her father grabbed the phone. He got hospital updates, called the other children, and secured travel arrangements and temporary employment for the store. They made their way down to Washington DC on a Saturday evening. They stayed at the Holiday Inn, a few blocks away from the hospital. Benevolence's siblings appeared a day later.

Everyone arrived as Benevolence began waking from her concussion. She was heavily sedated. She was hooked to blood pressure and heart monitors. Her right leg was in a cast suspended in the air. The swelling from her face was beginning to decrease.

Valentina helped Benevolence sit up. She propped her head on several pillows. A couple of days after the accident, Benevolence was talking comfortably. Her room looked like a botanical garden. Different types of floral arrangements were set everywhere, on the windowsill, on the table, and near the bed. Rosette stacked up the cards, while William and Francois arranged the new floral baskets.

"Bene, you need to eat. Your food is getting cold. You need to build up your strength."

Valentina felt her forehead and neck.

"Mummy, can I eat later? I just want to look around. I will have to take this medication afterwards. It makes me sleepy."

A tall, bald officer with brown eyes and a goatee walked inside of the room. He nodded to Benevolence's father. He whispered in Valentina's ear. She nodded and stepped back. William and Francois stood guard of their sister Rosette and their mother.

"Benevolence James?"

"Yes?"

"I am Officer Dickerson, from the fourth district. We have been waiting for a moment to speak with you about the accident five days ago. It has been labeled a 'hit-and-run.' We know an anonymous call went in to 911. It was a male voice. We think it was the suspect leaving the scene. Can you tell me anything that you remember about that night?"

"Um, there was this jeep . . . high beams . . . I couldn't see . . . I sped up. It was hailing outside. I couldn't see him. He hit me. Pushed me into the intersection. Pushed me into harm's way. I did not want to hit her. A tree . . . I swerved . . . I think I hit a tree. That's all I remember."

"Did you see the car speed away? Did you see the license tag number?"

"Yeah . . . some of it." Benevolence laid back to refocus; she tried to mentally force the memories back into her head.

"I can't remember."

Officer Dickerson wrote quickly. He flipped his pad and shoved it back into his pocket.

"I understand."

A throbbing pain forced its way into Benevolence's head.

"Here's my card. If you remember anything else, please give me a call."

He set it on her nightstand and smiled. He walked to the door when Valentina accosted him.

"Will you find this SOB, before she gets out?"

"Mrs. James, please calm down."

"No! My daughter is lying in the hospital because some crazy, drunk fool decided he wanted to play Speed Racer on the road! Who would do something like this? Who would be out to persecute my daughter like this?"

"Mrs. James, we're going to work as hard as we can to find out who did this to your daughter. She is one of us. We are looking for witnesses, anyone that might have seen something. Here's my card. We'll keep you informed."

Officer Dickerson gave Valentina his card.

"If you find out anything, you will let me know?"

Valentina took it as a token of promise forged between her and the police.

"Thank you, officer."

Later that afternoon, people flowed in and out of Benevolence's room. Rona stayed for three hours. Leah and Octavia came in as Rona was leaving. Leah noticed three men sitting out in the waiting room. Octavia walked in first. She waited for the conversation between the women to end before approaching.

"Hi, Minister James."

"Octavia. Leah. It is good to see you both."

"Mummy, Rosette. This is Leah and Octavia. Two of my mentees. Girls, this is my mother and my sister."

"How are you feeling?"

Leah scooted in a chair close to the bed.

"Not as groggy. My leg in the air is an interesting twist. They bring it down when I go to sleep."

"What happened?"

Octavia's instincts kicked in.

"Some fool hit her and ran away."

Rosette chimed.

"When we left you? At your poetry event?"

"Yes."

"Oh my God!"

Leah exclaimed.

"Did anyone see who did this? Has the police any leads?"

"They're working on it."

"Well, if you need a lawyer, I know a few folks you can talk to."

"Thanks, Octavia."

The nurse came in with a chart. She checked Benevolence's vitals.

"Visiting hours will be over in thirty-five minutes."

"Could I talk with you for a moment?"

Leah whispered to Benevolence.

Benevolence saw a look in Leah's eyes.

"Mummy, mind if I have a moment with the girls alone?"

Valentina looked at the girls. She huffed out some air.

"I really don't want to leave your side . . . but okay. The family will be right outside your door." She pointed for emphasis.

"Right out here, okay?"

"Okay."

They walked out of the door cautiously. Octavia sensed that Leah needed some privacy.

"I'm going to the cafeteria to get something to drink. Leah, do you want anything?"

"Could you get me some juice?"

"No problem."

Octavia closed the door. Leah paused. She updated Benevolence on her counseling session between Kendrick and Bishop Timms. She did not echo the ring match between Pastor Timms and Kendrick, but enough for Benevolence to form a picture.

"Has there been a point when you haven't felt this, Leah?"

"Yes . . . recently, earlier in the sanctuary this afternoon. Other times surprisingly, are with you and the girls. We met with Bishop Timms. Kendrick has issues he needs to work out. He criticizes me a lot verbally. I have known it for a long time. I have endured it for a long time. It wasn't always like this. For the first few years, we were just friends. It was wonderful how he supported me. How he encouraged me. He's been everything to me. Even after Daddy—, I needed Kendrick so much, that I ignore things. Since the engagement, I have been blind to everything. I can't do that anymore."

"So what do you want to do?"

"Right now, I don't know."

Leah got up from her chair. She smelled the daisies next to Benevolence's bed.

"I just want peace in my life. I want to be able to handle things on my own. I want to feel in control. I think . . . I might . . . go back to school."

"What about Kendrick? Your engagement? Do you love him?"

"Yes."

"Is that enough to marry him? With everything you have just said there seems to be this cloud of rejection that hovers over you. You needed him. He needed you. You both have some of the same issues. It sounds like he has issues that he has never really dealt with. You both need time to resolve these issues, before you become a family. The last time we talked, you were supposed to make an appointment to see a doctor. Have you done it?"

"I don't want to go by myself."

"Call one of the girls. Ask Octavia. I think she would go with you. That's if you feel comfortable."

Leah took Benevolence's hand and gave it a firm squeeze. Leah smiled to keep from crying.

"Benevolence, you've made such an impact in my life in the short time I've known you. Strangely, I feel closer to you than I do with my own family."

"Leah, sweetie, God has some beautiful things in store for you. You have had a lot of heartache. Unresolved grief. I believe God is giving you a chance to heal, His way. You have some decisions to make. Go to the doctor. Find out everything, and then go to God. He can use even this to bring you to the place He wants you."

Octavia knocked on the door. Leah wiped her tears with her hands and kissed Benevolence on the forehead. She squeezed her hand one last time, mouthed a thank-you, and walked out of the room. Octavia walked in. Leah intercepted her at the door.

"Here's your juice."

"Thanks. I'll drink it out here."

"Is she okay?"

"She's tired. I probably talked more than I should."

"Knock, knock." Octavia closed the door.

"I wanted to make sure you were okay."

"I'm going to be all right."

"Does anything hurt?"

Octavia sat in the empty chair near the bed.

"Do you want something to eat? To drink?"

"Not now. I will eat my dessert later. Can you prop me up? I feel stiff. I just need to stretch a little."

Benevolence noticed the tiredness in Octavia's face.

"You look exhausted."

"I'm okay. I am working a lot. Trying to get my caseload and research down."

"Is that all?" Octavia punched the pillow one more time before placing it behind Benevolence's head. She sat back down and drank more of her juice.

"How do you know if you're in the right career?"

Octavia caught herself.

"I'm sorry. You need your rest."

Benevolence thought about it a moment. She took her medication. She felt a flow of strength and energy run through her body. Her headache ceased.

"Well, that's not an easy question. It is probably one of the most essential questions you ask God after salvation. The answer is usually your first clue, your first quest into your destiny."

Octavia swallowed the last drop of juice.

"I think I made a mistake."

"At Huffman?"

"At everything. Something is gnawing at me. I just feel like there is more to life. More to me. Something bigger. Bigger than this. Bigger than where I am. I just don't know how I am supposed to get there."

The nurse walked in.

"Ms. James, you need your rest. Visiting hours are almost over. Let me check your vitals. Benevolence eased slowly back into her pillow.

"I needed rest a long time ago. I guess I have no choice but to take it now."

Chapter 27

"It's your season to come forth..."

"Good morning, Saints of God!" Minister Connor boasted.

"The presence of the Lord is in this place! Let your spirit reign among us. We, at Faith and Victory International are glad that you were able to come into the house of the Lord. The Lord wants you in His presence, seeing His power, witnessing His anointing. Hallelujah!"

The congregation echoed a 'hallelujah.' The burdens of many souls who came in depressed started to lift, awed from the heavenly presence that showered them from the pulpit.

The morning announcements came across the wide plasma screen like movie previews: Bible study, men's meeting, women's meeting, and youth retreat. All of the graphics, music, and voice-overs interweaved each other into the week's commercials.

"Technology is a wonderful thing, praise God. Now we've come to the better part of the service. A worshipful part of the service: it is offering time. Turn your Bibles to Malachi 3:10."

He read the scripture with a booming "James Earl Jones" voice:

"Test me in this,' says the Lord Almighty. 'And see if I will not throw open the floodgates of heaven and pour out so much blessing that you will not have room enough for it. I will prevent pests from devouring your crops, and the vines in your fields will not cast their fruit,' says the Lord Almighty. Then all the nations will call you blessed, for yours will be a delightful land."

Minister Connor closed the Bible.

"Children of God, God desires to bless you. He wants to fulfill your needs according to His riches and glory. God is faithful. When you abide in His word and his commandments, He will prosper you. Not just in money, but healing is available. Deliverance is available. Wisdom is available."

The musicians played two songs: "Softly and Tender" and "What a Mighty God We Serve." The last song turned into a five-minute jam session. People got out of their seats. Others were in the aisles. The musicians played on. The praise team stirred up a revival. All around the sanctuary, people danced. Fear vanished while the presence of heaviness and depression seemed bound and gagged. Spirits soon found themselves confounded and confused. A wind of renewal blew into the sanctuary, filling the entire building. Faith took her post, and peace eyed every entrance and exit. Excitement began building in the atmosphere, sending chills to those in the room and warmth to those needing His touch.

Leah came to church alone. So did Yasmine, Leah, and Octavia. Each of them, preoccupied with decisions, had a different set of consequences to bear. Unaware of each other, they sat in different pockets of the sanctuary. After the choir sang their special selection, Bishop Timms stood up and walked to the pulpit.

"What an awesome God we serve,"

He boasted. The congregation shouted amen.

"He is our rock, our salvation, our protector. He is our hope and our peace. He is our everything. Lord, we give you the highest praise. Father, as your people stand here praising you, reverencing you, let them know that you are here with them. Inhabit their praises, Lord. Let the joy of the Lord be their strength. Breathe on us, oh Lord. May we hide not from your presence, from your spirit. Grant us peace. Strengthen your people now, Lord. Even as the word comes forth, I pray the spirit of the Lord, the spirit of wisdom open their eyes, their minds, and open their hearts. Speak to their hearts. For we know that out it comes the issues of life. Position them to hear from you. Let them be hearers and doers of your word. Lord, let me say only that which you want me to say. I decrease, that you may increase in me. Bless your children, who hear your word and do your word. May your love be shone abroad in their lives. Shine your love on your people today as they come into your presence. I ask these things in Jesus' name. Amen."

His voice rang out unto the sanctuary.

"Turn your Bibles to Ephesians 4:1-8. Children of God, the world waits for you to come forth with the works that God has placed inside of you. Turn also to Ephesians 11-12, and 16. Saints, there is an agenda where your life is concerned. You see the devil comes to kill, steal, and annihilate hope. He is after your dreams. He is after your promise. It is his plan to make you doubt the one who is the giver of dreams." Several amens pierced the sanctuary.

"There are dreams that God has given you. Whether you want a satisfying and rewarding career, a loving and faithful husband who knows God, a business, or a fulfilling ministry, or even healthy and strong relationships, each of us has a dream in our heart. Whether it has been shared or unshared, something keeps us awake at night. There should be something that pushes us to be better. Or maybe it reminds us that we're not in the place God wants us to be."

Some "oohs" and "hmms" galloped like waves through the congregation. Octavia looked around, feeling the weight of those words press against her consciousness. She sat up. She stopped writing.

"The Holy Spirit has been around mankind for more than two thousand years, yet in the church, we don't talk about Him nearly enough. The Holy Spirit has a role, function and ministry in every believer's life. When you received salvation, God, in His sovereignty, placed specific gifts in you that you need to activate. He placed purpose inside of you. You have a unique assignment, a reason why you were created. Your task may take a lifetime to accomplish. Now, God knew your family history and he knew your childhood. He knew what drama would unfold when He wrote your story. He also knew that unless you seek a relationship with Him, the Holy Spirit would not have the opportunity to unveil your purpose or your spiritual gifts. You won't fully accomplish what the Master wants."

There was a holy pause, causing many to think and ponder its true essence. Yasmine shifted in her seat.

"Too many believers sit in church sad, depressed, broke, and confused. Too many believers are in the wrong careers, have bitter marriages, and broken relationships. They tolerate confusion, strife and apathy in their lives. Simply because they are not functioning in the role and purpose, the Creator intended. In Genesis and throughout the New Testament, we experience many roles of the 'Spirit of God,' the Holy Spirit. I am going to talk about some of these roles. It is time the church move into the next phase of glory!"

"Amen!" the elders and ministers echoed. The power of God began moving swiftly around the sanctuary.

"Jesus said in John 16:13: *Howbeit when he, the Spirit of truth, is come, he will guide you into all truth: for he shall speak of himself; but whatsoever he shall hear, that shall he speak: and he will show you things to come.*"

"One function of the Holy Spirit is to reveal to you things to come, the future. Some of you depend on the horoscopes for that." Some paused in reflection.

"There are Christians who get their palms read on a regular basis. They are on the 'psychic hotline,' or they get a letter from some clairvoyant saying riches are on their way to them . . . just send me this . . . and by this month, what I see . . . will come true. These are the works of the devil." Yasmine swallowed those words hard.

"One of the functions of the Holy Spirit is to comfort. Wisdom comforts those who feel weak, distressed, or depressed, those who need her care. Yes, I said "her," though there is no female or male person of the Holy Spirit, the nurturing attributes remind me of some of the goodness that God placed in women. Some of you have relied too much on the bottle, drugs, sex, work, shopping, or people to comfort you, and not the guidance of the Holy Spirit."

Leah, Octavia, and Simone, from different parts of the room, felt the truth marinate.

"Some of you have toxic relationships, people who are holding you back but you don't realize it. They have been there for years. Getting rid of them would be painful. You really cannot see how that will benefit you. You do not realize they are toxic. They are killing you. If you follow them, they will lead you to death. Well, Bishop, that seems harsh. I am not trying to kill myself. It is not all that. Saints, death, you see is a place of mediocrity. A place of complacency. A place of fear, false pride. If you follow them, you won't ever find the gifts lying dormant inside of you. You will be too busy with the cares of this world. Are you afraid to surrender? For others, you may be afraid to move higher because you have no clue where that will take you, in Him. Then there are others of you . . . pain has paralyzed you. The past was horrible, but the future is even more frightening. Therefore, you are stuck running in place. You are in toxic jobs. You go thru storm after storm and it drains you. You have some decisions to make. Fear has dominated your life. So has disappointment. You are afraid to surrender. You are afraid to lose control. You know God has been speaking, yet, you refuse to come near, nearer to the throne room, nearer to Him. There is a process that you will go through yet, you've been running for years."

The anointing grew stronger.

"Children of God can be toxic as well, don't get it twisted. I am not just talking about the heathen at school, or on the street. There are toxic Christians, who are carnal minded. They praise the Lord on Sunday, sin on Monday, and continue throughout the week. However, since they have not been caught, they deceive themselves by thinking they are okay. They are toxic!" Members squirmed in their seats. Others were stoic, color draining from their faces

"Saints of God, we need to allow the Spirit of Truth more entry into our lives. She has a ministry to accomplish. There are people that many of you should be ministering to. Some of you are gifted artists, writers, actors, directors, teachers, preachers, judges, political leaders and healers . . . But, you are not in the right place . . . You are not where you should be . . . Some of you are . . . in the right place, but it has been hell. God is purifying you, growing your character. He is sanctifying you. You are in a season of growth. You will have to confront your situation. It's toxic. Some of your views are toxic. You must confront them. Sit before God and have Him tell you what is next. A man plans his way, but the Lord orders his steps. If you don't let God reorder your steps, you won't move in His purpose, the divine plan that He has laid out for you."

The daggers of truth hit Simone in her heart. She gasped and closed her eyes.

"Some of you have been hurt. Deeply hurt. It was never your fault, but you have paid for it all your life. You look for comfort. You hold on. You hold dear to that past, but you need to let go. Change . . . it sounds wonderful, but scary. Can you do it? You will need the guidance of the Holy Spirit."

Leah's heart burst. Tears streamed uncontrollably down her face.

"Saints, God has allowed these circumstances to enter your life. The situations that happen are the result of the curse. Nevertheless, God has redeemed us from the curse. He can use all of the heartache, betrayal, abandonment, disappointment to his glory. He wants you to draw nearer to Him. He wants to reveal Himself to you. There is an anointing that God wants to release in your life. He wants to break the strongholds that have kept you from fully entering into his presence. He wants you to personally, witness the Holy Spirit, the spirit of grace, the spirit of supplication and the comforter. He wants you to seek his face. Seek Him in the morning, at noon, and in the evening. God wants to lift you out of despair's pit. He wants to lead you into the place of promise, the land of Canaan."

Bishop Timms gave the altar call. Men and women flooded the altar. There came another invitation. Pastor Timms rose up and walked to the pulpit.

"The presence of the Lord is here to heal. I believe the Lord wants to heal some of you." Octavia prayed softly.

"If after you hear this word, and you feel you need strength to do what God may require of you, come down to this altar right now."

Several more people walked down the aisle. Leah stood up and walked to the altar. Simone noticed. Octavia walked down what seemed the longest aisle to the tabernacle of prayer. As the ministers prayed, Leah could not stop crying. A hurricane of frustration flooded through Leah. She felt trapped under its whirlwind. Suddenly, a warmness cloaked her entire body. Leah shuddered. A hand touched her shoulder and brought her close. Pastor Deborah Timms whispered in her ear.

"Leah, you have a healing gift buried underneath all the pain. God wants to dig it out. He wants to use it. You've been trapped physically, emotionally, and mentally by words for years."

Leah wailed under the truth of that revelation.

"You are precious to Him. Your life is precious. The spirit of the Lord, His presence is here to heal you. He wants to make you whole. Today, you shall feel His presence in a new way. You shall feel His strength. Allow Him to lead you and love you from this point on."

Deborah Timms hugged Leah for a long time, until the crying and shaking stopped.

Chapter 28

"This recovery process feels like a thorn in my flesh..."

Benevolence walked slowly on the treadmill on a brisk and windy April afternoon. Six weeks after the accident, Benevolence recuperated slowly. She convinced her parents to go back to Martinique, while her brothers and sister left a few days later. Benevolence remained on sick leave, while the police searched for her attacker.

Benevolence went to physical therapy twice a week in southwest, convenient to her home, so she could walk home, when recommended, as her legs got stronger. Benevolence raised the incline on the treadmill from level four to level five. She felt shock waves ripple up and down her legs. Sweat trickled down her face.

"My heart feels like it's going to explode. How long have I been on here?"

"Almost eight minutes. Two more minutes left. We want you to warm up first.

"Can I slow down?"

"Keep it at a steady pace. You are doing great. This is just your second week so your body is getting used to activity. You'll get time to rest."

Benevolence focused her attention at the motivational pictures on the wall. The caption read *Success is like climbing a mountain—Full of new heights and new peaks.*

If this is a new height, I could have stayed in the valley for just a couple more days. Benevolence wiped her brow.

Dr. Isaac Morton, a white-haired therapist whose love for politics and film rivaled only by his successful therapy techniques, oversaw Benevolence's recovery. He was one of the district's best.

"How's my million-dollar patient?"

"Worth just about two cents right now... am I supposed to be sweating this hard?

"We've upped your exercise regimen just slightly. Your body is still getting used to the activity. You are making strides from a couple weeks ago. You are getting back strength in your right leg."

"I'm exhausted."

"You've lost two pounds. Our goal is get you back to 100 percent use of both legs. You will lose more weight. Roughly twenty-five to thirty pounds. You have had nothing but bed rest. We have to change that. Once we're done, we will give you a program that you can continue from home."

"How long will this be? The program, that is?"

"It depends. Three, four... maybe five more weeks. Don't worry. You're in good hands."

Benevolence panicked.

Five more weeks? I hope my insurance covers all of this. What about the girls? Should I even continue with them? Some job of mentoring I have been doing... They have spent more time caring for me than I have for them. I wonder how they are coping. Have they put their differences aside? Yasmine and Octavia... Lord, I hope so. What about Leah? Lord, I know you have something special planned for her. Help her, Lord. Simone... She has her heart set on Tavian... Lord, show her what you want her to see. Octavia... Lord, you have given her many gifts. It seems that dry bones fill her world. Show her how to speak life. Show her how to submit, to hear you. Show her your anointing. Put her where you want her to be and prepare her, Lord. Yasmine, she idolizes companionship. Separate her unto you, Lord. Sanctify her. Renew her mind. Prepare her for a godly mate and their ministry. Keep her, Lord.

Ring! Ring! Ring!

The timer buzzed for ten seconds.

"Benevolence, you can stop now."

Dr. Morton helped her down the treadmill and sat her on the table bed.

"Where were you just now? In a moment, your legs will feel like Jell-O. Here's your water. We'll start your leg stretches in a minute."

Benevolence took big swallows of her vitamin water.

"You know with the democrats in office, do you think America will get back on track? I wonder what Obama's or Clinton's plans are for health care, getting troops out of Iraq, and the economy. Can either one undo the damage done by the republicans and the current administration? Does either candidate have what it takes to be president? I do think Obama is the change that America needs. With all of the scandals going on, it's getting so that we can't trust anyone in public office anymore. What does that say about the way America is moving?"

Dr. Morton stretched her legs, taking the left leg slowly, easing it forward like an incline and back down again. Benevolence paused, happy to be lying down. She pondered the question some more.

"Well, it is only four months into the new year. Obama has a lot of ground to cover before the general election. I will be praying for him, specifically for wisdom."

"God help us all. At this rate, America is turning into a third-world country. Other countries are already passing us in education. Been doing that for years."

Dr. Morton moved the right leg in the same direction as before and set it down on the table bed for a quick rest.

"If America changes, it won't be just because of this administration. We're just not praying enough."

Chapter 29

"What's love really got to do with it..."

News of the engagement spread in the offices like wildfire. Colleagues were intrigued, elated. Others saw opportunity. Yasmine was now in the spotlight. She had to tread carefully; all eyes were watching. The engagement, however, was not all glamour and glitz. Still reeling from the shock of her parents' pending divorce, Yasmine panicked. She was frosty at work. Byron poked his head in as usual, but his tone was less than chipper.

"Yasmine, where are the prototype samples? We're supposed to ship them by one o'clock. Are they ready?"

"No. And they're not going to be at this rate."

"I thought you said they'll be ready by midmorning."

"Well, things happen."

"Can't you give me an estimate of what time they'll go out?"

"Can't you leave me alone to work on them? They will go out as soon as they are ready! Don't worry. They'll make deadline."

"What's with the attitude? You shouldn't make deadlines you can't meet."

"And, Byron, you're beginning to smell yourself."

"What does that mean?"

"It means that I bend over backwards and forwards to make you look good."

"What the client wants is what we provide."

"Prototype samples go out late all of the time. It is nothing new. You can get an extension."

"What if I don't want to?"

"Well, then that's your rep."

"Are you disobeying a direct order?"

"So now I'm being insubordinate?"

"Are you?"

"I'm just asking for a simple extension. Why are you being so difficult?" She kept the titration spinning for five different flasks.

"Yasmine, don't pull that manipulative crap today. I have deadlines. I got things riding on this too."

"I can't deal with you today. If you'll excuse me, I've got prototype samples to prepare."

Susan walked in. She engulfed in some of the tension raging in the lab.

"Yasmine, how are things going?"

"We'll finish this later."

Byron straightened his suit, smiled at Susan, and evaporated.

"Yasmine, what was that all about?"

"Deadlines. Stupid deadlines."

"Seemed more than just deadlines."

"It's nothing."

Susan made sure the door was completely closed.

"Rumor has it that you and boss man are engaged? Did I just witness a lover's spat?"

"No."

"What would you call it?"

"Being demanding."

"It's his job. He has a lot riding on this. It's a deal maker."

"And I don't?"

"You're the low man, rather woman on the totem pole. You are hissing at something different today. My star chemist doesn't seem to have all of her constellations in alignment."

"I don't believe in that astrology stuff anymore."

"Oh . . . it's just a figure of speech."

"Whatever."

Yasmine turned the titration down to a slow drip.

"Do you know what makes a good scent?"

Susan inquired. Yasmine turned to Susan. She continued.

"It's when you take a dry, ordinary mixture of aromas and you add a catalyst. You watch a reaction form and you wait for a chemical change. Sometimes, you know certain scents shouldn't even mix. You only put a little of it in the reaction, but then it stinks up everything and soon you can't get it off your clothes. Like smoke."

"Excuse me?" Yasmine had Susan's full attention.

"Ever wear bad perfume?"

"Yes. It smelled nice, but when I applied it on my skin, it didn't mix with my own scent."

"Were there signs?"

"I'm sure, but I didn't follow them."

Yasmine was slowly getting the hint.

"My parents are getting a divorce."

"I'm sorry."

Susan wanted to touch Yasmine's shoulder but thought better of it.

"No wonder you're so off. How long have they been married?"

"Close to twenty-five years."

"Whew! A lifetime of fragrances and scents. Listen, Yasmine, what you and Byron do is your own business, but, honey, he's a shark. He scopes out his prey, he feeds on them and moves on. Have you ever wondered if he's married? If he has a family somewhere else?"

"Don't you think I would have known that by now . . . Besides, I can protect myself."

Susan laughed.

"You can't see it. Poor girl, are you in love with him?"

Susan shook carefully one of the lacquer solutions in an Erlenmeyer flask.

"He asked me to marry him. What does that tell you?"

"I'm sure it's probably not your first marriage proposal. Do you love him? Do you know enough about him? I know you have your ways with men. I have watched you around here, but girl, you are in way over your head. You've met your match and you don't even know it."

Is Byron my match? I guess he is . . . Do I love Byron? I have always wanted to know what this feels like. Everything else seems great: our conversations, his companionship, his confidence, his spontaneity. I don't have to be in control. Not this time. I just can sit back . . . Is this what I want? It's gotta be. What else is there? I finally have someone to hold on to. We're alike. We're meant to be.

"Yes, I think I do. I do love him," Yasmine resolved.

"And have you told your parents?"

"I plan to soon, when things settle down."

"Divorces never settle down. They just finalize. Look, Yasmine, you are bright and young. You have a lot going for you here. You have put some strong effort into Cyprus the past four years and it has made you a superstar. There is room for management in your future, but this office romance is deadly. Watch yourself. You are not in control here. Not this time. Be careful."

Susan put the solution back on the counter. She walked toward the door.

"Try and get those prototypes out ASAP. No later than two o'clock."

Chapter 30

"Places of purpose are not always places that you understand . . ."

Octavia walked into Mr. Huffman's office on a cool April Wednesday with her resignation papers in hand.

Had it come to this?

She had endured seven months of corporate hostility. She had gotten used to the heavy caseload. She endured stares when she changed her hair, wardrobe, or presentation styles. She ignored the alliances, while forming a few of her own. However, she had hit a wall. She stood patient, she proved her talents, and her research skills got several lawyers winning cases; however, no one congratulated her. No one said anything. She wanted to let it go. She remembered her elementary teacher's words.

Octavia, this is a man's world. Women can only get but so far. You have to be better than the best. Be a team player, but you must be better than the men, if you plan on getting ahead—if you want to become powerful.

Octavia reminisced about the past Sunday's service. She pondered Bishop Timms' words. She could not forget her experience at the altar. Pastor Timms prayed with her. She replayed her words repeatedly in her mind.

Submit yourself to God's process. Submit yourself. God is requiring more of you. He will use you, your gifts and talents, but you must submit to his process. You must be willing to surrender control.

Octavia felt like she hit a brick wall. She had escaped one hostile environment and landed in another. The same cycle kept playing itself repeatedly without end.

Was this the sum total of my existence, my life? Surely, there is more to life. There is more for me than this . . . How did I get this far?

Octavia looked down at her resignation papers. She gripped them harder.

I have worked hard all my life, why isn't it adding up?

From the window, she could see Mr. Huffman reading briefs. Octavia knocked on the door. Mr. Huffman looked up, smiled, and beckoned Octavia to enter.

"Octavia, what can I do for you?"

"Mr. Huffman? Do you have a moment? I know you are extremely busy."

"Of course, Octavia, sit down."

Octavia surveyed his room: beautiful wooden chairs, leather sofa, refrigerator with bar television with DVD/VCR combo, and pictures of celebrities and awards adorned the walls.

Do I really want to leave this?

She cleared her throat.

"Mr. Huffman, you have been very good to me—showing me the ropes, letting me handle patent cases, labor cases, tax cases, contracts, copyright cases. It's been a very challenging seven months."

"Octavia, when we hired you, there were a lot of areas that could use your expertise. There were also areas that needed development. Civil, tax, labor, contract and patent are all vastly different. They fall under different umbrellas. You have done good work here. You take on many cases. Your research is impeccable. I can see you trying cases in court. Another few years, I think you have the potential to make partner. Typically, associates make it in six years, but I could see you doing it in a lot less."

Octavia's jaw almost dropped.

Partner? Me? I would be the first black female partner at Huffman & Associates . . . He is serious! All I have to do is hang on . . . Could I really do this? Associate sabotage . . . more one-hundred-hour weeks . . . more isolation . . . limited assistance . . . more promises . . .

"Mr. Huffman, that sounds great. Really, I believe you . . . but what about the current incentive program?"

"Uh, well, we're still finalizing it. I am sure we will have it out by early June. You have been doing well, Octavia. You are highly regarded around here. You're willing to take extra cases, willing to do what it takes."

"Yes . . . Mr. Huffman, everyone has to pull their own load."

"And it hasn't gone unnoticed, by me. You are doing some strong work, Ms. Kalu. I know it has been rough. Hang in there. Things will work itself out. Not sure why I'm saying this, wine goes through many stages before it becomes something we all admire when we drink it."

Octavia wanted to hand over her papers.

Do it, and get out of here. Save yourself.

She pulled the papers out of the folder from her lap. She moved her neck from side to side and cleared her throat.

"Octavia, you're in training. I think for something awesome. Just hang in there . . . When change comes, Octavia, you will know. Just let me know, if there's anything that I can do."

Huffman smiled. Octavia slowly shove the papers back into her folder.

"Thanks for your time, Mr. Huffman."

They shook hands. Octavia walked out of the office and closed the door behind her. She lingered on the door for a brief moment.

Why didn't I do it? I must be a masochist or something. Only a fool would continue at the pace I have been going.

Octavia felt her face flush and tears sting her eyelids.

"Lord, I can't continue like this. I really can't."

June.

It was a soft whisper, heard as the wind whistled through the trees outside. She heard it again as she walked slowly back to her desk.

Wait until June, Octavia.

She opened her bottom drawer and placed the resignation letter with the folder inside the drawer. She made her way to the research library to retreat and think.

Chapter 31

"God's works must go through fire in order to come out golden..."

The women agreed to meet at Benevolence's home after her physical therapy session. Sessions typically last for two hours. Dr. Morton agreed to do a one-hour session and pace out the other hour. Everyone took a half day to pitch in on what they deemed "Benevolence Day." They enacted a coupon system, where they would complete various services for their minister while she was at physical therapy.

Leah brought Benevolence in her car, brimming with aroma from the restaurant. The others were busy cleaning, dusting, and mopping nooks and crannies of the house. Octavia and Simone straightened the bedroom. Octavia removed the sheets from Benevolence's bed.

"Octavia, be careful with those sheets. Put them on delicate cycle."

"Okay. What are we eating this time? I haven't done a lick of work and already I am starving. Is Leah bringing food?"

"Yeah, she is. She will bring it here first, then swing by and pick up Benevolence. Yasmine, please vacuum the living and dining rooms."

Yasmine poked her head into the door and held it.

"Where's the vacuum?"

"It's in the closet, in the hallway."

Simone pointed. Suddenly, a small brilliant light flashed before her eyes.

"Whoa! Yasmine, what is that on your finger?"

Simone ran out after Yasmine. She pulled Yasmine by the hand and sat her on the bed. Octavia fluffed the pillows. She stopped fluffing. The doorbell rang. Leah walked through the door. The women left the bedroom and stood at the top of the stairs.

"We have less than two hours to get this place in tip-top shape. Are you guys hot or is it just me?"

Leah brought the food into the kitchen.

"Yasmine's engaged!"

"To herself or is there really a man involved?"

Octavia snorted.

"He's real. He's definitely real."

Yasmine waved her hand in Octavia's face. Octavia playfully swatted it down. Leah put the food in the kitchen. The women came down the stairs and met at the sectional. Leah sat next to Yasmine and pulled her hand. She examined it suspiciously.

"How long have you been keeping this secret?"

Leah interrogated.

"Five weeks . . . since the accident. I wanted things to settle down. Didn't seem like the right time to tell anyone."

"When's the wedding?"

Simone asked.

"We have not set a date yet, we're still planning."

"Have you told your parents yet?" Octavia cross-examined.

"Nope."

Yasmine belted out nonchalantly.

"Girl, why is everything on hold? I figured you would have shouted it from the mountaintops by now." Octavia continued.

"My parents are getting a divorce."

Yasmine chuckled. She noticed no one shared her amusement.

"It's not like anyone died. They are splitting up after twenty-five years. I guess it was time. People need something new, new horizons to explore."

"You make it sound like some new expedition. Are you okay about it? About the divorce? Come to think of it, my parents have been together for about that long."

Octavia piped. Simone confessed to everyone from across the sectional.

"My father left my mother when I was seven."

Simone had no emotion in her voice. Leah still held Yasmine's hand, surveying the ring.

"My father would still be married to my mother if he were still alive."

A well of emotions began bubbling. Yasmine blocked away tears. She changed the subject.

"Minister James has been losing weight. She looks great."

"Yeah, she said the doctor's aim was twenty-five to thirty pounds, but she is pushing herself to forty."

"Is she pushing too hard?" Octavia looked over at Leah.

"I don't know, but if anyone can come back from this, it would be Minister James."

"What about her job? What about her medical benefits? She's been out a long time."

Simone got up and dusted the pictures on the coffee table and near the sectional.

"I'm sure she's fine," Leah reassured.

"It's an insurance matter. We shouldn't worry. But her clients, those women . . . I wonder . . . I bet they miss her. They miss having her to talk to. She has some mail. We will give it to her when she gets here. Did everyone finish reading *God's Masterpiece*?"

Simone pondered loudly. The women nodded their heads.

"Do you think we have divine moments? Split decisions that determine the next step to our destiny?" Leah inquired.

"I think we do. I just don't think we are taught to recognize them. I think they hide in our worst circumstances."

Octavia surrendered.

"Why does it seem to be our worst circumstances? Why not our best?" Simone challenged.

"Because sometimes, it takes the bottom to drop out of our lives to see what God really wants us to see. I also think that we could see them in our best circumstances. We just need training on how to make good decisions. We need to be consistent in making them, at least for me; I need to be more consistent."

Leah resolved.

"It's not fair!"

Yasmine started crying. No one moved. No one knew what to do. They had never seen Yasmine lose her control. Simone found some tissues for Yasmine and sat on the other side of her on the sectional. The food was warming in the oven, but there was still vacuuming, mopping, and dusting left to do.

"What's not fair, Yazz?" Simone handed her a tissue.

"I've always thought my father would tell my mother the truth."

Yasmine sniffed.

"I always thought that if he could show her who he really was, she could have a choice . . . a choice to love him."

"You don't think she had a choice? You don't think she may have already known?"

"I don't really want to talk about it, not now."

"Yasmine, if not now, then when?"

Simone put her arm around Yasmine. A tearful Yasmine looked around. For the first time, she saw women looking back at her, not looking as competitors or jealous "hoochie mommas," but as kind, loving faces that wanted to comfort.

"I'm not sure . . . I just need time to think. I am not even sure about the engagement. Everything is swirling in my head right now."

"Is it still that office romance? Girl, be careful. Make sure you don't get burned."

Octavia warned. Leah glared at Octavia. She took Yasmine's hand.

"I think we've all had a lot to think about. We all have boyfriends, fiancés, careers, and situations that are weighing heavy on us. I am glad we started praying for each other. I am glad I have my prayer partner."

Leah smiled at Octavia.

"I think the best thing we can do is listen to the Holy Spirit. Just like in the book, God's masterpieces go through a lot of heat, in order to become the kind of artwork that people will admire for years to come. I guess we all have our fiery furnaces to sit in. The important thing is that we remember we don't sit alone. Let's finish up and eat. Minister James will be here in a little while. I'm sure she'll be hungry."

Chapter 32

"Some things must happen in life in order to make sure you receive..."

Several hours later, the women were all in the living room, watching Tyler Perry's *Why Did I Get Married?* While Benevolence rested upstairs. Everyone took breaks checking in. Yasmine went upstairs to give Benevolence some juice. She handed Benevolence her cup and sat down on the sofa. Benevolence set her cup down on the nightstand next to the remote. She looked at Yasmine with her hands in her lap.

"When were you going to show me the ring?"

"I was going to show you. I just wanted to wait until you were stronger."

She put her hand closer to Benevolence so that she could get a good view of the rock.

"Do you love him?"

"Why is everybody asking me that?"

Yasmine drew her hand back.

"Is it that difficult to answer?"

Benevolence raised an eyebrow.

"No."

"Well?"

Benevolence smoothed over the blanket. She motioned Yasmine to sit in the space.

"My parents are splitting up."

"Does that affect your answer?"

They were now face-to-face.

"No, not really... shouldn't it?"

"Have you talked to your father?"

"No." Yasmine turned away.

"I know he probably asked for it. He's been cheating for years."

"Before you make any judgments, talk to him, talk to them both."

"Why?"

Yasmine turned back to Benevolence.

"Because you're not going to find peace until you do."

Twenty minutes later, Octavia came in with a stack of mail.

"You have a few letters from the correctional facility."

"I'll open them later."

"I almost quit my job a few days ago."

"What? I thought you loved it. That's all you ever talk about."

"Minister James, I'm tired. I have been working one-hundred-hour weeks for a long time. They gave me all different kinds of cases: patent, copyright, tax, labor, and contract. I cannot specialize like that. Some of those cases don't even belong to me. Everyone is always watching me, my hair, my wardrobe, my attitude. It's as if they're waiting for me to crack. The environment is hostile. I don't get many aides to help me. I am stuck doing everything: the research, the legwork. They have stretched me. I really don't know how much more I can take. Some days, I wonder why I get up in the morning."

"Stay till June."

"What?"

Octavia heard June again. It was much louder than a whisper.

"Stay till June. You will have the summer off. Don't lawyers take vacation? You will get your rest. However, I suspect, before you do, you need to finish some things. Don't worry. Things will lighten up, you'll see."

It was nine o'clock in the evening. Simone came in with her coat on her arm.

"Do you need anything? The girls are leaving."

"I'm good, thanks."

"I broke up with Tavian."

Benevolence turned the television on mute.

"I thought by now that I'd have my career, my husband, and my 2.5 kids."

"You've held on tight to that dream. You ever consider giving it to God?"

"Yeah, but I wasn't quite sure that He would give it back."

Simone kissed Benevolence on the cheek and closed the door. Benevolence stretched for twenty minutes before going to bed. She pressed the button for her voice mail: three messages.

"Benevolence, heard you were recovering. Come back to the lounge when you are better. Got a spot for you. You were a hit. People dig you. Too many been asking when you will be back. Hope I don't have a one-hit wonder. Just kidding. Anyways, give me a call. Jerry."

Click.

"Benevolence, this is your mother and auntie. We are just checking up on you. Please pick up the phone. We know the girls were supposed to come over and help you out. They are wonderful. Okay, call your mother before you go to bed. Good night."

Click.

"Benevolence James, my name is Darius Henderson of Soteria Publishing. I had the pleasure of seeing you perform a few months ago, and I am interested in finding out if you have any projects you were currently working on. I was informed of your situation, and I understand if you aren't able to talk now. Please call (601) 773-4499 when you get a chance. I look forward to hearing from you."

Darius Henderson. What a voice.

Benevolence pressed repeat button on the voice mail a few times, just to make sure that she was hearing correctly. She chuckled.

Okay. So now, I got a suitor.

She opened the stack of letters left on the nightstand. She peered through each of them until she found one letter with Arlington County stationary.

Officer James,

> *This is LaTasha. I begged one of the other COs to get this to you. I told her, I just wanted to say hello. They gave me flack, but that's all I wanted to do. Not sure if she is going to go through with it, but just in case . . . I figured I would try it. Been thinking a lot lately. The girls still act like bit—oh sorry, I know you don't like that kind of language. I took your advice. I decided to form a team. Even without you here, I know you know what's been going on. I figure I could brush up on my game, practice my "hook" shot. We don't have a name yet. Those other teams? Scrubs. I have seen their game. Ain't s—. Sorry, that slipped. Been reading too. Psalms 25. It helps me, sometimes. It has been weird here lately. Girls all up in people's face. I'm trying to lie low. I stay on the court when I'm done with my duties. I practice when they let me. You better yet? Probably. I know it's hard. I would not be trying to come back. I feel ya´. We are just a bunch of chickenheads. Anyways, get better. Oh, my mom called. She tried to apologize. Says she sees things clearer now. He tried it with my younger*

sister. She kicked him out. Said if he ever came around her or her daughters again, that she would cut his penis off. Sounds like she meant it. Wish she had done that three years ago. Said she wants to come see me. I did not return her letter. She sent letters. Should she come? I mean it ain't like I care or anything. Come and visit when you are "off vacation."

LaTasha.

Benevolence put the letter close to her heart. She sighed.

You are my chickenhead! Lord, you are definitely moving. I don't know where things are going, but you are definitely moving.

Chapter 33

"I am choosing to become better, not bitter..."

Bishop Timms greeted his love-starved congregation on the Sunday morning. The last few months, an outpouring of love, faith, and healing rippled like Niagara Falls through the sanctuary and throughout the building. Members filled the seats of Faith and Victory weekly like die-hard fans at a Redskins game.

"Faith and Victory today, we are going to be blessed by one of our covenant pastors, Pastor Ibrahim Jacobs of Zion Praise Ministries. Give him a warm welcome, an FVI welcome."

As many of the members stood clapping in their seats, Octavia, Simone, Leah, and Yasmine sat together in the sixth row of the center aisle, close enough to the front, behind the ministerial row, close to the anointing. A short thirty-something man with deep chocolate skin, full lips, and a beautiful bone structure with glasses commanded the pulpit in his brown pinstriped suit.

"Good Morning, Faith and Victory International!"

Pastor Ibrahim greeted in a regal African accent.

"I am honored to be before you. I thank your Bishop for inviting me here today. I bring greetings from Zion Praise. I know I didn't come alone. Some of my elders and members are here."

They began to scream.

"Hey! Zion Praise is here!"

He raised his fist in the air, acknowledging their support.

"Before we get into the word, permit me to pray."

He closed his eyes and pressed his hands together.

"Father, precious Jesus. You are our teacher. Our guide. Please teach us your word so that we may be living vessels of honor towards you and the people you place in our lives. Let us realize that we have treasure in earthen vessels. Let today's word penetrate that which has been broken, torn apart, and disrupted."

The girls looked at each other. No one said a word.

"I am sorry that the message I have is not a feel-good message, but God has asked me to come because He has been trying to reach you. You see, you are about to graduate to the next level in God, but before you get to the promotional exercise and walk across the stage, you must pass your final exam!"

Shouts bellowed from the different corners of the sanctuary.

"Your past can be powerful. Some people believe it is what made them who they are. Their family life, learning conditions, childhood experiences, past failures, or relationships, all form this full picture of their life. Believers can make an exit, an exodus if you will, from their past. Then, leave their baggage in the spirit realm. You see, whenever you try to break free from the past, some of the elements of your present will make your past look good."

Several heads nodded.

"Saints, we are uniquely made for a purpose. We will spend the rest of our lives, trying to pursue our purpose. Some of us may be more in our purpose than others. However, we should strive to reach and finish our assignment. The reason we were created. You say, Pastor, what if we do not know what we are suppose to do, eh? How can we go where we are supposed to go?"

Pastor Ibrahim sipped a glass of water, wiped his brow, and opened his Bible.

"Please turn with me to Colossians 3:12-14. I will be reading from the New International Version. My message is entitled 'Forgiveness—Choose to Become Better, and Not Bitter.' Tell your neighbor on the left, I choose to come better, and not bitter. Then turn to your neighbor on the right.

Colossians 3:12-4 says, Therefore, as God's chosen people, holy and dearly loved, clothe yourselves with compassion, kindness, humility, gentleness and patience. Bear with each other and forgive whatever grievances you may have against one another."

He left the Bible open to that passage.

"Sometimes, when we walk with God, we have this perception that we come into the kingdom of God, all our struggles, God will just zap it away. We bop along, eh—"

Pastor Ibrahim moved his shoulders up and down in rhythm.

"We dance along in life, eh, and try to live the way God wants us to. We may fall. We sin. We cuss, but as long as we are in this kingdom, we are working to become more like Him. How do the saints say, 'God understands my heart.' What does that mean, oh?"

The congregation laughed at Pastor Ibrahim's mannerisms.

"I think it means I can not be like Jesus. He was perfect. So, while I am trying to get there, please, Lord, just excuse this fornication here and there. Excuse this cussing here and there. Excuse this jealousy here and there. Excuse this anger, here and there. Excuse this greed, this worry, this fear, this strife, this adultery, this lying, this homosexuality here and there."

"Ho!"

One of the Zion Praise members screamed. Saints fidgeted in their seats.

"You see, there are things in your life, people in your life, and circumstances that will cause you to lose direction, determination, and depth needed to reach your assignment. What is it that God wants you to face? Is it disappointment? Is it betrayal? Is it oppression, depression? What is it?

"In each of us, there is something. What is the thing that we believe in more than we believe God? Fear follows us in the shadows of our lives. It tries to prevent us from passing our final exam. Some of you do not even know what I am talking about. If nothing is going on now, don't worry, it will soon come. If you feel under duress now, call on God to give you strength and grace. There will be more tests. It will come in all different shapes and sizes, in all forms of questions: multiple choice, fill in the blank, problems, and essay."

Everyone laughed. Octavia turned to Simone and smiled.

"Turn to Matthew 18:21-35, 5:23-24."

Pastor Ibrahim delivered the passage like a griot telling an African story.

"Lord, how many times shall I forgive my brother, oh, when he sins against me? Up to seven times? And you see Jesus' response. Let me translate . . . I bet Jesus sat next to this young fellow, put his hand on the young man's shoulder and told him: 'I tell you, oh, not seven times, but seventy-seven times.' Forgiveness is hard concept. It seems impossible after you become citizen of the kingdom. Sometimes, you feel most of the pain is inflicted by Christians and not the world, not the heathens. Some heathens know how to treat you better than Christians do. Maybe, your parents hurt you. A brother, a sister, a boss, a boyfriend, a girlfriend, a wife, or a husband. Maybe it was an accident . . . an injustice . . . or altercation. We find ourselves in a place where we are bitter. We feel we have the right. They disappointed us, betrayed us—God curse them, oh! Avenge us oh, we feel.

"We may even want to return to the comfort of the past, but we know we cannot."

Octavia chewed on his words.

"Instead this is what we must do. We must reach out to God in prayer. We must reach past our circumstances, and grab hold of the healing of God's word. Let me disclose to you some myths about forgiveness.

Number one: forgiveness is not pretending everything is fine. Too many people do that. Number two: forgiveness is not accepting behavior because you feel the person will never change, so you begin to condone it. Number three: forgiveness is not forgetting just enough of the past, so you can deal with it. When you forgive, you have to release the offense. You have to release the offender. It is imperative you do this, or you may risk missing your divine season. Hear me, saints; this is for the sake of your future."

"Amen!"

Pastor Timms and the presbytery board praised.

"And just like a final exam has comprehensive parts . . . So healing comes in different stages. First, believe. Believe you can do this. You can walk this process out. You will go through denial, where some of you are now. You refuse to believe what is happening. You refuse to look at the situation. Next, you will go through self-blame. Everything is your fault because there is something wrong with you. You always attract these kinds of situations. Then self-pity follows: you are the victim, you have suffered, but you are angry, indignant about your problems. Next, you come to a realization, that there are truths that you must face. Take a good look at yourself. Come to those truths. Forgive yourself and your offenders. You will survive, you will move forward, further than where you are. You begin to discover new things. Finally, there is healing. Restoration. Recovery. You relinquish the past, the power it had on you and move on to your future. You are filled with vitality, new strength, a new resolve."

Sighs echoed across the sanctuary. Hope and her army arose, positioning themselves in different corners of the sanctuary. Angels swooped across the sanctuary.

"Let me warn you, saints, the world's way to forgive is avoidance. It is forgetting but not releasing. Don't take the world's way. Take the narrow road. I prophesy today, God will manifest Himself in a powerful way through your obedience to forgive. Some of you are the sacrificial lamb. Through you, God will remove the curse. You will walk in His blessing. If you do what He says, in a year's time you will be completely different. God wants you to see His love. His love blots out the sins of the past. Saints, forgive. Go through the process. Pass your exam and you will experience breakthrough."

Chapter 34

"The higher the gloss ... the cheaper the merchandise ..."

Leah sat down in the section of blue chairs in the waiting room at the doctor's office. She wiped her sweaty, clammy palms on her black wrap suit and crossed her legs. Moments later, she uncrossed her legs. She looked around and fumbled around for a tissue to dry her hands. Octavia sat down next to Leah.

Most of the people here look normal. Just goes to show—if you want, you can easily pass under the radar.

Octavia took out some papers from her briefcase. She glanced at Leah's hands. She knew the truth about being detected. Once it is out there, you cannot go back.

"Leah, you okay?" Octavia gave her a nudge on the elbow.

"I really hate hospitals."

"We won't be here long. I promise."

The nurse came out of the triage, looked at her clipboard, and called out a few names.

"Leah Decruz?"

Leah dropped her purse. Octavia bent down and picked it up. Leah and Octavia's eyes met. Octavia cocked her head to the left in the nurse's direction. Leah paused. Octavia cocked her head again. Leah stood up straight. She grabbed her coat and followed the nurse into a long sky blue hallway. The nurse stopped in front of an opened door. The view of a decorated office filled with cherry wood furniture, TV-VCR combo, and an examining table gave Leah some comfort; it seemed inviting. Leah walked in slowly.

"Dr. EnBregado will be back in just a moment."

The nurse closed the door.

"Quaint office."

Octavia commented as she paced the room. Her eyes landed on the gallery of credentials that were hung meticulously on the wall. Leah walked over to the examining table. She stared at her reflection in the television monitor. She raked her hands through her hair.

"You think he records all of his patients?"

"How do you know it's a 'he'?"

Someone knocked on the door, and the door creaked open. Octavia mouthed an "I told you so" to Leah and walked toward the five feet eight inch, dark-haired, honey-colored woman with rimmed glasses, and shook hands.

"Dr. EnBregado, I'm Octavia Kalu."

"Good to meet you. Thanks for coming."

Octavia retreated to the back of the room as Dr. EnBregado greeted Leah.

"Hello, Leah."

A childlike presence washed over Leah. She was slow to speak, afraid that whatever unwanted thoughts hovering in her mind might spew out of her mouth before she could forget to coat them.

"Leah, why don't you sit down? Let's talk. Is that okay?" Leah nodded. The doctor went to her desk and sat down. Leah laid her coat on the brown plush chair opposite from the desk and sat down.

"Dr. EnBregado, I think the last time I went to an office such as yours, the doctor said that nothing was wrong. After twenty-five years, I think it's time for a second opinion."

Leah pulled out a balled-up sheet of paper from her coat pocket.

"I don't trust myself to speak. Therefore, I made a list. I like who I am. At least, I have tried. I work in the restaurant business, as a manager. My father's restaurant, but things could probably be worse. Well, here's the list.

I daydreamed a lot in class when I was younger. Teachers called me lazy, but have enormous amounts of potential . . . Got an 800 on the verbal college boards, but couldn't get my papers in on time so I got Cs in English . . . have many changing interests . . . . Have lots of ideas floating in my head, but can't seem to structure them so that I can make things happen. My home, restaurant desk, is always cluttered . . . I am eternally forgetful . . . Have a hard time finding the right way to say things so I choose the first thing that comes out . . . have always felt that I think differently from other people, my friends, my family . . . relationships have been difficult to manage . . . Um, no matter how organized I try to be, I always mess up. I don't do housework. I hop around from one activity to the next. I organize myself around the restaurant so that I have things to think about."

Leah took a deep breath. Tears began welling up in her eyes. Octavia fumbled in her briefcase for some tissue. She hesitated, walking over to the desk.

"Leah, do you want to stop?"

"Yes ... I mean no ... I need to get through this ... I feel that I have to drive myself to get into things ... but inwardly, I feel desperate. People try to reassure me but it does not help. There is something inside of me that needs to change ... I am easily hurt and rejected ... It's like on the inside, I'm trying to tell myself I'm not stupid. I need things to calm me down otherwise, I go crazy. But if you were to just look at me, you wouldn't know any of this."

"Leah, how long did it take you to write this list?"

"It took me forever," Leah said between sniffles.

"A few years. I kept it in my journal. Every time something happened, when I remembered to do it, I would jot it down. I am sure that there was more to write but this is all I have. They're all over the house. I would always lose them so I always made about a dozen copies. I have piles of papers everywhere. My assistant helped to put it all down on one sheet of paper."

"Octavia, can you come and sit next to Leah, please? Leah, that was bold of you to read all of the items on your list. Can I see the list?"

Dr. EnBregado took the list and perused it. She took off her glasses. She approached the topic more like a friend giving advice than a clinician.

"Thank you, Leah. It took a lot of courage to do what you just did. I want you to know that. Judging from your list you gave, these are symptoms of adult ADD. Have you ever heard of Attention Deficit Disorder?"

Leah recalled the magazine that she almost picked up from the drugstore. Now she wished she had bought it.

"Sort of."

Octavia gave Leah some tissue. She wiped her eyes. Leah nodded a thank-you to Octavia.

"Leah, you have ADD. They misdiagnosed you as a child. Back then, it was hard to diagnose. It was more common in boys than girls. Over the years, new clinical research has made early diagnosis more successful. There is treatment. But there are a few life style changes you will also have to make."

Leah broke down, crying. Octavia tried to comfort her friend. She felt so out of touch with the situation. She battled her own thoughts. She held Leah and let her cry. More nebulous clouds of burdens drifted from Leah's spirit.

"Dr. EnBregado, thank you. Just knowing that there was something real going on inside of me and that I'm not crazy ... You don't know what this means for me."

"Leah, we can start you on medication, and some psychotherapy. I have some concerns about some of the things on the list—constantly have to convince yourself that you're not stupid. Are there people in your life who are sending you negative messages?"

Images of Kendrick, her mother, and others flashed into her mind, but Kendrick flashed more than the rest. Leah did not respond.

"Leah, we have family sessions, informational sessions that help loved ones understand what it is and how they can help. We can set up some sessions in the next couple of weeks. I am going to give you some information to read which include tips on life management. I am also going to write you a prescription. This will help you put some things in order. We will be monitoring you to see how these first few days go."

Octavia drove Leah to Kendrick's town house in a comfortable silence. Leah wanted to tell Kendrick everything. Hope sprang from her heart.

This could change things for us. Kendrick could come to the family sessions. So could Shah, Mommy, and Victor . . . I'm not sure how to do that yet . . . we can work things out . . . we come to church together again . . . go forth with wedding plans . . . next October will soon be here . . . sooner than we know it . . . Maybe the girls could be my bridesmaids . . . Benevolence could help . . . I haven't begun planning anything . . . But things might change . . . just have to get Kenny to the sessions. He can see . . . he can really see me. Love me . . . all of me. Leah wanted Kendrick to see what his words were doing to her, their relationship, and their future. She realized at that moment how much she wanted to work things out.

Octavia realized that she uncovered another layer of herself, allowing herself to feel someone else's pain and not overanalyze. She allowed herself to be a friend, not expecting anything in return. Octavia allowed her mind to process the day. She parked in front of Kendrick's house.

"Do you want me to wait?"

"No, I am going to stay and wait for him."

She gave Octavia a hug.

"Tavie, thank you so much," Leah whispered in her ear and got out of the car. Octavia drove off. Leah used her spare key and opened the door. As soon as she walked into the immaculate castle, she took off her shoes and went to the kitchen. She opened the refrigerator. It was packed with fruits, vegetables, juices, pasta, and cooking wines.

I will surprise him with dinner but first I need a nap. It has been a long, emotional day.

Leah went over to his bedroom. She took off her wrap suit and hung it on the chair. She went over to the drawer to get her pajamas. She had been in Kendrick's house sparingly over the last few months. She forgot where he kept her things. He kept receipts and papers on the top of the drawer. She looked into the first drawer. His cologne and scent leaped out. She closed it back hard; trying to remember which drawer was her official drawer. Receipts and papers fell to the ground. Leah panicked. She did not want Kendrick to think she was spying on him. She tried to put the papers back in order. She picked up a yellow carbon receipt from Joe's Auto body shop in Maryland. The bill was for $975.00. The list included a paint job, bodywork, and broken headlights.

Leah looked at the receipt in detail.

I do not remember Kendrick telling me about an accident.

She looked at the date of the receipt. Her body stiffened. The urge to sleep jerked right out of her body.

I cannot believe this.

She wanted to grab a smoke. She had been endeavoring to quit since the deliverance service a few weeks ago.

Leah stacked all of the papers neatly on the cabinet drawer, folded the yellow carbon receipt into its already-made creases, and placed it into her purse. She wrapped her suit back onto her body and sat in the chair. Suddenly, the room appeared darker at two o' clock in the afternoon. Leah stood up from the chair. She dialed her BlackBerry.

"Tavie, it's me . . . Leah. On second thought, can you come back and get me . . . from Kendrick's house?"

She left Kendrick's house and walked out to the nearest bus stop. She opened her purse. She pulled out her Virginia Slim pack. One cigarette left. Leah sighed. Her hands started to shake. She threw the pack in the trash and drew up her lighter.

Chapter 35

*"Train a child up in the way they should go . . .
and hopefully they will not depart from it . . ."*

Yasmine's mother made a surprise trip to DC. For two weeks, they went shopping, to cafes, theatres, spas, and more shopping. It was the most therapeutic two weeks of Yasmine's life. Yasmine had lunch with her mother at La Madeline's in Rockville.

"Mom, are you okay?"

"Yazzy, never felt better. These are all on your father's tab."

"What are you going to do next? When you leave here?"

"See the world. I may try tae kwon do or yoga. I want to live! Breathe new places. See new things. I've been waiting to live, waiting for a chance."

"What does that mean?"

Yasmine sipped her frappachino.

"Yazzy, don't be stupid. Your father has been cheating for years. I have had proof for years. I've denied it, ignored it, and condoned it—I've done everything under the sun, to keep myself from the truth."

"You never said anything."

"I loved him. I fell in love with him. When we were dating, it wasn't like that. He used to give me all of his attention. When things changed, I never challenged it. I dealt with him and the lies my own way."

"So you asked for the divorce?"

"He didn't fight it. We both knew. He is even settling out of court. Too much media. He has to keep his empire together. A man with that much zeal and charisma in one area can have a total lack of self-control in another. I have a house in northern California. It is quaint. I am renting right now. I will be doing a bit of traveling until everything is finalized. I have a slush account. Not exactly hurting for money. I made the necessary provisions years ago." Yasmine felt a buzz on her hip. She picked up her cell phone and smiled.

"Who is that, baby?"

"It's Byron, your future son-in-law."

"What? You are engaged? That is wonderful! Why didn't you tell me?"

"I was going to . . . then everything happened with you guys."

"Yazzy, listen . . . you are my baby girl, but you are also your father's child. You are a lot like him. Vibrant, charismatic . . . but there were some things I should have been more firm on."

"Mom, I'm fine."

"We spoiled you. You wanted for nothing. Took advantage of everything . . . Do you love this guy? Does he love you? Are you ready for this? It's a big step."

"Mom, I'm old enough to make my own decisions."

"Yes, you are . . . What I really want to know is . . . are you old enough to learn from your mistakes?"

Yasmine walked into the office from lunch. Colleagues eyed her and shook their heads. She looked around. People stared. Some smirked; others looked at her.

Why are people looking at me? Was that pity?

Yasmine shrugged it off. She pulled out a catalogue from her purse. *Byron will love this dress, I am just going to show him some samples.* Yasmine knocked and walked into Byron's office unannounced.

"Byron . . ."

"Yeah, Dallibeth, you know how I . . . oh my god . . ."

Byron was in his swivel chair, holding the head of a longhaired beauty toward his midsection. Yasmine dropped her purse. The catalogue fell to the floor.

"What was that . . . Yasmine! Uh . . . Dallibeth, stop, get up, don't stop, ah, get up!"

Yasmine picked up her purse and her bag. She fixed her hair, did an about-face, and strutted out of the office into her lab. She turned classical music loud. She stared at computer simulations.

You are not going to cry . . . you are not going to get upset . . . you're going to change course . . . everyone has at least one indiscretion.

Byron walked into Yasmine's office.

"Yasmine, turn the music down."

Byron skipped over to her desk. He extended his hand over to her computer when he caught a glance of her face. He pulled his hand back.

"Don't touch my desk."

"We need to talk."

"About what?"

Byron scratched his head, took a deep breath, and stepped back a few feet from Yasmine's space.

"Yasmine, this isn't going to work out."

"What do you mean?"

Yasmine continued to stare at the computer screen.

"You're too young to understand what a man like myself really needs."

"What the hell are you talking about?"

Yasmine whipped around the computer to face Byron. He jumped.

"Look, we took things a little fast . . . really fast . . . I guess I took things fast. You're tantalizing, but bottom line, there's nothing substantial here."

"That's not true. We're a lot alike. We like the same things. We love the Lord."

Byron coughed. Yasmine continued.

"We are ambitious, outgoing, persistent, and we see life as exciting. Isn't that enough?"

"That's not my criteria . . . anymore. I see things different now. Look, right now, your parents are splitting up. You are a basket case unraveling. You're affecting things . . . work, for example."

"No it hasn't," Yasmine whined.

"Yazz, c'mon. You are not the superstar you once were. People are catching up. New products. New developments. New moves. Look, keep the ring. I am not ready to make the commitment. I am not there yet. You understand. It's not you . . . it's me."

Oh my god. That is my line. He used my line against me. The bastard.

Yasmine turned red.

"So did you suddenly become clearer from your little rendezvous, a few minutes ago? Who was that heifer, anyway?"

"Don't you call my wife, a heifer."

"Your wife!" Yasmine almost screamed. She stood and faced him. Yasmine wished she were strong enough to throw a punch.

"You're full of it! Trying to run a game on me . . . I know the game. I have played the game. I don't get played."

"Did it ever occur to you, that we're just too much alike? Sooner or later, this would have run its course."

Byron swaggered out of her office and out of her life, closing the door behind him.

News spread that Byron had broken up with Yasmine. Water-cooler talk was that he reunited with his wife. He had taken Yasmine's prototype and planned to sell it to his next profit venture, the highest bidder. Cyrus Pharmaceuticals was seeking legal action. All of the drama made Yasmine puke. Soon everything just seemed old and sour: her job, the condominium, her lacquer perfumes, and even Cadence. Yasmine moped around the condominium, finding reasons not to venture out into the outside world. She flicked channels with the remote. Cadence returned from the store with a few groceries.

"Yasmine, what are you doing?"

"Watching TV."

"You're flicking channels."

"I can't find anything interesting."

"Yazz, stop trying to run away and talk to me."

"I'm not running away, I'm sitting right here."

Cadence plopped down beside Yasmine and yanked the remote.

"Yazz, you're hurting. Talk to me."

"Why? To tell you what you already know? That he was a con man. He was selfish, only wanting to fulfill his needs. That he was just like me. That eventually, I would get what I deserved . . . right in my face . . . at my job."

"Yazz, I'm sorry."

"I was just a temporary fix . . . some young thing."

"Are you going to leave your job? Don't do anything crazy."

"Why not? Actually, I feel like doing something crazy. I've been holding back . . . for a while now. Why not? I've got money saved. I can always find another job."

"What about unemployment? If you quit, you won't be eligible."

"These people would probably be ecstatic. Let someone else be a superstar for a change. I am tired. I just want to be free. Free from everything. Cadence, come with me!"

Yasmine took Cadence's hands. Cadence snatched them back.

"Nope. One of us has to be sane."

"That's just it. We do not. Aren't you tired of rescuing me? You enable me. That's it. I give you permission to leave me be."

Cadence got up from the sofa and went back into the kitchen.

"I forgot the oranges, and melons that I need for the fruit salad. I need to go back to the store."

"You stay here. I'll go. I feel stale. I need some fresh air."

Yasmine walked in the Giant supermarket store near Maryland Avenue, in grey sweatpants, blue NYU hoodie, blue baseball cap, and blue-grey sneakers.

She picked up a green basket and walked to the fruit section. Patrons poured into the supermarket chain like a tidal wave. Lines stretched fifteen feet. Folks shuffled in and out of the sections.

Honey Bunches and oats were also on sale two for $5.00. Fruit cocktail, soda, and V8 blends were also on sale. Yasmine piled all the sale items into her cart. She dragged herself to the fruit section. Honeydew and cantaloupe were on sale. She shook several melons, checking for ripeness. Several patrons came over to the melon section, shaking and using their own clues for ripeness. One patron walked by and picked up a melon. He set his basket next to Yasmine's basket and proceeded to look for the right melon to massage. Yasmine took her melon and dumped it into her neighbor's basket. She looked up.

"I am so sorry. I thought it was my basket. I hope I didn't smash anything."

She took her melon out of the basket and peeked around it. The patron looked into his basket after she finished and then at Yasmine and smiled.

"Nope. I think you're safe."

Yasmine saw a twinkle in his eye, yet no glow surrounded his body. She put the melon into the basket and strolled off.

"Excuse me, um . . . how do you know when you've pick the right one?"

"Huh?"

Yasmine turned back around.

"The melon . . . how did you know when you picked the right one."

"Oh . . . I don't know . . . I shook them and felt the texture . . . looked at the colors. Not anything too specific."

"Sounds confusing."

"Brother . . . you don't know the half of it."

"Can't you help me pick mine?"

What an unusual request. I need to get out of here. The last thing I need is to be figuring out how to pick melons with a perfect stranger.

"I've got to go."

Yasmine picked her basket and did an about-face away from melon aisle.

"It won't take that long . . . C'mon, please . . ."

It was the way he spoke, confident, reassuring, yet tender. Yasmine walked back over to the section and looked at the pile of melons as if they were a shelf of favorite fragrances.

"What about that melon?" The stranger pointed.

"Too bright," Yasmine retorted.

"And that one?"

"You'll have to feel it."

He shook several melons and settled on two cantaloupes and one honeydew that sat in front of the pile.

"Thanks. I really appreciate it." He smiled.

"Don't mention it."

Yasmine began walking in the opposite direction.

"You know there is a real method to picking the right one. It's really just a matter of picking . . . in the right season . . . Thanks for your help."

The stranger walked off in the other direction. Yasmine stopped. She didn't turn around. In that moment, she knew he was not talking about melons.

Chapter 36

"You are under divine advisement..."

Simone was driving down Columbia Rd. Her cell phone rang, and she put her earpiece on.

"Hello?"

"Hey, what's going on?"

"It's June tenth and I'm officially on summer break . . . I can't complain. I am picking decorations for our graduation party. What's up?"

"Just called to say hello. Something is up here. Like Yasmine says, people are smelling themselves."

"Are you okay?"

"Yes, surprisingly. I have tried to fight them by sending memos back and forth. I have kept conversations poignant and brief. One of the associates knew what was going on. She wanted me to call EEOC, but I didn't. She has helped me when she could. The air here has gotten thick. The brook has been running dry. My time is running out."

"I thought you said you weren't quitting."

"I'm not. There were days when I thought about it, but for the past month, I had a resolve to work here . . . endure the workload, the laughs, the lack of respect, even my mentor's blindness to it all. Funny, I pray for everyone in this office. I do. I don't feel hate anymore towards them or anyone. Sounds crazy, right?"

"Yep, but you don't sound any more crazy than me. I've decided to breakup with Tavian for good."

"I thought you said things were great. Or like you prophesized you'll be walking down the aisle by this time next year."

"Well, there are some matters that Tavian has to take care of. I don't try to think about matrimony. Not anymore. We haven't seen each other in weeks since we all went to Dance Place."

"Whoa, that was weeks ago. Are you okay with that?"

"Nope."

"When is everything going down?"

"Not sure. I am going to let him make the first move for a change. I have stopped initiating. Hey, I'm near downtown. I'll stop by. Think you can get away for lunch?"

The phone buzzed.

"Simone, I have a meeting. I'll call you back."

Octavia walked into her mentor's office. All of the partners were sitting there. It reminded her of her interview almost a year ago.

"Octavia, sit down."

Her mentor looked conflicted. He folded his hands. He took big breaths and let them out in slow sighs.

"We are changing the way we do business. The law firm is moving in different directions. We have done well in the past, but we have taken some hits in recent years. In order to move in the current direction, or rather new direction, we have to make some changes. We understand, Octavia, you have done excellent work for us. I know there have been some rough patches, but you have been able to smooth them out. I can honestly say that you have braved the circumstances like no other young attorney that we have come across. We have prepared a severance package. You are also eligible for unemployment. We have tried to make special accommodations. If you need recommendations, I will be happy to provide them."

"Mr. Huffman, when will this take into affect?"

"Two weeks from today or you can forfeit the two weeks. We have already added the salary into the severance package."

"So today is my last day?"

"You've done excellent work. The cases will be transferred to some of the other associates. We will provide the same care that you have provided."

"Will I have time to clean out my desk?"

"Yes, whichever offer you decide to take. I assume you're taking the second?"

"Yes."

"Well, it's . . . it's been a pleasure, Ms. Kalu."

None of the other partners could look Octavia in the eye as she shook their hands, except her mentor who looked as if he would cry at any moment.

Freedom . . . I am free. Delivered . . . like this? Wow.

"Thank you, Mr. Huffman."

As Octavia walked out of the conference room, the news broke. Octavia took thirty minutes to clear her things. Her phone rang.

"You ready for lunch?"

"Even more than you know. Can you park?"

Chapter 37

"It's time for you to open your eyes..."

Tavian sat in the bleachers for ten minutes. He checked the contents in his black Nike bag.

Everything looks good.

He took out the wrapped package out of the bag and held it at eye level. He looked across the green field at the orange and blue track. He could almost imagine a blue tent pitched in the left corner of the field. His memories took him back to the very beginning, the beginning of where he met his first love. He clutched the package tightly, leaving an imprint on the wrapping.

Aaw, man ... let me put this back.

He placed it back into the bag. He took out the pink rose. He smelled it and closed his eyes.

If life could be as sweet and simple as this pink rose ...

He carefully laid the rose in a narrow place in the bag. He stood up and shook himself straight while pacing back and forth. He smoothed out his long-sleeved striped alligator shirt and cleared off any remaining pollen off his pants. He checked his watch.

She should be here any minute ... I might have one more chance ... I have to make this right ...

Tavian's business world had its cycles, but nowadays he cruised through business. He was not cashing in on U.S. imports, so he focused on his export market. Tavian had made a name for himself traveling from China to Egypt to Australia, picking up precious relics for the online market. He could smell new opportunities opening. Seasons changing. He even sensed his own dawning. However long it took him to gain his confidence in the business world, to tap into his genius, he needed double the amount in his personal life. He regretted not being the brother he needed to be for his sisters or the uncle his nieces and nephews needed. The man Simone wanted. He hoped he could communicate that . . . to show Simone and not just tell her.

I am going to be thirty soon . . . Am I ready to make the biggest commitment of my life?

Tavian started pacing down the bleachers again.

Simone walked onto the orange track from the corner of the field. She looked around the center of the football field.

What is he up to . . . Why are we here?

Simone zipped her jacket. A strong breeze blew by.

I wonder what he thinks this will accomplish . . . Resurrecting old memories . . . it's kinda romantic . . . Well, it started here it might as well end here . . .

Simone walked over to the high jump pit and kicked some dirt forward. Her thoughts faded into flashbacks of crowds roaring, baton exchanges, and whistles blowing, and ringing bells signifying the final lap.

Tavian saw his vision of loveliness. He checked his breath, sprayed Listerine mint in his mouth, and combed his hands through his curly hair. He gently swung the Nike bag over the fence and hopped onto the grassy field.

Still very agile.

He walked up behind Simone. Fearing he would scare her, he decided to give her a heads-up.

"Simone! I am right behind you . . . just a foot."

Simone snapped out of her trance. She turned around. She hadn't seen him in weeks. She wanted nothing more than to be in his strong arms at that moment.

Tavian saw her staring at him. Her gaze was so intense it drew him, yet made him feel uneasy.

Is she still angry? She looks angry.

He cleared his throat, stopping about five inches behind her. Simone adjusted her purse from her left shoulder to her right and shoved her hands in her jacket pocket.

"Hey, Monie."

Tavian wanted to embrace her but thought better of it. If she refused him, the rejection might kill his whole plan.

"Hey."

Simone half-smiled. She wanted to hug him, be closer to him, but she refused to initiate it. She willed her hands from moving out of her pocket.

"Can we go somewhere and talk?"

"Tavian, we're in an empty field. Take your pick. You can't get much more alone than this."

Oh, boy. This is going to be difficult.

"Yeah, well, I was hoping we could sit down and talk. Get everything out and into the open."

Finally, the man speaks. It's your show, you lead.

"Okay. You lead."

Tavian walked in front, with his Nike bag slung over his shoulder. They walked up to the second row of the bleachers.

"Wait."

Tavian pleaded before Simone sat down. He took off the Nike bag, set it on the side next to him, and brought out a green and white tablecloth. He placed the tablecloth neatly on the bleachers, allowing room for him and Simone to share comfortably. He gestured for Simone to sit down.

"I have a few symbolic tokens."

He took out the square-shaped slightly indented package and handed it to Simone.

"Open it."

Simone smiled. Gifts were a good start. She wasn't sure where he was going with the gestures, but she decided to play along. She smiled quizzically while ravaging the package. Her smile quickly faded.

"What in the hell is this . . . I mean . . . what is this, Tavian?"

"It's an ice pack. It's not exactly the ice pack I took from you years ago, but it's the ice pack I'm giving back to you."

Simone shook her head.

"Okay. I'm sorry, I don't get it."

"At first, neither did I. My world is a bit frosty, sort of like this ice pack. If you put me in the microwave, I warm up and do all I can to heat you. If you put me in the freezer, I freeze. I do what I can to freeze you. But if you use both ways, I think it's okay, but then gel starts oozing out of me."

"You've lost me."

"It has taken me a long time to figure out my life, or rather my heart. Like this ice pack, I didn't know whether I was supposed to be totally hot, cold, or both. I've been totally cold. Not because I wanted to be, but because it was the only temperature I knew. You know that my father died when I was young. My uncles were womanizers, my sisters had cheap replicas for boyfriends and my mother did the best she knew how under the circumstances. My culture engages in the excess: food, women, and money."

"Whose culture doesn't these days?"

"I had no one to show me anything. There were no role models. No one to talk to about things that make men who and what they are. I had to figure things out on my own. If you haven't noticed, I have not been the brightest bulb in the pack when it comes to this arena. I don't imagine any man is, but I think people pick clues faster than I have. I had to lose you in order to realize how much you really mean to me."

"Tavian, we've been down this road before, what makes this trip any different? I asked you this question a very long time ago, and I think I'll ask it again, 'cause I think maybe this time you might have an answer. Do you want a woman or a wife? There is a difference. It's someone who will stand by you as you pursue the path that God has laid out for you. It's someone to pray you from sickness to life. It's someone who will encourage you when the world suddenly reminds and remembers the black side of you, and treats you as such. It's someone who will keep your heart when your issues seem to spill all over the interstate highway. As much as I want you to succeed and be the man that God has called you to be, I need you to want that for me. Are you willing to pray through storms for me? Pray me through sickness? Be the father to our children that you wish you had?"

"Monie, that's a tall order."

"Not if you let God back into your life. I am not asking you to be Superman. I am asking you to find out what God wants you to do. Where does He want you to go? Will you allow Him to take over and be your father? Tavian, there is so much inside of you that I see, that I need, but it will never come out unless, you discover it."

Simone took Tavian's hand.

"You trust me. If you would allow yourself, you could trust God. If you are ready to do that, then maybe we can move forward."

Simone released his hand. She stood up and walked down a bleacher so that they faced each other at eye level.

"I need you to seek God for yourself. I need you to recommit your life back to Him and pursue something real with Him. He needs to be directing your paths and not me. Life requires risks, but love requires more risks. I can't wait another ten years. You brought us back to this track, where we first met. This race can start and end here, it's your choice."

Tavian leaned back into the bleacher. His mind was whirling with decisions.

"Tavian, I love you, but I am prepared to run this race by myself."

Tavian leaned forward. He knew he should do something, say something. He tried to stand up, but Simone hushed him quiet. She cupped his face, stared into his eyes, and kissed him tenderly. She took her purse and walked down the bleachers into the field and out of his sight. He stared at her silhouette. He did not move; he froze. He held on tight to every single second, every moment of that kiss. He looked at the green and white tablecloth and then the Nike bag. Suddenly, he remembered. He pulled out the last token of his gesture from the bag. A pink rose. He smelled it. He laid it in the spot where Simone sat, in the center of the cloth. As he set the rose down, two petals fell to the ground.

Chapter 38

*"Though freedom is scary, it is the closest choice
that we have to dominion..."*

Faith and Victory International sponsored a personal safety class as part of their outreach campaign. News reports have spread across the nation about domestic violence, with the number of deaths occurring from domestic abuse rising sharply. Two separate incidents of domestic abuse occurred close to home and gained local attention: One case reported a boyfriend dousing his girlfriend with gasoline in a store before setting her on fire. Another case involved a Silver Spring woman recovering from second- and third-degree burns when her ex-boyfriend set her house on fire.

With such frightening accounts coming back to the congregation, the leadership decided to combat the epidemic with the word and action. Sista Power Incorporated, a nonprofit program in the metropolitan area, hosted a personal safety class in the sanctuary at Faith and Victory on a Saturday afternoon. Pastor Deborah Timms, wearing a white tank top, a green and white Adidas sweat suit, and white K-Swiss tennis shoes, spoke in front of the mixed group.

"Victorious women of Faith and friends, I am so excited to see you all today!"

Benevolence stood in the audience, making her debut months after her accident. She walked with a cane for support. She joined the other deacons in the audience.

"As a part of our Stop the Violence campaign, we are educating our families on domestic violence and how you can help. Today, Women of Faith Ministries has sponsored this personal safety class for our community, our men, women, and children. You will all be broken up into groups. Kids will all work together. Let me introduce you to our trainer, Mister Keita Kerim."

Yasmine, who had been under self-imposed house arrest for several weeks, dragged Octavia out, who since her exodus from Huffman & Associates slept away most of her days and nights.

"When is this going to be over?"

Octavia moaned while stretching her arms.

"Not for a while, so wake up!" Yasmine nudged her side.

"Hey! Stop that, before I report you."

Octavia looked across the groups.

"Where's the rest of the clan? I know you didn't just drag me?"

"They're here somewhere. I'm sure they're coming."

Simone walked in determined not to break down from her emotional standstill with Tavian the night before. While she finally felt that Tavian saw the whole picture, she was not sure that he would do right by her. She needed to clear her mind. She brought both hands to her face and rubbed her temples, forcing herself to focus on the present moment.

"Good Morning."

The six-foot forty-something caramel-skinned trainer, who sported a fresh fade and full back features, greeted his audience.

"I am very proud to be a part of Sista Power Inc. I have been with the organization for four years and the impact that we have seen in the communities have been life changing! I am sure that almost everyone here has had a friend, family member, or co-worker who has been personally affected by domestic violence. What we do is educate the public about personal safety. We do more than just talk about statistics; we will give you the skills and techniques needed to handle yourself in a potential situation."

Leah sauntered in fifteen minutes late, wearing an orange sweat suit with her black mane tied in a ponytail. She kept the secret about the receipt. Her worries tailgated her mind for several days. She needed a diversion.

Did Kendrick really hit Benevolence? My Kendrick? What would make him do such a thing? How am I going to tell her? He could have killed her . . . I need to go to the police . . . This can't be . . . my fiancé . . . The man I want to spend the rest of my life with . . . could do this . . . This is too much to absorb at once. First, I have ADD and now this . . .

She looked at her watch, while rummaging through her bag.

Good . . . Got it.

Since taking her new medication, Leah felt brand-new. The psychotherapy sessions have also been a plus. The to-do lists have been easier to start and finish. The house is livable more than three days a week. Even restaurant duties have developed into a joy. Leah checked her inventory earlier and restocked supplies on her own for the first time ever. She smiled at the thought. She blended into one of the groups forming as they started the breakout sessions.

"Okay folks, here is a checklist of public safety tips we want to know and practice. Tip number one: look around your surroundings before unlocking your car or truck. Tip number two: look at your surroundings when driving, walking in a parking garage, before unlocking the door at home, hotel or dorm room and definitely when using public transportation."

After thirty minutes, another trainer, wearing a dark blue Save-a-Sista t-shirt and jeans, bent his back then placed his hands in a triangular formation over his mouth.

"Switch groups!"

A petite black woman with a curly afro rallied her group of twenty together on the floor like a football huddle. Octavia and Yasmine fell into the group. Leah waved them hello from her circle.

"We are going to talk about relationships and myths about domestic violence in children, teenagers and adults. We will talk about warning signs, triggers and how best to protect yourself mentally and emotionally. Does anyone know what domestic violence is?"

One child raised his hand. He looked at the adults first before daring to speak.

"It's when yo´ father be beefing with yo´ mother. Then he be trying to 'pimp slap' her so she act right." He smiled, looked at the angry faces, and frowned himself into silence.

"Okay. You are correct. Domestic violence is violence in the home. It occurs when adult children fight with one another or with another family member. It also occurs when one partner who is intimate with another partner displays abusive, violent, or threatening behavior towards that partner. Who is most affected by domestic violence?"

A little girl raised her hand.

"My mom . . . she wanted to come but she was scared, so she stayed home. I came with my aunt and sisters."

Many nodded and groaned in agreement.

"Is it mostly women?"

A teenaged girl raised her hand.

"It seems all over the world women are being affected by domestic violence. It just seems worse than it is here . . . if you could call it worse."

"Domestic violence can happen anywhere to anyone of any race, religion, culture or economic status. It really does not matter . . . Domestic violence affects both partners, their children, other family members, friends and colleagues.

Domestic violence can occur in ANY intimate relationship, including same-sex relationships and including by women towards men. However, in most domestic violence incidents, a man commits an act against a woman. Domestic violence is dangerous. Too often, conflicts cause injury or even worse, death. There is a common perception in many societies that domestic violence is the woman's fault. Women, this is a big lie! While this perception is changing, men and women often share this belief. In some cultures, women still are not allowed to make choices about who they will marry and whether or not they will stay in a relationship. Do you know what? Things are changing. Organizations all around the globe are working together to create laws and change cultural perceptions that tolerate or condone domestic violence. Here's another question: is there any way that we can be warned that our partner might be dangerous?"

The adults looked around. Many were helpless to answer, trying to think back to their own situations. Octavia and Yasmine looked at each other and then down on the floor. The trainer got up and distributed some kid-friendly pamphlets.

"I want everyone to go around the room and read either a tip or discovery from the pamphlet." She pointed to Yasmine.

"Can you go first?"

"Some of most important personal safety skills we want students to learn include assessing the person's behavior and being aware of potential danger signs, getting centered to calm themselves down so that they can think clearly and make safer choices instead of panicking or escalating the argument. Protecting themselves emotionally rather than being triggered or coerced by the mean things someone says." Leah volunteered to read the next tip in her group.

"Protecting themselves physically without fighting back. Creating a safety plan for how to leave and for how to get help."

"Using verbal self-defense tactics to defuse a potentially violent interaction. What are verbal self-defense tactics? Do they really work?" one woman asked.

"That's a good question. We will show you some tactics in the next segment and show you how to say and use them. Can we get another volunteer?" Octavia raised her hand to read in her circle.

"Paying attention to warning signs while dating or courting . . . Here are some useful questions that we encourage you to consider while dating: Does he treat you as if you belong to yourself or does he act possessive of you? Does he seem positive about the attention you get from others OR does he seem jealous of it? Does he insist that you do nothing affectionate or sexual towards him unless you truly feel like it, or does he try to pressure you into doing more than you want?" Simone read in a different circle somewhere in the room.

"Does he encourage you to spend time with friends and family OR does he try to separate you from others who are important to you? Does he take full responsibility for his behavior OR does he tell you he cannot help himself because he loves you so much? Does he encourage you to be independent OR does he try to get you to be dependent on him? Does he do his full share of the work in the house and with money OR does he expect you to pay for him or to do most of the work?"

"Thank you. See, women are often taught, that a man being possessive, jealous, demanding, needy, or wanting them all to himself means that he cares. The real truth is that a man believing that a woman is his property is dangerous."

Benevolence read from her radical circle.

"One excellent predictor of someone's future behavior towards any of us is that person's behavior towards others. Useful assessment questions, how does he act towards others? What does he do when he is mad at someone or upset about something?"

Leah read aloud in her group one last time, her tone changing with each question.

"Does he take responsibility for his share when things go wrong with another person, or is his story that everything is the other person's fault? Does he try to make women feel sorry for him because of all the hard luck he has had with other people?"

Leah felt shaky. Tears were welling up in her eyes.

"Miss, are you okay?"

Everything was hitting too close to home.

If only I could find the girls . . . find Benevolence . . .

"Switch groups!"

A Save-a-Sista timekeeper belted forth. Leah jolted up and scanned the room. She needed support for this last session. Suddenly, a hand grabbed hers.

"Hey . . . I thought we all should be together for this last one."

Benevolence squeezed Leah's hand tight. Leah felt her heart shift gears from pain to hope.

"Let's go find the others and make our own power circle."

Soon people were looking for other people. Neighbors looked for neighbors, deacons for deacons, ministers for ministers, sisters for sisters, and brothers for brothers. Everyone wanted to be near someone familiar.

"Wow!"

Keita Kerim exploded.

"There is power building in here! People have moved from all across the sanctuary to find people they know. Folks, this is our most engaging session yet!

We are going to give you some everyday safety tips. We are going to teach you some skills, give you verbal defense tactics. We are also going to do some role-play scenarios. By the time you leave, you will be different from when you came. You will be stronger. First, take a bathroom break and a snack break. We will resume in fifteen minutes."

The women gave each other a warm hug. No one had seen each other for two weeks. The difference was noticeable. They huddled in a small group by the water cooler.

"Ladies, I am so glad to see you guys. It hasn't been that long, has it?"

"It seems like it." Octavia continued.

"Anyway, it's good to see you guys."

"Guess what?"

Leah piped in. She had not found a way to tell the girls anything. The moment seemed right.

"I have ADD."

"What's that?" Yasmine got a cup of water.

"It is adult Attention Deficit Disorder. It's a biophysical condition kids have. They cannot sit still, or pay attention. It is hard to focus, to organize, things like that. Kids grow up with it but hopefully, it is less mild."

Simone chimed in, picking up a paper cup from the cooler.

"The doctor gave her medication and she has been going to therapy. The doctor says an intervention will be done to integrate family and friends if Leah so chooses, right?"

Octavia tried to reassure everyone about Leah's progress.

"You knew?" Yasmine said surprised.

"I asked Octavia to go with me," Leah interrupted.

"I told her not to say anything. I needed time to sort through some things."

She looked directly at Benevolence.

"Is there more? More that you want to tell us?"

Benevolence read Leah's eyes and her thoughts.

"All right folks, let's begin."

The trainer's voice broke the stare between Leah and Benevolence.

"Everybody pair up. We want all the kids in one group . . . all the teenagers in another group. Men and women can mix into the other groups. Pick a partner and we want you to sit down facing your partner."

Benevolence grabbed Leah. Leah helped her sit on the floor. The youth trainers started first.

"We tell our young women who are dating, even if someone is wonderful to you, it is a danger signal if he is mean or threatening to others or if he blames others instead of taking responsibility. We want you to act as if you are extremely allergic to any sign of possessiveness, emotional coercion or threat. Remember that you do not owe loyalty or love to someone who endangers you. We want you to know some practices to use for when you are dating: First, we want you to take the power out of the words, 'stuck-up bitch.' Next, we want you to stand up. Supposed your partner says I want you to go to the pool house with me. We want to you say in a relaxed, but firm voice, 'No thank you, I am not interested,' and walk away. Let's practice." The kids practiced peer-pressure techniques and other dating scenarios.

"Here are a few more that we like: say clearly and firmly, 'I do not want to go out with you.' Everyone repeat clearly and firmly. Now, I want you to practice pushing your partner away from you and saying firmly, 'I am going home now.' Let's practice."

The kids were assertive, strong, and confident. The girls seemed more forceful than the boys.

"Finally, I want you all to sit down and pretend you are driving a car. Decide who will drive. Suppose the person driving says something really mean and nasty. Here's what I want you to say: 'Take me home. My parents or roommates know where I am. Take me home NOW! Ladies, do not give in. Do not let anyone make you feel guilty for not liking him or her. Remember, ladies, that saying in a loud firm voice, 'my no means no!' These strong words will shut those potentially violent situations down. Let's switch partners."

"Okay, now for our adults, we have some verbal tactics we want you to practice. If someone is trying to harm you, we want you to identify a safe place to go for the moment. We also want you to memorize your safe question, which is, 'Is there a neighbor, family member or friend I can take my children to stay with until things cool down?' If you are by yourself, you can say, 'Can I stay here for a moment until things cool down.' Let's practice."

As the couples started practicing, Leah said her safe question to Benevolence.

"Can I stay here a moment until things cool down?"

"Leah, do you have something you need to share?" Benevolence whispered.

"Is that part of my safe question?"

Leah did not know how to open her can of worms, but Benevolence was not going to budge until the worms spilled onto the floor. The trainers continued.

"Next, I want you to do what we call, leaving with love. It is dangerous to scream, 'I hate you and I never want to see you again!' Instead, go to a safer place while saying quietly and warmly, 'I love you and I want us all to be safe. I will come back when you feel better.' Let's practice."

As Leah repeated her lines, Benevolence continued her own safe statements.

"Leah, whatever it is . . . I can handle it. I will not be mad. We can handle it together. You and me. No one else has to know. If that is what you want."

The trainer continued. He walked from circle to circle.

"Here's another tactic: distraction. Have a plan ready if someone is about to blow up. A distraction could be someone important to your abusive partner who you have asked to expect a call so you can say, 'Your brother or sister called with some exciting news,' and be able to count on the person coming through. A distraction could be to bring up a topic that will get him to focus on outside problems, like politics. A distraction could be having a favorite food."

Leah said her distraction lines to Benevolence for practice. Distractions were not enough to throw Benevolence off her informational quest.

"Yes, it is my fault. All my fault, I fought with him before it happened. I left and drove home."

Leah said, blinking her tears away. Benevolence came closer. Close, but not close enough to stop the confession. Benevolence whispered so the other pairs would not hear.

"What's your fault? Leah, what are you trying to say?"

Leah took a deep breath, trying to stop the flurry of tears that refused to quit running down her face.

"Here's one more tactic: offer a face-saving way out. Some people will fight to the death to preserve their image of themselves as being powerful and in control. We do not want anyone doing that. Instead of arguing, it can be more effective to agree with an abusive partner who is being unreasonable in order to buy some time and calm the situation down."

"Minister James, I think I know who hit you . . . earlier this year."

Chapter 39

*"When you get tired . . . allow Him to show you
the essence of who you are . . ."*

It was rearing the end of June, and graduation was days away. There were weeks of e-mails filled with checklists and other lists. E-mails included the designated functions and responsibilities: silverware, entertainment, guest lists, video, program, and party favors. Benevolence excitedly generated fresh ideas for the list while refining others. The decorations had been picked out. The Evite guest list trickled up and down. Benevolence typed an e-mail to one of the vendors after reading her morning memos. She had been fully functional at work for several weeks. Benevolence confined herself to desk duty and paperwork until she no longer needed her cane. Most of her caseload transferred temporarily to a visiting psychologist. Today, Benevolence was on a different agenda. She wanted to make sure the award certificates were ready. She called one of the vendors.

"How are you coming with the custom-made, engraved plaques?"

"They'll be ready, don't you worry, Miss James."

"Thanks, Cornelius. Talk to you later."

Benevolence hung up the phone and continued down her to-do-list. The phone rang.

"Hello?"

"Benevolence, this is your uncle. We want to check and see if you needed anything for the party."

"Yeah, some prayers please . . . too many details. Did Mummy asked you to call? She checking up on me?"

"I can call my favorite niece without her help. She wanted to make sure you wouldn't be overdoing it. You are still recovering, you know. Let me know if you need help with anything."

"Okay, I can e-mail you a partial list."

"Benevolence, how are the police doing on your case? Did they catch the imbecile who hit you?"

Benevolence jolted, remembering Leah's words.

Kendrick did it. I am so sorry . . . He was the one who hit you . . . I have proof . . . I am going to the police . . . I don't want anything else to happen because of me.

"Uncle, I believe they are going to crack the case soon. They have a suspect."

"Bene, who? Did you tell your mother and father?"

"They are questioning new folks. I have to go. I have a ten o' clock appointment."

Benevolence made another phone call.

"Hello?"

"Darius, it's me."

"Hey, baby . . . what's up? How's everything coming for graduation?"

"It's coming. Can I see you? This afternoon? My last session ends at two. Can we meet at our spot?"

"Sure. What's wrong? What happened?"

"I'll explain it when I see you . . . thanks, bye."

Benevolence strolled through the corridors of the facility.

It seems like ages since I've been here. Have things really changed? Will I know? What about LaTasha?

Benevolence opened the door to the counseling room and waited eight minutes.

Well, I guess things haven't quite changed.

LaTasha walked in, her swagger more bouncy than Benevolence ever noticed. Upon seeing Benevolence, LaTasha actually ran over and gave Benevolence a hug as best as her handcuffed hands would allow, all under the CO's watchful eye.

"Supervisor James?"

"I'm all right."

She nodded to him. As soon as LaTasha returned to her chair, a safe distance away, he moved back to his position by the door.

"How have you been, Ms. James?"

Benevolence wrote nothing in her folder. She sat to get a good look at LaTasha. Her face was rounder, and she was gaining weight. Her hair was getting longer.

"Good. Better."
"What's been going on?"
Benevolence shot out questions.
"Did you get my letters?"
LaTasha spewed forth questions of her own.
"Yes, yes I did. I read them."
"Well, the tournament is in a few days. We beat all the other groups. They were scrubs anyway, except the Pasadena crew. We're meeting them in the finals."
"Pasadena, I've never heard of them before."
"They're a new bunch of girls, but their leadership is old school around here. They be trying to run things."
"Are they recruiting?"
"Mostly. But I'm lying low. Trying to focus, trying to practice. My mother came by last month. She said she wasn't making any promises, but maybe she can get off early to come to the game."
"That's progress."
"Well, what about you, Ms. James? What is going on? You look hot! In a respectful CO kind of way. You have lost what, ten pounds?"
"No, close to twenty. Working on a few more . . . but it's coming."
"Well anyways, you look good. You can get a date now. No offense, but you looked worn out. I guess I would be mean and worn out too, having to deal with us hopeless, chickenheads all day."
"You're not hopeless."
"Some are. I am not one of them . . . I'm just saying. Don't they have some GED programs in here?"
"Yes?"
"Well I was thinking—"
LaTasha brought her hands up to the table and leaned forward as if she was telling Benevolence a secret.
"If I knew how many credits I needed to graduate, I could take some classes, you know. Nothing big. Thought maybe I needed to looked at finally graduating from school, you know. Think about college. Life beyond this place. I am up for parole in a few weeks. Figured I've spent enough time in here."
"Really?"
Benevolence noticed power, revelation, and conviction coming from her voice.
"Yeah . . . just been thinking . . . I'm ready for a change. Something different. I want to play again. Still got the skills that God gave me. It's still there. I've been sleeping on it, but it's still there. He's been showing me a lot of things. I've been learning a lot . . . about Jesus, I mean."

The guard knocked on the door.

"Time's up."

"LaTasha, you're making real progress."

"You coming to my game?"

"Wouldn't miss it, but I can only stay the first half."

"Just as long as you make it."

LaTasha got up and swaggered out. There was no mistaking this moment. Breakthrough had entered the meeting.

Eleven o'clock in the morning and a disheveled Octavia grumbled through her morning devotions as she stared through her bedroom ceiling. Some mornings, personal prayer and worship was a joy, while other days it was nonexistent. Three weeks after her termination, Octavia fumbled for a plan. She stared at the twirling ceiling fan. Her bones ached. She had a headache, and she had to concentrate hard to stare at the fan. Thoughts spun their own web in her mind.

Nothing I do ever seems to pan out ... Why did I want to become a lawyer again ... I could go back to temping ... You don't make partner temping ... idiot. Octavia got up slowly. The months of working eighty-hour weeks had finally taken its toll. Fatigue rolled all over her like a fog. The phone blared in Octavia's ear. She jumped. She nearly crawled to the receiver to stop its deafening rings.

"Hello?" Octavia moaned out.

"Octavia, this is your mother. Are you still asleep?"

"I just woke up."

"It is past eleven."

"Thank you."

"Octavia, what is wrong? You have not called. You have not come by. Your sister said that she has tried to call you but no answer. Are you still thinking about work?"

"I have a headache, Mommy."

"Why don't you come over? Daddy will be glad to see you. We can fix you something to eat. I know you haven't been eating."

"I can't, Mommy."

"Why not? You should not be there by yourself. You need to be outside getting fresh air."

Shame lay next to her, reading a law brief. Octavia thought of the other times that she was unemployed; she, in some ways, caused it. This one was different. Though she felt vindicated, it still hurt. It hurt like hell. It pierced the confines of her dignity and her heart.

"Mommy, I need to sort things out. I can't come yet. Besides, I know Daddy is disappointed. I will never be the type of lawyer that he can be proud of."

"Don't say that . . . your father is very proud of you. He talks about you all of the time, his first daughter. He knows that you have had a rough time, but it doesn't mean that he is not proud of you for trying."

The phone beeped.

"Mommy, hold on . . . I have another call . . ."

Happy for a moment to change subjects, she clicked over.

"Hello?

"Hello . . . Octavia Ka . . . lu?"

The voice on the other end sounded foreign and robotic.

"This is ENR Services. We are calling to find confirm—"

"Could you hold on please? I have another call."

"Mommy, I have to go. I have another call."

"Tavie, don't sit in the house all day. Get out. Do something."

"Okay, Mommy. I'll talk with you later. Bye."

Octavia switched her tone and demeanor to the other call.

"Sir, not sure how you got this number but I am on the National Do Not Call List. Kindly take my name off your list and your neighbor's and the rest of the entire department . . . because I know you have a million lists . . . So kindly take my name off and do not call here again unless you want legal action taken. I hope I have made myself clear. Have a pleasant day."

Click.

That felt good . . .

For a brief moment, she had an outlet to spew her venom. It gave her a quick burst of energy. She got up and went into the living room. She looked at her mail. Bills, junk mail, postcards, and more bills filtered the table. Octavia picked up the bills when a small mailer with a theatre-set background fell to the floor.

Think you are America's next director? Think you have what it takes? Apply now! Howard University's Masters in Fine Arts program. Octavia stared at the black face seated in the director's chair. She threw the mailer in the corner and went to the kitchen. She washed down the orange juice from the carton and ate a bagel. She picked up a banana and collapsed on the sofa, flicking the cable channels while massaging down a headache.

After catching the last thirty minutes of the *Price Is Right,* she detected the warning levels of her "funk meter" rising and journeyed to the bathroom. She stared into the mirror while brushing her teeth. Bags appeared under her eyes. She had one tiny crease forming on her forehead.

I look like an old hag . . . and for what? Some pipe dream of a partnership from a law firm. Failure. You should have done business, even theatre. Something with maybe a little more shelf life . . .

Octavia spit out the toothpaste and rinsed. She got into the shower, hoping to wash away the fog of fatigue that had been showering her for weeks. The faucet rained out cold droplets before evolving into a steamy waterfall.

I guess I should be used to life bringing me persecution by now . . . but I have yet gotten to the 'be of good cheer' part. My time at Huffman was ending I knew that . . . But, God, why do I feel like this? So worthless . . . I work hard and no one notices . . . All my sweat and tears always make someone else look amazing . . . God, I know you got me . . . I have trusted you before, but, man, this sucks! I am tired of going through transitions. I'm tired of things not working out. I'm supposed to be graduating in a few days. I should be moving into a new season. There should be bigger and better things awaiting me . . . This is not fair . . . What is it that you want me to do? I give up! I give up doing things my way. Whatever you want me to do, I'll do it. I'm just done.

Twenty minutes later, Octavia marched out of her condominium with her purse in hand under a clear June sky. She took her mother's advice to escape outside from the grips of despair that seemed to be dwelling around her soul.

Benevolence parked her car. Darius was sitting on a park bench, in a white shirt, brown tie, and brown slacks. He waved, then got up to greet his princess.

He looks scrumptious! What exactly did I do to deserve this gift? Thank you, Jesus.

Benevolence retreated slowly from her car.

"Hey, Bene, I got you."

"Thank you."

"Do you want to sit by the bench?"

"Please."

Darius walked arm and arm with his beauty by his side. He led her to the bench with her cane. She sat down. She laid the cane along the edge.

"You didn't sound like yourself."

"Darius . . . there's something I've been keeping . . . a secret . . . but I am getting angrier with each day I hold it."

"What is it? Is something wrong with the girls or family?"

"Not quite."

Benevolence could no longer hold in her anger. She patted her gun and breathed deeply.

"Leah knows who hit me. She told me."

"That's good news! The police should be questioning them right?"

"I don't know."

"What do you mean, Bene?" Darius turned toward Benevolence. He held her hand.

Benevolence picked up her cane.

"It was her fiancé that hit me. It was Kendrick."

Darius's face burned with anger. He stood up.

"Why didn't you tell me this earlier?"

"I didn't know what to do with the information myself. I don't have any proof."

"Does Leah?"

"I think so. I just feel so . . . violated. I just met him at the restaurant. I only knew of him from Leah. I sensed that their relationship wasn't the best but this—"

On impulse, Benevolence took her left hand and patted for her gun. Darius noticed.

"Bene, what are you doing?"

"He hit an officer. He should pay for it."

Darius took her cane, laid it down, and cupped both of her hands into his. He kissed them.

"Bene, he will pay. I promise you, he will."

"How do you know? I am not sure that Leah will make that decision. This will cost her. She has a lot to lose."

"I know because God sees everything. He is a righteous judge. I bet this has torn apart his life, not to mention his relationship with Leah. I cannot imagine Leah knowing this and not sharing it with the police. Especially if she has proof. That doesn't sound like the young woman that you've been mentoring. If he wants to bully someone, I'll show him who he can bully."

Darius raised his fists, looking like a lighter, muscular version of George Foreman. Benevolence laughed.

"Bene, let me pray for you. You can't keep this anger. This hurt. His actions caused harm, but look at what God did afterwards. Your life has changed. I care about the woman I see right now. I won't let anything or anyone harm you. Let me pray for you. God is your advocate. He will do right by you."

Darius cupped her hands again and prayed. Deliverance swooped down from the trees and encircled the bench several times. Benevolence cried into Darius's arms. He gently kissed her tears away.

Chapter 40

*"There is a way that seems right to a man,
but in the end . . . you're crazy!"*

Caribbean DeLite was the spot for the graduation ceremony. At two o'clock in the afternoon, patrons entering the restaurant tried to peek unsuccessfully at the new space available for eating. The hostess detoured patrons to other tables. The renovated, tan-colored private dining area was complete and unveiled just in time. It sported a cozy, comfortable, and delightful setting for thirty-five guests, mostly close friends, co-workers, family, and church members. A celebration of a spiritual journey traveled by these five women was now for the most part complete.

"Whoa! Is it finally finished?"

Octavia beamed at how spacious the room appeared. Happy for a reason to be dressed up and out of the house, Octavia determined that she would enjoy herself. The women sat dressed in white at their own guest-of-honor table in the center of the room. The table had a special red overlap with white napkins and silver crystal. The bar became the gift setting. It reminded Octavia of an initiation of a different kind, a long time ago. Leah surveyed the room and its décor with pride.

"Yeah. Now I can breathe. We have already started advertising for big events and special occasions. I am happy to say that we will christen it tonight with our graduation."

"Hey, Yasmine, are you going to introduce us to your parents?" Yasmine stood near the gift table, inspecting all of the latest entries.

"When they get here, although, I'm not sure that they're coming together. The divorce will be final soon."

"Simone, is your family here? Is Tavian coming?"

"Mom couldn't make it but my uncle and sister are here. I am not sure about Tavian."

"Leah, where's Kendrick? Is your family here?"

"My mom and Shah are over there." Leah pointed across the room. "Victor couldn't make it. Kendrick? He may be tied up. We'll see. I left him a note. Hey, guys, I have something to tell you so don't leave later okay?"

Benevolence rose from the head table seated with her parents, her sister Rosette, Jules, Rona, Darius, Bishop and Pastor Timms, and Deacon Baylor. She was twenty-eight pounds lighter, 150 percent stronger, and on top of the world. She approached the podium and lifted the microphone. She looked out into her audience.

"I am so glad you all could be here today. Today is filled with so many blessings, so many opportunities, and so many decisions. These women and I went on a journey. I thought I would assume the primary role of mentor and teacher, but I found that oftentimes, it was they, who taught me. They taught me a lot about new friendships, consistency, patience and perseverance even through pain. It was much more than we could have gotten from the readings alone. I have honestly learned a lot."

She smiled at each of them.

"I hope each of them did too. I am dedicating this poem to my girls and every woman who desires to break out of her shell. I call it 'Stretch.'

If there ever was, a story left untold
Ask the Master, but he will let the pieces unravel and unfold;
Characters came into view, some dynamic, some small,
Yet, life has a way of making everyone seem four feet tall.
Four women, having different views, different hues, different cues.
Each played their instruments, all with a different tune.
Some off-key, others off-pitch, noisy sounds clanging together.
Too many soloists, no musicians, any real harmony was severed.
Meanwhile, a plan was stewing to get the band to play
With the conductor missing, there would be a short delay.
Yet the Master Conductor stepped in; he suddenly changed the song.
Soon the musicians stretched to figure out each new part
Who would end and who would start?
The big show was coming; they had to get ready,
Rehearsals rocked back and forth, but soon they became steady
Now the show is here, but not the one you see.
For it's the art and struggles of musicianship that finally brought harmony."

Benevolence looked at the flowers blossoming in front of her.

"Thank you. I love you, guys."

She blew them a kiss and sat back down. The crowd buzzed and roared in fanfare. As Benevolence sat down, she hugged her mother and father.

"We are proud of you."

They echoed softly. Benevolence looked over at LaTasha, in street clothes, accompanied by a correction officer. LaTasha was recovering from a stab wound. She was in good spirits. She smiled. Benevolence beamed her smile over to her uncle, Rona, and Jules before settling in her seat. Darius took her hand. She beamed all over. He kissed her cheek when she sat down.

The night continued with moments of reflection. Yasmine talked about her soup-kitchen experiences. Simone remembered many car conversations with Octavia. Leah called many referee moments between Octavia and Yasmine. The girls laughed. Actually, everyone had a different catfight that involved Octavia and Yasmine. Everyone agreed that Yasmine's witty words had a way of triggering an avalanche of attitudes when caught off guard. The women exchanged gifts and cards with each other. Benevolence's family shared words of wisdom.

"Hello, ladies, I first want to thank you for being there for my Bene in her time of need. And though the police have not locked up the fool that hurt her, I am thankful that she is alive, safe and is looking good!"

Valentina gave her daughter a big kiss on the cheek.

Pastor Timms spoke.

"Ladies, this is indeed a great day. I sense that God and the angels are smiling down at you today. Not only because of the work He was able to accomplish in you, but because you stuck through the process. There were hurts, there were disappointments, but instead of isolating yourselves, you stuck together. You learned to rely on each other. This is just the beginning. You may go your separate ways from here, but know that you have sisters that you can count on. You've got a sister circle full of power."

The crowd bellowed amen.

Leah told her mother and sister about her ADD. Her mother cried. She remembered the warnings. She remembered her late husband's words. Her mother realized what role her own treatment of Leah played in their current relationship. She asked Leah for forgiveness. Shah and Leah spent a few days together for some needed bonding. Leah told her family about Kendrick. She spoke of the abuse, accident, and her plans. Leah stayed clear of Kendrick. He called several times and came over several more, but the interference by her new assistant manager kept him at bay. He knew something was up.

Simone noticed Tavian slipped inside. She felt strong enough for the first time in her life to release herself from the coveted role Tavian once played in her life. She had made a decision, and she would stick with it.

Octavia wondered about her new life of freedom, her own personal surrender. What would it bring? She would have to rely on the leading of the Holy Spirit. Where would it take her? If it was anything like this process, she was going to be in for it. She had spent all of these years, over one hundred thousand hours, studying, excelling, but in the end, she never really had control. For the first time in her life, she was going to find out what this narrow path leading to life really entails.

Yasmine's parents sat at the same table, barely facing each other. It was important to show up for Yasmine's sake, but they no longer kept pretenses. They were no longer even friends.

Daddy looked older. Tired. He could finally be free. Did freedom mean loneliness? Daddy would never be alone, but the way in which he interacted with his wife, he won't find that again . . . so accepting . . . so loving.

As Yasmine looked over at her parents, at that moment, a revelation hit her.

I don't want to manipulate my way to love. I can't keep such a tight grip of my heart. I cannot control others, I can only control me.

Everyone greeted the women at the end of the ceremony. Rona and Jules made their way to the table. As the waiters helped clear the tables, the women gathered for photographs. With Leah on one end, Benevolence, Octavia, and Yasmine in the middle, and Simone on the other end, continuous sounds of snapshots rolling highlighted the end of one season and the beginning of another.

A courier rode over to the restaurant.

"I have a package for Kendrick O'Riley. Are you him?"

"Nope."

"Sorry, specific instructions. He has to sign for it. Just doing my job."

"I'll get him."

Rage slammed the door in a red fury. Kendrick came in out of the kitchen, engaged in an intense argument with one of the chefs. He bumped into the hostess.

"Yes, what the hell is it?"

"You have a package."

"You couldn't take care of it? What the hell do I pay you for?"

"Sir, the courier has specific instructions. You are the only one who can sign for it."

Kendrick walked to the front lobby. Kendrick scribbled his name on the clipboard and stormed off.

"Jerk. I feel sorry for you."

The courier walked off. Kendrick went to his office. It was a paper envelope with a typed white label. When he opened it, another envelope lay inside with handwriting that he immediately recognized. He opened the envelope. He sat down.

Dear Kendrick,

> *I have loved you for a long time.*
>
> *You were there when no one else could have been. You were my teacher, guiding your student into the food business. You shepherded every order, inventory, employee until I could manage things. Only, I never really could manage things. I would forget inventory, inspector visits, and orders. Employees came and went. It was rough. I sucked. Everything would have closed down if not for you. Family helped, but you were my anchor. Little did I notice, however, I was beginning to sink. Sink from fears. Sink from insults. I tried to say it was the pressure of being the best, being a famous restaurateur's son. You were running two businesses. Yours and mine. I was your apprentice. You took delight in molding me. It took years of love and of care. Years of mistakes. We both made them. Ten years of business, friendship and love. I hoped we could move to the next level. The next phase. I always knew there was something different about me. I have adult ADD. Adult Attention Deficit Disorder. You said that about me a few times. I wish I knew then. I have wanted you to look past my faults. You've been my anchor. Now we're not moving forward. Your words torment me. First by accident, then on purpose. Your moods cascaded me from coast to coast. I thought by protecting me, you anchored me. Now, baby, I am sinking. I have shrunk back into a desolate place. I need to be free. I thought I could love you enough to move the anchor forward. You've been everything to me . . . for a long time. I forgive you. The fights. The words spoken . . . the taunts. Even the accident. You were hurting too. I guess I never realized how much. I forgive you. But I am sinking and I have to let go. I love you. I always will, but I'm letting go of my anchor.*
>
> *Leah.*

Kendrick wiped the tears streaming down his face. The door knocked. "I'm busy!"

Kendrick cleared his throat. The door knocked again. The door opened wide. Two officers, one male and the other female, appeared. The male officer called out,

"Kendrick O'Riley?"

Kendrick wiped his eyes; he did not even look up.

"You are under arrest, for aggravated assault, assault, with the attempt to do harm and fleeing the scene of an accident. You have the right to remain silent. Anything you say will be used against you in the court of the law."

The female officer handcuffed Kendrick and escorted him out of the restaurant with all of the patrons and chefs watching.

Chapter 41

*"Part of the quest of life is to realize the potential
God has for you and be satisfied there..."*

A year after the graduation, the women met for their own reunion. Octavia and Yasmine drove with company to BWI airport. They met Leah and Simone on a week rendezvous to Martinique for a very joyous occasion: Benevolence's wedding.

"Yazz, girl, if this is not the best excuse for a vacation, I don't know what is! Didn't you just start your new job? They let you go on a vacation?"

"Yeah, Tavie. I made it sound more like a family emergency, but they were cool about it. Onyx Research is in the 270 corridor. They work on herbal perfumes, but have other products on the pipeline. They are currently doing brain research and the effect smell has on the brain. It's cool to see the kinds of opportunities they've been coming up with. I am still learning the ropes, but research is gearing up for the summer so this week is perfect. How is graduate school? How are your classes? How's show business?"

"Girl, the transition was crazy but now... I thank the Lord. Now I get it! Man, the Holy Spirit knew what she was doing. I can use everything I learned at Huffman. I actually love directing."

"Excuse me... Yazz, where's Martinique?" Dominick flipped through his traveler's map. Dominick Wadley, Yasmine steady beau, had an innocence about him that refreshed her. Dominick found her in one of the aisles at the grocery store. They exchanged e-mails and phone numbers, but Dominick did not call her until a few weeks later. They have been courting ever since.

"Isn't it near Guyana or is that Grenada? Octavia, do you or Silas know?"

"Hey, we are from Africa not the islands."

Silas snickered.

"I bet your guess would be better than ours."

Silas laughed as he made the right turn onto the beltway.

"Silas, shut up." Octavia laughed.

"Don't pay Silas any attention. It's near St. Martin and Jamaica. When we get to the airport, we can get a better map."

Forty minutes later, Silas parked the car. The couples met up with Leah and Simone in line at reservations. Octavia greeted them both with hugs.

"You guys look great! Leah, you have twists!"

"It is different. I look very ethnic. I worry more about my classes now. They have been kicking my butt. I am handling it though."

"Simone, is Tavian here?" Octavia saw extra baggage.

"He went to the bathroom. He will be right back. And who is this?"

Dominick stuck out his hand.

"Hello. I'm Dominick. Yazz has told me so much about you."

He shook Simone's hand.

"Leah Decruz . . . Caribbean DeLite, right? I order carryout a lot from there. It is a pleasure."

"Yasmine, where have you been keeping him?" Leah joked.

"Nowhere. He keeps me. He does what he feels comfortable doing. I only suggest things."

"What church do you attend?"

"I go to church in northeast DC. The Children's Bread International with Pastor and First Lady Jacobs."

"How's the service? I bet it is off the chain!"

"They are anointed!"

Dominick said with pride. He loved his church home. Tavian walked back to the line, and everyone made introductions. The line moved very quickly.

"Hey, folks, this is a beautiful reunion, but can we get our luggage on board so that we'll have some clothes on the island. I mean we can also be like Adam and Eve. You know that was in Africa right? Where's my video camera? I might get some inspiration."

Everyone laughed.

"I'm so sorry, that y'all will have to put up with him. He's been like this since the first day we met."

"Where was that?" Yasmine asked.

"On set of a pilot television show they plan to run on NBC.

I was working as a production assistant. He was one of the cinematographers. I think they may have dropped him in the bushes when he was a baby." Octavia snickered.

"Hey, don't make fun of the bushes . . . that is an insult to my people."

"What people? You were raised in the States."

Octavia nudge Silas playfully in the stomach. He bent over faking the pain but rose back up laughing.

"I went back . . . a few times . . . I know MY people."

"Does everyone have their passport?"

Simone interrupted.

"Just checking, wouldn't want anyone missing their flight."

They boarded the eleven o'clock flight going to the JFK airport to New York. At one thirty, they boarded Air France. They arrived in Martinique around five o'clock in the evening. After about an hour in customs, the group walked outside and beheld a breathtaking view of the tropical island, as the yellow-orange sun cast a shadow of yellow rays on the forest green grassland. The air was brisk and fresh. People were waving for taxis, in French. There were gardens of hibiscus, frangipani, and orchids growing along the sidewalk. Silas brought out his digital camera.

"Wow!" Yasmine gasped.

"This place is beautiful! Nick, don't you think so?"

"So, this is where your mentor is from? Nice."

"Man, if the flowers look this good I am afraid to see the women," Silas whispered. The brothers slapped fives. Tavian laughed.

"Brother, don't be afraid, we got you. We will endure this together."

"What are you guys laughing about?"

Octavia snooped. The guys hushed up.

"Silas is scared of flowers," Dominick offered.

"Man, whatever." Octavia reasoned.

"They're bonding. Let them have their moment." Simone suggested.

"Uh-huh, whatever. I know Silas. His eyes are like his camera. He likes to pan-scan the view."

"Girl, you are stupid." Leah laughed.

"We need to be looking for Benevolence or her family."

Yasmine looked over near the taxicab and saw a familiar face. There were a group of people speaking half Creole and half French, and they were walking in her direction. Benevolence's sister, Rosette, greeted the group.

"Hello! We are so glad that you are here, able to see the island. We will all gather at the house. You will have time to change before the rehearsal dinner. Each one of you will stay with us. Don't worry. We don't live too far from Mummy. You came in time for Sugarcane Festival. You plan to stay a week, no? There is much to see and much to do. We must give you a tour. My sister will be so glad you are here. She has been a wreck. Never seen her like this."

Rosette shook her head and made sounds with her mouth.

"Scary. Everybody ready? Let us go."

She whispered in Creole to Francois; they laughed and got into their respective cars. Rosette, Octavia, and Silas lead the way. Francois, Yasmine, and Dominick rode in the other car, leaving William, Leah, Simone, and Tavian following closely behind them. The forty-minute ride through the southern tip of Martinique revealed coconut palm trees, white sandy beaches, and plantation farms. Rosette drove like a tour guide, gesturing and giving pieces of the island's rich history.

"The H. M. S. Diamond Rock is a sort of Caribbean Gibraltar rising 183 meters from the sea. The British used the Le Roche de Diamant as a sloop of war in an 1804 sea battle. We will also pass the Le Marin, a well-equipped marina, and an ancient Jesuit-style church dating to 1766. Our coves, peninsulas and white sand beaches around Sainte-Anne, the Plage des Salines and Cap Chevalier, are considered among the most beautiful in the Caribbean."

They arrived at a two-story lake-view house. Palms shaded the front porch. Big windows brought in the natural sunlight. A floral garden of hibiscus, frangipani, and orchids surrounded the landscape. The house had three bedrooms and three bathrooms. The backyard was a small farm filled with fruit trees and gardens. Rosette parked the car. William and Francois arrived a few minutes later. Rosette entered. She kissed her cousins and laughed aloud. The air was a mixture of jambalaya, rum, flowers, and spices. Benevolence's home revealed stately furniture, which featured a small fireplace. Some African choral music was playing on the radio.

"Put your things down and say hello to Mummy. Meet our cousins. I will get Benevolence. She is probably on the farm."

Octavia, Leah, and Simone looked at each other. They smiled, thinking the same thing. Change the language, and this looked a lot like their own family gatherings. Darius came out of the kitchen.

"Hey! So glad y'all made it."

Darius wore a peach cotton shirt that emphasized his cantaloupe-colored skin and off-white linen pants. He relished his surroundings. His voice picked up hints of island Creole dialect. He hugged everyone.

Benevolence and Rona came through the back door.

"Hey, everybody!"

They hugged everyone and made introductions to the rest of her cousins and future in-laws. One hour later, after changing and freshening up, everyone stood at the dining room table. Smaller tables adjoined the main table for the additional guests. The children ate in the parlor and living room. Patrick James, Benevolence's father, said the blessing over the meal.

"Lord, we thank you on this very special occasion, that you found favor with our daughter and her husband-to-be. We thank you for saving her for him. We thank you for their life and we thank you for the life of our family. You have kept us. We praise your name. We thank you for the family of the groom and friends who have come to join this blessed occasion. We pray for peace to rule in this house, love to flow from room to room and new friendships to form. Bless the food and the fellowship in Jesus' name. Amen."

The days passed quickly. The visitors watched the Sugarcane Festival. Dancers marched the streets. Salsa and calypso filled the air. It was a spectacle—'Martinique' style.

Hours disappeared, and soon the wedding day dawned.

Benevolence was in her old room. Rosette was holding a white gown while the makeup artist was applying her makeup and fixing her hair.

"Bene, please sit still. Do you want a cross on your face?"

"Sette, my nerves are dancing all over the place."

"Jesus, calm my sister down please. You have all items for the blessing ceremony?"

"I hope so."

"Bene, don't worry. Everything is going to be fantastic. Just don't faint out there. Though I'm sure your husband-to-be won't mind catching you."

Fifty-five minutes later, Valentina walked in as Rosette zipped the back of Benevolence dress. She was a curvy size fourteen in all the right places. She stood at the door looking at her through the full-length mirror. The photographer walked in, snapping new photos.

"Oh my goodness!"

Valentina clasped her hand over her mouth.

"Thank you, Jesus, for this very special day. Bene, you look so beautiful!"

"Mummy, don't make me cry! Rosette do you have my tiara?"

"Yes."

"Give it to Mummy."

Valentina walked toward the bed. Rosette handed the tiara. She left the room so that they could have some time alone. The photographer took more photos.

Benevolence sat on the edge of the bed, facing the mirror. Valentina walked to her right side and stroked her hair. The photographer got the moment quietly before slipping out of the room.

"I am so proud of you . . . of the woman you've become. You are so strong, so brave. Darius is a very special man. He will be very blessed. I thought when you went off to college I would lose you to America. Nevertheless, you kept your roots and your family near. You have made me so proud."

"Mummy . . ."

Benevolence could not back her tears.

"Bene, don't cry. Don't worry. I will fix it. First, let me crown you." She placed the tiara neatly on Benevolence's head. She took some tissue and blotted masterfully any smudged areas. She placed the veil over Benevolence's face. The door knocked gently.

"It's time to go," Rosette warned.

"Ok," Valentina assured.

"The girls want to see you."

Valentina left and closed the door slightly. Another knock and everyone entered the room one by one. They all gasped simultaneously.

"You better not make me cry," Benevolence warned.

"You look so beautiful," Octavia offered.

"Wow!" Leah and Simone exclaimed.

"You are glowing!"

Yasmine gave Benevolence a hug.

"We're not going to be long. We just wanted to see you. We also wanted to thank you for all that you've brought to our lives . . . for all the advice, prayers and love. We learned more about you than you think. We love you and we want you to know that you will always be a part of our lives. Thank you for inviting us to share this special moment with you."

Yasmine hugged her again and stood near the window.

"You, girls, have brought so much to my life. When I met you guys, I was drained. I felt drained from life, from work and I needed some new oil poured on me. I fought God for asking me to mentor you, because in my mind, I had nothing to give you. I was on empty. Strangely every encounter we had, I gained strength. I never thought you guys would work things out. You were all so different. Through God's own plan and timing, He worked things out. You are such a blessing to me . . . every one of you. Your strengths, your gifts, God used them to help me in my time of need. I love you guys, as if you were my own flesh and blood. I pray that God will continue to bless you and keep your friendship together."

Benevolence hugged Leah, Simone, Octavia, and Yasmine.

"Let's go. I'm ready."

Benevolence stepped out of the room holding her dress, ready to march into a new season. Her vision of happiness awaited her: a beautiful man stood dressed in a white tuxedo, waiting her arrival. Family and friends cheered as waves flowed toward the shore. Sacred vows of love will be shared under a gazebo. All while basking under a picturesque island sun.